A PLUME BOOK

CITY OF THIEVES

DAVID BENIOFF is an author and screenwriter. He adapted his first novel, *The 25th Hour*, into the feature film directed by Spike Lee. He also adapted the bestseller *The Kite Runner* and wrote the screenplay for *Wolverine*, in theaters fall 2008. Stories from his critically acclaimed collection *When the Nines Roll Over* appeared in *Best New American Voices* and *The Best Nonrequired American Reading*. He lives in Los Angeles with his wife and daughter.

Praise for *City of Thieves*

"A wonderful tale. Russian enough for me, and absolutely delightful."   —Martin Cruz Smith, author of *Gorky Park* and the Arkady Renko series

"*City of Thieves* is flat-out great. Benioff's screenwriting chops are in full force here—the plot careens along with cinematic verve—but that's expected. The surprise is Benioff's understated wisdom and tenderness."
                                                        —*Men's Journal*

"How Lev, a gawky Jewish teenager, and Kolya, his strutting sidekick, salvage their humanity—as elusive a treasure as the farm-fresh eggs that could ransom their lives—makes this novel, with all its wartime horrors, as heartening as survival itself."   —*O, The Oprah Magazine*

"David Benioff's second novel features a snappy plot, a buoyant friendship, a quirky courtship, an assortment of menacing bad guys, an atmosphere that flickers between grainy realism and fairy-tale grotesquerie, and a grim but irrepressible sense of humor. Really, everything a reader could hope for in a buddy story set during the German army's siege of Leningrad during World War II. [A] well-crafted tale."   —*Los Angeles Times*

"A gripping, at times gory, but ultimately sweet story . . . it has the phenomenal twists of, yes, a great movie."
—*New York Magazine*

"You don't have to be a lover of war literature or a fan of historical fiction to appreciate *City of Thieves*. Author and screenwriter David Benioff's second novel . . . crosses genre lines . . . to become a story with universal appeal. Virginal seventeen-year-old protagonist Lev Beniov possesses a Woody Allen–esque charm. . . . [*City of Thieves*] is as riveting as the *Odyssey*, and, like Homer, Benioff is a master of rising and falling action."   —*BookPage*

"Novelist and screenwriter Benioff's glorious second novel . . . is a wild, action-packed quest, and much else besides: a coming-of-age story, an odd-couple tale, and a juicy footnote to the historic World War II siege of Leningrad. This gut-churning thriller will sweep you along and, with any luck, propel Benioff into bestseller land."
—*Kirkus Review* (starred)

"[A] hard-to-put-down novel . . . a wry and sympathetic observer of the devastation around him, Lev is an engaging and self-deprecating narrator who finds unexpected reserves of courage at the crucial moment and forms an unlikely friendship with Kolya, a flamboyant ladies' man who is coolly reckless in the face of danger. Benioff blends tense adventure, a bittersweet coming-of-age, and an oddly touching buddy narrative to craft a smart crowd-pleaser."   —*Publishers Weekly* (starred)

"With deftly sly humor, respect for the agony of warfare, and dialogue that elevates the boys-to-men story beyond its typical male ribaldry, this second novel (after *The 25th Hour*) by screenwriter Benioff (*The Kite Runner*) deserves a bright spotlight in most libraries to attract readers young and old to its compelling pages."
—*Library Journal*

"A high-spirited adventure."   —*Booklist*

David
Benioff

City of
Thieves

A Novel

A PLUME BOOK

PLUME
Published by the Penguin Group
Penguin Group (USA) Inc., 375 Hudson Street, New York, New York 10014,
U.S.A. • Penguin Group (Canada), 90 Eglinton Avenue East, Suite 700,
Toronto, Ontario, Canada M4P 2Y3 (a division of Pearson Penguin Canada
Inc.) • Penguin Books Ltd., 80 Strand, London WC2R 0RL, England •
Penguin Ireland, 25 St. Stephen's Green, Dublin 2, Ireland (a division of
Penguin Books Ltd.) • Penguin Group (Australia), 250 Camberwell Road,
Camberwell, Victoria 3124, Australia (a division of Pearson Australia Group
Pty. Ltd.) • Penguin Books India Pvt. Ltd., 11 Community Centre, Panchsheel
Park, New Delhi – 110 017, India • Penguin Group (NZ), 67 Apollo Drive,
Rosedale, North Shore 0632, New Zealand (a division of Pearson New
Zealand Ltd.) • Penguin Books (South Africa) (Pty.) Ltd., 24 Sturdee Avenue,
Rosebank, Johannesburg 2196, South Africa

Penguin Books Ltd., Registered Offices: 80 Strand, London WC2R 0RL, England

Published by Plume, a member of Penguin Group (USA) Inc. Previously
published in a Viking edition.

First Plume Printing, January 2009
10 9 8 7 6 5 4 3

 REGISTERED TRADEMARK—MARCA REGISTRADA

LIBRARY OF CONGRESS CATALOGING-IN-PUBLICATION DATA

Benioff, David
City of thieves: a novel / David Benioff.
p. cm.
ISBN 978-0-670-01870-3 (hc.)
ISBN 978-0-452-29531-5 (pbk. internat'l)
1. Grandparent and child—Fiction. 2. Reminiscing in old age—Fiction.
3. Russians—United States—Fiction. 4. Saint Petersburg (Russia)—
History—Siege, 1941–1944. 5. Domestic fiction. [1. Survival—Fiction.] I. Title.
PS3552.E54425C58   2008
813'.54—dc22   2007042784

Printed in the United States of America
Set in Palatino
Original hardcover design by Francesca Belanger

For Amanda & Frankie

and if the City falls but a single man escapes
he will carry the City within himself on the roads of exile
he will be the City

Zbigniew Herbert

At last Schenk thought he understood and began laughing louder. Then suddenly he asked in a serious tone, "Do you think that the Russians are homosexuals?"
    "You'll find out at the end of the war," I replied.

Curzio Malaparte

City of Thieves

My grandfather, the knife fighter, killed two Germans before he was eighteen. I don't remember anyone telling me—it was something I always seemed to know, the way I knew the Yankees wore pinstripes for home games and gray for the road. But I wasn't born with the knowledge. Who told me? Not my father, who never shared secrets, or my mother, who shied away from mentioning the unpleasant, all things bloody, cancerous, or deformed. Not my grandmother, who knew every folktale from the old country—most of them gruesome; children devoured by wolves and beheaded by witches—but never spoke about the war in my hearing. And certainly not my grandfather himself, the smiling watchman of my earliest memories, the quiet, black-eyed, slender man who held my hand as we crossed the avenues, who sat on a park bench reading his Russian newspaper while I chased pigeons and harassed sugar ants with broken twigs.

I grew up two blocks from my grandparents and saw them nearly every day. They had their own small insurance company, working out of their railroad apartment in Bay Ridge, catering primarily to other Russian immigrants. My grandmother was always on the phone, selling. No one could resist her. She charmed them or she frightened them, and either way, they bought. My grandfather manned the desk, doing all the paperwork. When I was small, I would sit on his lap, staring at the stump of his left index finger, rounded and smooth, the top two knuckles so cleanly severed it seemed he'd been born without them. If it was summer and the Yankees were playing, a radio (after his seventieth birthday, a color television my dad bought him) broadcast the game. He never lost his accent, he never voted in an election or listened to American music, but he became a devout Yankees fan.

In the late nineties, an insurance conglomerate made an offer for my grandparents' company. It was, according to everyone, a fair offer, so my grandmother asked them to double it. There must have been a good deal of haggling, but I could have told the conglomerate that haggling with my grandmother was a waste of time. In the end they gave her what she wanted and my grandparents, following tradition, sold their apartment and moved to Florida.

They bought a small house on the Gulf Coast, a flat-roofed masterpiece built in 1949 by an architect who would have become famous if he hadn't drowned the same year. Stark and majestic in steel and poured concrete, sitting on a solitary bluff overlooking the Gulf, it is not the house you'd imagine for a retired couple, but they didn't move south to wither in the sun and die. Most days my grandfather sits at his computer, playing chess online with old friends. My grandmother, bored by inactivity within weeks of the move, created a job for herself at a commuter college in Sarasota, teaching Russian literature to tanned students who seem (based on my one classroom visit) constantly alarmed by her profanity, her heavy sarcasm, and her word-perfect memory of Pushkin's verse.

Every night my grandparents eat dinner on the deck of their house, looking out over the dark waters toward Mexico. They sleep with the windows open, the moths battering their wings against the mesh screens. Unlike the other retirees I've met in Florida, they're not worried about crime. The front door is usually unlocked and there is no alarm system. They don't wear their seat belts in the car; they don't wear suntan lotion in the sun. They have decided nothing can kill them but God himself, and they don't even believe in him.

I live in Los Angeles and write screenplays about mutant superheroes. Two years ago I was asked to write an autobiographical essay for a screenwriting magazine, and midway through I realized I had led an intensely dull life. Not that I'm complaining. Even if the summary of my existence makes boring reading—school, college, odd jobs, graduate school, odd jobs, more graduate school, mutant superheroes—I've had a good time existing. But as I struggled through the essay I decided I didn't want to write about my life, not even for five hundred words. I wanted to write about Leningrad.

My grandparents picked me up at the Sarasota airport; I stooped to kiss them and they smiled up at me, always slightly bemused in the presence of their giant American grandson (at six foot two I'm a giant next to them). On the way home we bought pompano at the local fish market; my grandfather grilled it adding nothing but butter, salt, and fresh lemon. Like every dish he made, it seemed incredibly easy to do, took him ten minutes, and tasted better than anything I'd eaten that year in LA. My grandmother doesn't cook; she is famous in our family for her refusal to prepare anything more complicated than a bowl of cereal.

After dinner my grandmother lit a cigarette and my grandfather poured three glasses of homemade black currant vodka. We listened to a choir of cicadas and crickets, stared out at the black Gulf, and slapped away the occasional mosquito.

"I brought a tape recorder with me. I thought maybe we could talk about the war."

I thought I caught my grandmother rolling her eyes as she flicked her ash onto the grass.

"What?"

"You're forty years old. Now you want to know?"

"I'm thirty-four." I looked at my grandfather and he smiled at me. "What's the matter? You guys were Nazis? You're hiding your Nazi past?"

"No," he said, still smiling. "We weren't Nazis."

"You thought I was forty years old?"

"Thirty-four, forty—" She made her *pshh* sound, always accompanied by a dismissive wave of the hand, slapping away the stupidity. "Who cares? Get married. Find a wife."

"You sound like every other grandmother in Florida."

"Ha," she said, a little wounded.

"I want to know what it was like. What's so horrible about that?"

She nodded at my grandfather while pointing the burning tip of her cigarette at me.

"He wants to know what it was like."

"Darling," said my grandfather. Just that, nothing else, but my grandmother nodded and stubbed out her cigarette on the glass-top table.

"You're right," she told me. "You want to write about the war, you should."

She stood, kissed me on the top of my head, kissed my grandfather on the lips, and carried the dishes inside the house. For a few minutes we sat there quietly, listening to the waves breaking. He poured us fresh vodkas, happy to see I'd finished mine.

"You have a girlfriend?"

"Uh-huh."

"The actress?"

"Yeah."

"I like her."

"I know you do."

"She could be Russian," he said. "She has the eyes.... If you want to talk about Leningrad, we talk about Leningrad."

"I don't want to talk. I want you to talk."

"So, OK, I'll talk. Tomorrow?"

He kept his word. For the next week we sat together every day on the concrete deck and I recorded his stories. A few hours in the morning, breaking for lunch, then again in the afternoon—my grandfather, a man who hated to speak more than two consecutive sentences in mixed company (meaning in the company of anyone other than his wife), filled minicassette after minicassette with his words. Too many words for one book—truth might be stranger than fiction, but it needs a better editor. For the first time in my life I heard my grandfather curse and speak openly about sex. He talked about his childhood, about the war, about coming to America. But mostly he talked about one week in 1942, the first week of the year, the week he met my grandmother, made his best friend, and killed two Germans.

When he was finished telling his stories, I questioned him about various details—names, locations, weather conditions on certain days. He tolerated this for a while, but eventually he leaned forward and pressed the Stop button on the tape recorder.

"It was a long time ago," he said. "I don't remember what I was wearing. I don't remember if the sun came out."

"I just want to make sure I get everything right."

"You won't."

"This is your story. I don't want to fuck with it."

"David—"

"A couple of things still don't make sense to me—"

"David," he said. "You're a writer. Make it up."

You have never been so hungry; you have never been so cold. When we slept, if we slept, we dreamed of the feasts we had carelessly eaten seven months earlier—all that buttered bread, the potato dumplings, the sausages—eaten with disregard, swallowing without tasting, leaving great crumbs on our plates, scraps of fat. In June of 1941, before the Germans came, we thought we were poor. But June seemed like paradise by winter.

At night the wind blew so loud and long it startled you when it stopped; the shutter hinges of the burned-out café on the corner would quit creaking for a few ominous seconds, as if a predator neared and the smaller animals hushed in terror. The shutters themselves had been torn down for firewood in November. There was no more scrap wood in Leningrad. Every wood sign, the slats of the park benches, the floorboards of shattered buildings—all gone and burning in someone's stove. The pigeons were missing, too, caught and stewed in melted ice from the Neva. No one minded slaughtering pigeons. It was the dogs and cats that caused trouble. You would hear a rumor in October that someone had roasted the family mutt and split it four ways for supper; we'd laugh and shake our heads, not believing it, and also wondering if dog tasted good with enough salt—there was still plenty of salt, even when everything else ran out we had salt. By January the rumors had become plain fact. No one but the best connected could still feed a pet, so the pets fed us.

There were two theories on the fat versus the thin. Some said those who were fat before the war stood a better chance of survival: a week without food would not transform a plump man into a skeleton. Others said skinny people were more accustomed to eating little and could better handle the shock of starvation. I stood in the latter camp, purely out of self-interest. I was a runt from birth. Big nosed, black haired, skin scribbled with acne— let's admit I was no girl's idea of a catch. But war made me more attractive. Others dwindled as the ration cards were cut and cut again, halving those who looked like circus strongmen before the invasion. I had no muscle to lose. Like the shrews that kept scavenging while the dinosaurs toppled around them, I was built for deprivation.

On New Year's Eve I sat on the rooftop of the Kirov, the apartment building where I'd lived since I was five (though it had no name until '34, when Kirov was shot and half the city was named after him), watching the fat gray antiaircraft blimps swarm under the clouds, waiting for the bombers. That time of year the sun lingers in the sky for only six hours, scurrying from horizon to horizon as if spooked. Every night four of us would sit on the roof for a three-hour shift, armed with sand pails, iron tongs, and shovels, bundled in all the shirts and sweaters and coats we could find, watching the skies. We were the firefighters. The Germans had decided rushing the city would be too costly, so instead they encircled us, intending to starve us out, bomb us out, burn us out.

Before the war began eleven hundred people lived in the Kirov. By New Year's Eve the number was closer to four hundred. Most of the small children were evacuated before the Germans closed the circle in September. My mother and little sister, Taisya, went to Vyazma to stay with my uncle. The night before they left I fought with my mother, the only fight we'd ever had—or, more precisely, the only time I ever fought back. She wanted me to go with them, of course, far away from the invaders, deep into the heart of the country where the bombers couldn't find us. But I wasn't leaving Piter. I was a man, I would defend my city, I would be a Nevsky for the twentieth century. Perhaps I wasn't quite this ridiculous. I had a real argument: if every able-bodied soul fled, Leningrad would fall to the Fascists. And without Leningrad, without the City of Workers building tanks and rifles for the Red Army, what chance did Russia have?

My mother thought this was a stupid argument. I was barely seventeen. I didn't weld armor at the Works and I couldn't enlist in the army for close to a year. The defense of Leningrad had nothing to do with me; I was just another mouth to feed. I ignored these insults.

"I'm a firefighter," I told her, because it was true, the city council had ordered the creation of ten thousand firefighting units, and I was the proud commander of the Kirov Fifth-Floor Brigade.

My mother wasn't forty years old, but her hair was already gray. She sat across from me at the kitchen table, holding one of my hands in both of hers. She was a very small woman, barely five feet tall, and I had been afraid of her from birth.

"You are an idiot," she told me. Maybe this sounds insulting, but my mother always called me "her idiot" and by that point I thought of it as an affectionate nickname. "The city was here before you. It will be here after you. Taisya and I need you."

She was right. A better son would have gone with her, a better brother. Taisya adored me, jumped on me when I came home from school, read me the silly little poems she wrote as homework to honor martyrs of the revolution, drew caricatures of my big-nosed profile in her notebook. Generally, I wanted to strangle her. I had no desire to tramp across the country with my mother and kid sister. I was seventeen, flooded with a belief in my own heroic destiny. Molotov's declaration during his radio address on the first day of the war (OUR CAUSE IS JUST! THE ENEMY WILL BE BEATEN! WE SHALL TRIUMPH!) had been printed on thousands of posters and pasted on the city's walls. I believed in the cause; I would not flee the enemy; I would not miss out on the triumph.

Mother and Taisya left the next morning. They rode a bus part of the way, flagged down army trucks for rides, and walked endless miles on country roads in their split-soled boots. It took them three weeks to get there, but they made it, safe at last. She sent me a letter describing her journey, the terror and fatigue. Maybe she wanted me to feel guilty for abandoning them, and I did, but I also knew it was better with them gone. The great fight was coming and they did not belong on the front. On the seventh of October the Germans took Vyazma and her letters stopped coming.

I'd like to say I missed them when they were

gone, and some nights I was lonely, and always I missed my mother's cooking, but I had fantasized about being on my own since I was little. My favorite folktales featured resourceful orphans who make their way through the dark forest, surviving all perils with clever problem solving, outwitting their enemies, finding their fortune in the midst of their wanderings. I wouldn't say I was happy—we were all too hungry to be happy—but I believed that here at last was the Meaning. If Leningrad fell, Russia would fall; if Russia fell, Fascism would conquer the world. All of us believed this. I still believe it.

So I was too young for the army but old enough to dig antitank ditches by day and guard the roofs by night. Manning my crew were my friends from the fifth floor—Vera Osipovna, a talented cellist, and the redheaded Antokolsky twins, whose only known talent was an ability to fart in harmony. In the early days of the war we had smoked cigarettes on the roof, posing as soldiers, brave and strong and square-chinned, scanning the skies for the enemy. By the end of December there were no cigarettes in Leningrad, at least none made with tobacco. A few desperate souls crushed fallen leaves, rolled them in paper, and called them Autumn Lights, claiming the right leaves provided a decent smoke, but in the Kirov, far from the nearest standing tree, this was never an option. We spent our spare minutes hunting rats, who must have thought the disappearance of the city's cats was the answer to all their ancient prayers, until they realized there was nothing left to eat in the garbage.

After months of bombing raids we could identify the various German planes by the pitch of their engines. That night it was the Junkers 88s, as it had been for weeks, replacing the Heinkels and Dorniers that our fighters had gotten good at gunning down. As wretched as our city had become in daylight, after dark there was a strange beauty in the siege. From the roof of the Kirov, if the moon was out, we could see all of Leningrad: the needlepoint of the Admiralty tower (splashed with gray paint to obscure it from the bombers); the Peter and Paul Fortress (spires draped with camouflage netting); the domes of Saint Isaac's and the Church on Spilled Blood. We could see the crews manning the antiaircraft guns on the rooftops of neighboring buildings. The Baltic Fleet had dropped anchor on the Neva; they floated there, giant gray sentries, firing their big guns at the Nazi artillery emplacements.

Most beautiful were the dogfights. The Ju88s and the Sukhois circled above the city, invisible from below unless they were caught in the eyes of the powerful searchlights. The Sukhois had large red stars painted on the undersides of their wings so our antiaircraft crews wouldn't shoot them down. Every few nights we'd see a battle spotlit as if for the stage, the heavier, slower German bombers banking hard to let their gunners get a bead on the darting Russian fighters. When a Junkers went down, the plane's burning carcass falling like an angel cast from heaven, a great shout of defiance rose up from rooftops all across the city, all the gunners and firefighters shaking their fists to salute the victorious pilot.

We had a little radio on the roof with us. On New Year's Eve we listened to the Spassky chimes in Moscow playing the "Internationale." Vera had found half an onion somewhere; she cut it into four pieces on a plate smeared with sunflower oil. When the onion was gone, we mopped up the remaining oil with our ration bread. Ration bread did not taste like bread. It did not taste like food. After the Germans bombed the Badayev grain warehouses, the city bakeries got creative. Everything that could be added to the recipe without poisoning people was added to the recipe. The entire city was starving, no one had enough to eat, and still, everyone cursed the bread, the sawdust flavor, how hard it got in the cold. People broke their teeth trying to chew it. Even today, even when I've forgotten the faces of people I loved, I can still remember the taste of that bread.

Half an onion and a 125-gram loaf of bread split four ways—this was a decent meal. We lay on our backs, wrapped in blankets, watching the air-raid blimps on their long tethers drifting in the wind, listening to the radio's metronome. When there was no music to play or news to report, the radio station transmitted the sound of a metronome, that endless tick-tick-tick letting us know the city was still unconquered, the Fascists still outside the gate. The broadcast metronome was Piter's beating heart and the Germans never stilled it.

It was Vera who spotted the man falling from the sky. She shouted and pointed and we all stood to get a better look. One of the searchlights shone on a parachutist descending toward the city, his silk canopy a white tulip bulb above him.

"A Fritz," said Oleg Antokolsky, and he was right; we could see the gray Luftwaffe uniform. Where had he come from? None of us had heard the sounds of aerial combat or the report of an AA gun. We hadn't heard a bomber passing overhead for close to an hour.

"Maybe it's started," said Vera. For weeks we'd been hearing rumors that the Germans were preparing a massive paratrooper drop, a final raid to pluck the miserable thorn of Leningrad from their advancing army's backside. At any minute we expected to look up and see thousands of Nazis drifting toward the city, a snowstorm of white parachutes blotting out the sky, but dozens of searchlights slashed through the darkness and found no more enemies. There was only this one, and judging from the limpness of the body suspended from the parachute harness, he was already dead.

We watched him drift down, frozen in the searchlight, low enough that we could see that one of his black boots was missing.

"He's coming our way," I said. The wind blew him toward Voinova Street. The twins looked at each other.

"Luger," said Oleg.

"Luftwaffe don't carry Lugers," said Grisha. He was five minutes older and the authority on Nazi weaponry. "Walther PPK."

Vera smiled at me. "German chocolate."

We ran for the stairway door, abandoning our firefighting tools, racing down the dark stairwell. We were fools, of course. A slip on one of those concrete steps, with no fat or muscle to cushion the fall, meant a broken bone, and a broken bone meant death. But none of us cared. We were very young and a dead German was falling onto Voinova Street carrying gifts from *das Vaterland*.

We sprinted through the courtyard and climbed over the locked gate. All the streetlamps were dark. The entire city was dark—partly to make the job tougher for the bombers and partly because most of the electricity was diverted to the munitions factories—but the moon was bright enough to see by. Voinova was wide open and deserted, six hours into curfew. No cars in sight. Only the military and government had access to gasoline, and all the civilian autos had been requisitioned during the first months of the war. Strips of paper crossed the shop windows, which the radio told us made them more resistant to shattering. Maybe this was true, though I had walked by many storefronts in Leningrad where nothing remained in the window frame but a dangling strip of paper.

Out on the street we looked into the sky but could not find our man.

"Where'd he go?"

"You think he landed on a roof?"

The searchlights were tracking the sky, but they were all mounted on top of tall buildings and none of them had an angle to shine down Voinova Street. Vera tugged on the collar of my greatcoat, a vast old navy coat inherited from my father and still too big for me, but warmer than anything else I owned.

I turned and saw him gliding down the street, our German, his single black boot skidding over the frozen pavement, the great canopy of his white parachute still swollen in the wind, blowing him toward the gates of the Kirov, his chin slumped against his chest, his dark hair flecked with crystals of ice, his face bloodless in the moonlight. We stood very still and watched him sail closer. We had seen things that winter no eyes should ever see, we thought we were beyond surprise, but we were wrong, and if the German had drawn his Walther and begun shooting, none of us would have been able to get our feet moving in time. But the dead man stayed dead and at last the wind gave out, the parachute deflated, and he slumped to the pavement, dragged another few meters facedown in final humiliation.

We gathered around the pilot. He was a tall man, well built, and if we had seen him walking around Piter in street clothes, we would have known him at once for an infiltrator—he had the body of a man who ate meat every day.

Grisha knelt and unholstered the German's sidearm. "Walther PPK. Told you."

We rolled the German onto his back. His pale face was scuffed, the skin scraped on the asphalt, the abrasions as colorless as the intact skin. The dead don't bruise. I couldn't tell if he had died frightened or defiant or peaceful. There was no trace of life or personality in his face—he looked like a corpse who had been born a corpse.

Oleg stripped off the black leather gloves while Vera went for the scarf and goggles. I found a sheath strapped to the pilot's ankle and pulled out a beautifully weighted knife with a silver finger guard and a fifteen-centimeter single-edge blade etched with words I could not read in the moonlight. I resheathed the blade and strapped it to my own ankle, feeling for the first time in months that my warrior destiny was at last coming true.

Oleg found the dead man's wallet and grinned as he counted out the deutsche marks. Vera pocketed a chronometer, twice as big as a wristwatch, that the German had worn around the sleeve of his flight jacket. Grisha found a pair of folded binoculars in a leather case, two extra magazines for the Walther, and a slim hip flask. He unscrewed the cap, sniffed, and passed me the flask.

"Cognac?"

I took a sip and nodded. "Cognac."

"When did you ever taste cognac?" asked Vera.

"I've had it before."

"When?"

"Let me see," said Oleg, and the bottle went around the circle, the four of us squatting on our haunches around the fallen pilot, sipping the liquor that might have been cognac or brandy or Armagnac. None of us knew the difference. Whatever it was, the stuff was warmth in the belly.

Vera stared at the German's face. Her expression held no pity, no fear, only curiosity and contempt— the invader had come to drop his bombs on our city and instead had dropped himself. We hadn't shot him down, but we felt triumphant anyway. No one else in the Kirov had come across an enemy's corpse. We would be the talk of the apartment bloc in the morning.

"How do you think he died?" she asked. No bullet wounds blemished the body, no singed hair or leather, no sign of any violence at all. His skin was far too white for the living, but nothing had pierced it.

"He froze to death," I told them. I said it with authority because I knew it was true and I had no way to prove it. The pilot had bailed out thousands of feet above nighttime Leningrad. The air at ground level was too cold for the clothes he was wearing— up in the clouds, outside of his warm cockpit, he never had a chance.

Grisha raised the flask in salute. "Here's to the cold."

The flask began to circle again. It never got to me. We should have heard the car's engine from two blocks away, the city after curfew was quiet as the moon, but we were busy drinking our German liquor, making our toasts. Only when the GAZ turned onto Voinova Street, heavy tires rattling on the asphalt, headlights stabbing toward us, did we realize the danger. The punishment for violating curfew without a permit was summary execution. The punishment for abandoning a firefighting detail was summary execution. The punishment for looting was summary execution. The courts no longer operated; the police officers were on the front lines, the prisons half full and dwindling fast. Who had food for an enemy of the state? If you broke the law and you were caught, you were dead. There wasn't time for any legal niceties.

So we ran. We knew the Kirov better than anyone. Once we got inside the courtyard gates and into the chilled darkness of the sprawling building, no one could find us if they had three months to search. We could hear the soldiers shouting at us to stop, but that didn't matter; voices didn't frighten us, only bullets made a difference and no one had pulled a trigger yet. Grisha made it to the gate first—he was the closest thing to an athlete among us—he leaped onto the iron bars and hoisted himself upward. Oleg was right behind him and I was behind Oleg. Our bodies were weak, muscles shrunken from lack of protein, but fear helped us scale the gate as quickly as we ever had.

Near the top of the gate I looked back and saw that Vera had slipped on a patch of ice. She stared up at me, her eyes round and fearful, on her hands and knees as the GAZ braked beside the body of the German pilot and four soldiers stepped out. They were twenty feet away, their rifles in their hands, but I still had time to pull myself over the gate and disappear into the Kirov.

I wish I could tell you that the thought of deserting Vera never entered my mind, that my friend was in danger and I went to her rescue without hesitation. Truly, though, at that moment I hated her. I hated her for being clumsy at the worst possible time, for staring up at me with her panicked brown eyes, electing me to be her savior even though Grisha was the only one she had ever kissed. I knew that I could not live with the memory of those eyes pleading for me, and she knew it, too, and I hated her even as I jumped down from the gate, lifted her to her feet, and hauled her to the iron bars. I was weak, but Vera couldn't have weighed forty kilos. I boosted her onto the gate as the soldiers shouted and their boot heels slapped on the pavement and the bolts of their rifles snapped into place.

Vera went over the top and I scrambled up behind her, ignoring the soldiers. If I stopped, they would gather around me, tell me I was an enemy of the state, force me to kneel, and shoot me in the back of the head. I was an easy target now, but maybe they were drunk, maybe they were city boys like me who had never fired a shot before in their lives; maybe they would miss on purpose because they knew I was a patriot and a defender of the city and I had snuck out of the Kirov only because a German had fallen twenty thousand feet onto my street, and what seventeen-year-old Russian boy would not sneak outside to peek at a dead Fascist?

My chin was level with the top of the gate when I felt the gloved hands wrap around my ankles. Strong hands, the hands of army men who ate two meals every day. I saw Vera run inside the Kirov, never looking back. I tried to cling to the iron bars, but the soldiers dragged me down, tossed me to the sidewalk, and stood above me, the muzzles of their Tokarevs jabbing at my cheeks. None of the soldiers looked older than nineteen and none seemed reluctant to splatter the street with my brains.

"Looks ready to shit himself, this one."

"You having a party here, son? Found yourself some schnapps?"

"He's a good one for the colonel. He can ride with the Fritz."

Two of them bent down, grabbed me under the armpits, yanked me to my feet, guided me to the still-idling GAZ, and shoved me into the backseat. The other two soldiers lifted the German by his hands and boots and swung him into the car beside me.

"Keep him warm," one of them said, and they all laughed as if it were the funniest joke ever told. They squeezed into the car and slammed the doors.

I decided I was still alive because they wanted to execute me in public, as a warning to other looters. A few minutes before, I had felt far more powerful than the dead pilot. Now, as we sped down the dark street, swerving to avoid bomb craters and sprays of rubble, he seemed to be smirking at me, his white lips a scar splitting his frozen face. We were going the same way.

2

I f you grew up in Piter, you grew up fearing the
Crosses, that gloomy redbrick stain on the Neva, a
brutish, brooding warehouse of the lost. Six thousand convicts lived there in peacetime. I doubt a
thousand were left by January. Hundreds impris-
oned for petty crimes were released into Red Army
units, released into the meat grinder of the German
Blitzkrieg. Hundreds more starved in their cells.
Each day the guards dragged the skin-draped skel-
etons out of the Crosses and onto sledges where the
dead were stacked eight high.

When I was small, it was the silence of the prison
that frightened me most. You walked by expecting
to hear the shouts of rough men or the clamor of a
brawl, but no noise escaped the thick walls, as if the
prisoners inside—most of them awaiting trial or a
trip to the gulag or a bullet in the head—hacked out
their own tongues to protest their fate. The place
was an antifortress, designed to keep the enemies
inside, and every boy in Leningrad had heard the
phrase a hundred times: "You keep on with that
and you'll end up in the Crosses."

I had seen my cell only for a second when the
guards shoved me inside, their lamps shining on
the rough stone walls, a cell two meters wide and

four meters long, with bunk beds for four and all of them empty. I was relieved at that, I didn't want to share the darkness with a stranger with tattooed knuckles, but after a time—minutes? hours?—the black silence began to feel tangible, something that could get into your lungs and drown you.

Darkness and solitude generally didn't frighten me. Electricity was as rare as bacon in Piter those days, and my apartment in the Kirov was empty now that Mother and Taisya had fled. The long nights were dark and quiet, but there was always noise somewhere. Mortars fired from the German lines; an army truck motoring down the boulevard; the dying old woman upstairs moaning in her bed. Awful sounds, really, but *sounds*—something to let you know you were still in this world. That cell in the Crosses was the only truly silent place I'd ever entered. I could hear nothing at all; I could see nothing. They had locked me in death's waiting room.

As siege-hardened as I believed I was before my arrest, the truth was that I had no more courage in January than I had in June—contrary to popular belief, the experience of terror does not make you braver. Perhaps, though, it is easier to hide your fear when you're afraid all the time.

I tried to think of a song to sing, a poem to recite, but all the words were stuck inside my head like salt in a caked shaker. I lay on one of the top bunks, hoping whatever heat existed within the Crosses would rise and find me. Morning promised nothing but a bullet in the brain and yet I longed for daylight to seep inside. When they dumped me in the cell, I thought I had seen a sliver of barred window near the ceiling, but now I couldn't remember. I tried counting to a thousand to pass some time but always got lost around four hundred, hearing phantom rats that turned out to be my own fingers scratching the torn mattress.

The night was never going to end. The Germans had shot down the fucking sun, they could do it, why not, their scientists were the best in the world, they could figure it out. They had learned how to stop time. I was blind and deaf. Only the cold and my thirst reminded me that I was alive. You get so lonely you start longing for the sentries, just to hear their footsteps, smell the vodka on their breath.

So many great Russians endured long stretches in prison. That night I learned I would never be a great Russian. A few hours alone in a cell, suffering no torture other than the darkness and the silence and the absolute cold, a few hours of that and I was already half broken. The fierce souls who survived winter after winter in Siberia possessed something I did not, great faith in some splendid destiny, whether God's kingdom or justice or the distant promise of revenge. Or maybe they were so beaten down they became nothing more than animals on their hind legs, working at their masters' command, eating whatever slop he threw down for them, sleeping when ordered and dreaming of nothing but the end.

At last there was noise, footsteps, several sets of heavy boots clomping in the corridor. A key turned in the lock. I sat up in bed and cracked my skull against the ceiling, hard enough that I bit through my lip.

Two guards—one of them holding an oil lamp, the prettiest light I ever saw, better than any sunrise—escorted a new prisoner, a young, uniformed soldier who glanced around the cell like a man viewing an apartment he's considering for rent. The soldier was tall and stood very straight; he towered over the guards, and though they had pistols in their holsters and the soldier was unarmed, he seemed ready to give orders. He held his Astrakhan fur hat in one hand and his leather gloves in the other.

He looked at me just as the guards left, shutting the cell door and bolting it from the outside, taking their light with them. His face was the last thing I saw before the darkness resumed, so it stuck in my mind: the high Cossack cheekbones, the amused twist of the lips, the hay-blond hair, the eyes blue enough to please any Aryan bride.

I sat on the bed and he stood on the stone floor and from the perfect silence I knew neither of us had shifted position—we were still staring at each other in the darkness.

"Are you a Jew?" he asked.

"What?"

"A Jew. You look like a Jew."

"You look like a Nazi."

"I know. *Ich spreche ein bisschen Deutsch,* too. I volunteered to be a spy, but nobody listened to me. So, you are a Jew?"

"Why do you care?"

"Don't be ashamed of it. I don't have a problem with Jews. Emanuel Lasker is my second-favorite chess player. Just a rung under Capablanca. . . . Capablanca is Mozart, pure genius; you can't love chess and not love Capablanca. But Lasker, nobody's better in the endgame. You have any food?"

"No."

"Put out your hand."

This seemed like some sort of trap, a game children played to snare morons. He would slap my palm or just let it hang there till I realized my stupidity. But no offer of food could be refused, even the least likely, so I stretched my hand into the darkness and waited. A moment later a sliver of something cold and greasy sat on my palm. I don't know how he found my hand, but he did, without any fumbling.

"Sausage," he said. And then, after a pause, "Don't worry. It's not pork."

"I eat pork." I sniffed at the sausage and then nibbled off a bit. It was as far from real meat as ration bread from real bread, but there was fat in it, and fat was life. I chewed on the sliver as slowly as I could, trying to make it last.

"You chew loudly," he told me, a reprimand from the dark. I heard the creak of bedsprings as he sat on one of the lower bunk beds. "And you're supposed to say thank you."

"Thank you."

"You're welcome. What's your name?"

"Lev."

"Lev what?"

"What do you care?"

"It's just manners," he said. "For instance, if I introduce myself, I say, 'Good evening, my name is Nikolai Alexandrovich Vlasov, my friends call me Kolya.'"

"You just want to know if I have a Jewish name."

"Do you?"

"Yes."

"Ah." He sighed happily, pleased to hear his instincts confirmed. "Thank you. Don't know why you're so afraid of telling people."

I didn't answer. If he didn't know why, there was no point explaining it.

"So why are you here?" he asked.

"They caught me looting a dead German on Voinova Street."

This alarmed him. "The Germans are already on Voinova? So it's begun?"

"Nothing's begun. He was a bomber pilot. He ejected."

"The AA boys got him?"

"The cold got him. Why are you here?"

"Sheer idiocy. They think I'm a deserter."

"So why didn't they shoot you?"

"Why didn't they shoot *you*?"

"Don't know," I admitted. "They said I was a good one for the colonel."

"I'm not a deserter. I'm a student. I was defending my thesis."

"Really? Your thesis?" It sounded like the dumbest excuse in the history of desertion.

"An interpretation of Ushakovo's *The Courtyard Hound*, through the lens of contemporary sociological analysis." He waited for me to say something, but I had nothing to say to that. "You know the book?"

"No. Ushakovo?"

"Miserable how bad the schools have gotten. They should have you memorizing passages." He sounded like a crotchety old professor, though from my one look at him I would have guessed he was twenty. "'*In the slaughterhouse where we first kissed, the air still stank from the blood of the lambs.*' First line. Some say it's the greatest Russian novel. And you've never heard of it."

He sighed extravagantly. A moment later I heard

a strange scratching sound, as if a rat were sharpening its claws on the mattress ticking.

"What is that?" I asked.

"Hm?"

"You don't hear that noise?"

"I'm writing in my journal."

I could see no farther with my eyes open than with them closed and this one was writing in his journal. Now I could tell the scratching was a pencil on paper. After a few minutes the journal slapped closed and I heard him stuff the book into his pocket.

"I can write in the dark," he said, punctuating the sentence with a light burp. "One of my talents."

"Notes on *The Courtyard Hound*?"

"Exactly. How's this for strange? Chapter six: Radchenko spends a month in the Crosses because his former best friend . . . Well, I don't want to give it away. But I have to say, it seemed like fate when they brought me here. I've been every other place Radchenko visited—every restaurant and theater and graveyard, the ones that are still around, anyway—but I've never been inside here. A critic could argue that until you spend a night in the Crosses, you can't understand Radchenko."

"Pretty lucky for you."

"Mm."

"So you think they'll shoot us in the morning?"

"I doubt it. They're not preserving us for the night just to shoot us tomorrow." He sounded quite jaunty about it, as if we were discussing a sporting event, as if the outcome wasn't particularly momentous no matter which way it went.

"I haven't had a shit in eight days," he confided.

"I'm not saying a good shit—it's been months since I've had a good shit—I mean no shit at all for eight days."

We were quiet for a moment, considering these words.

"How long do you think a man can last without shitting?"

It was an interesting question and I was curious to know the answer myself, but I didn't have one for him. I heard him lie down, heard him yawn happily, relaxed and content, his piss-stained straw mattress as comfortable as a feather bed. The silence lingered for a minute and I thought my cell mate had fallen asleep.

"These walls must be four feet thick," he said at last. "This is probably the safest place in Piter to spend a night." And then he did fall asleep, shifting from speech into snores so quickly that at first I thought he was faking.

I've always envied people who sleep easily. Their brains must be cleaner, the floorboards of the skull well swept, all the little monsters closed up in a steamer trunk at the foot of the bed. I was born an insomniac and that's the way I'll die, wasting thousands of hours along the way longing for unconsciousness, longing for a rubber mallet to crack me in the head, not so hard, not hard enough to do any damage, just a good whack to put me down for the night. But that night I didn't have a chance. I stared into the blackness until the blackness blurred into gray, until the ceiling above me began to take form and the light from the east dribbled in through the narrow barred window that existed after all. Only then did I realize that I still had a German knife strapped to my calf.

3

An hour after dawn two new guards opened the cell door, rousted us from bed, and clamped handcuffs on our wrists. They ignored my questions but seemed amused when Kolya asked for a cup of tea and an omelet. Jokes must have been rare in the Crosses, because it wasn't such a good joke, but the guards grinned as they shoved us down the hallway. Somewhere someone was moaning, a low and endless moan, a ship's horn heard from a great distance.

I didn't know if we were heading for the gallows or an interrogation chamber. The night had passed without sleep; save for a swig from the German's flask, there hadn't been a sip to drink since the rooftop of the Kirov; a lump the size of an infant's fist had swelled where my forehead had cracked the ceiling—it was a bad morning, really; among my worst—but I wanted to live. I wanted to live and I knew I could not face my execution with grace. I would kneel before the hangman or the firing squad and plead my youth, detail my many hours served on the rooftop waiting for the bombs, all the barricades I had helped to build, the ditches I had dug. All of us had done it, we were all serving the cause, but I was one of Piter's true sons and I didn't deserve to die. What harm had been done? We drank a dead German's cognac—for this you want to end me? You want to tie rough hemp around my skinny neck and shut down my brain forever because I stole a knife? Don't do this, comrade. I don't think there is greatness in me, but there is something better than this.

The guards led us down a stone staircase, the steps beaten smooth by hundreds of thousands of boot heels. An old man with a heavy gray scarf wrapped twice around his throat sat on the far side of the iron bars that blocked the bottom of the staircase. He gave us a gummy grin and unlocked the gate. A moment later we walked through a heavy wooden door into the sunlight, emerging from the Crosses intact and alive.

Kolya, unimpressed by our apparent reprieve, scooped up a palmful of clean snow with his shackled hands and licked it. The boldness of the maneuver made me jealous, as did the thought of cold water on my tongue. But I didn't want to do anything to anger the guards. Our escape from the Crosses seemed like an odd mistake and I expected to be shoved inside again if I did something wrong.

The guards escorted us to a waiting GAZ, its big engine grumbling, exhaust pipes spewing dirty vapor, two soldiers sitting in the front seat watching us with zero curiosity, their fur-lined hats pulled down low on their foreheads.

Kolya hopped into the backseat without waiting for an order.

"Gentlemen, to the opera!"

The guards, standards diminished by years of

working the Crosses, gave Kolya another good laugh. The soldiers did not. One of them turned and inspected Kolya.

"You say another word and I'll break your fucking arm. It were up to me, you'd already have a bullet in your head. Fucking deserter. You"—and this was addressed to me—"get in."

Kolya's mouth was already open and I knew violence was on the way; the soldier did not look like a bluffer and Kolya, clearly, was incapable of heeding a simple threat.

"I'm not a deserter," he said. With his manacled hands he managed to push up the left sleeve of his greatcoat, the left sleeve of his army sweater, the left sleeves of the two shirts beneath it, and offered his forearm to the soldier in the front seat. "You want to break the arm, break it, but I'm not a deserter."

For a long count nobody spoke—Kolya stared at the soldier, the soldier stared back, and the rest of us watched and waited, impressed by this match of wills and curious to see who would win. Finally, the soldier conceded defeat by turning away from Kolya and barking at me.

"Get in the car, you little cunt."

The guards grinned. This was their morning's entertainment. They had no torture scheduled, no teeth to wrench, no nails to pluck from a screaming man's nail beds, so they got their fun watching me, the little cunt, scurry into the backseat next to Kolya.

The soldier drove very fast, caring not at all about the slicks of ice on the road. We sped along the banks of the frozen Neva. I had my collar upturned so I could hide my face from the wind that blasted in beneath the canvas roof. Kolya didn't seem bothered by the cold. He stared at the spire of the Church of John the Baptist across the river and said nothing.

We turned onto the Kamennoostrovsky Bridge, the old steel of its arches rimed with frost, the lamp-posts bearded with icicles. Onto Kamenny Island, slowing only a bit to circle around a bomb crater that had shattered the center of the road, pulling into a long driveway lined with the stumps of lime trees, and parking in front of a magnificent wooden mansion with a white-columned portico. Kolya studied the house.

"The Dolgorukovs lived here," he said, as we stepped out of the car. "I suppose none of you have heard of the Dolgorukovs."

"A bunch of aristocrats who got their necks snapped," said one of the soldiers, gesturing with the barrel of his rifle for us to walk toward the front door.

"Some of them," admitted Kolya. "And some of them slept with emperors."

In the daylight Kolya looked like he could have stepped out of one of the propaganda posters pasted on walls throughout the city; the angles of his face were heroic—the strong chin, the straight nose, the blond hair that fell across his forehead. He was a fine-looking deserter.

The soldiers escorted us onto the porch, where sandbags had been piled four feet high to form a machine-gun nest. Two soldiers sat near their gun, passing a cigarette between them. Kolya sniffed the air and stared longingly at the hand-rolled butt.

"Real tobacco," he said, before our armed guides pushed open the front door and herded us inside.

I had never been inside a mansion before, had only read about them in the novels: the dances on the parquet floors, the servants ladling soup from silver tureens, the stern patriarch in his book-lined study warning his weeping daughter to stay away from the lowborn boy. But while the old Dolgorukov home still looked magnificent on the outside, the revolution had come to the interior. The marble floor was tracked with a thousand muddy boot prints, unwashed for months. The smoke-stained wallpaper curled away from the baseboards. None of the original furniture had survived, none of the oil paintings and Chinese vases that must have lined the walls and rested on teak shelves.

Dozens of uniformed officers hurried from one room to the next, hustled up a curving double staircase missing its balustrade and all the balusters, probably torn down for firewood weeks ago. The uniforms were not Red Army. Kolya noticed me staring.

"NKVD. Maybe they think we're spies."

I didn't need Kolya to tell me the men were NKVD. Since I was little I had known what their uniforms looked like, with their peaked blue-and-maroon caps and their holstered Tokarevs. I had learned to dread the sight of their Packards idling outside the gates of the Kirov, the Black Ravens, waiting to carry some unlucky citizen away from his home. The NKVD arrested at least fifteen men from the building while I lived there. Sometimes those taken returned after a few weeks, their heads shaved and their faces pale and lifeless, avoiding my eyes in the stairwell as they limped up to their apartments. The broken men who came home must have known how rare and lucky they were, but they took no apparent joy in their survival. They knew what happened to my father and they could not meet my eyes.

The soldiers kept prodding us forward till we entered a sunroom at the very rear of the house, the tall French windows offering a fine vantage of the Neva and the grim, stolid apartment buildings of the Vyborg section on the far side of the river. An older man sat alone at a simple wood desk set down in the middle of the sunroom. He had a telephone receiver nestled between his face and his shoulder so he could scribble with a pen on a pad of paper as he listened.

He glanced at us as we waited at the entryway. He looked like an ex-boxer with his thick neck and crooked, flattened nose. The shadows below his hooded eyes were deep, as were the furrows that crossed his forehead. His gray hair was shaved very close to the scalp. He might have been fifty years old, but he looked like he could rise from his chair and beat us all down without mussing his uniform. Three metal stars shone on the collar tabs of his jacket. I didn't know precisely what three stars signified, but they were three stars more than anyone else in the mansion.

He tossed his pad of paper on the desk and I could see that he hadn't been taking notes, as I'd thought, but simply drawing X's, over and over again, till the entire sheet of paper was covered with them. For some reason this frightened me more than his uniform or his brawler's face. A man who drew pictures of tits or dogs seemed like a man I could understand. But a man who drew nothing but X's?

He was watching us, Kolya and me, and I knew that he was judging us, condemning us for our crimes and sentencing us to death, all while listening to a voice traveling across wires.

"Good," he said at last, "I want it done by noon. No exceptions."

He hung up the phone and smiled at us, and the smile was as incongruous on his face as the man and his plain wood desk were in the gorgeous sunroom of the old noble house. The colonel (for I assumed now that this was the colonel the soldiers had spoken of the night before) had a beautiful smile, his teeth surprisingly white, his brutal face shifting instantly from menace to welcome.

"The deserter and the looter! Come, come closer, we don't need the cuffs. I don't think these boys will cause any trouble." He gestured to the soldiers, who reluctantly pulled out their keys and removed our manacles.

"I'm not a deserter," said Kolya.

"No? Go," he ordered the soldiers, not bothering to look at them. The soldiers obeyed, leaving us alone with the colonel. He stood and walked toward us, the pistol on his waist holster slapping against his hip. Kolya stood very straight, at attention for the officer's inspection, and I, not knowing what to do, followed his lead. The colonel kept coming until his battered face nearly touched Kolya's.

"You're not a deserter and yet your unit reported you missing and you were picked up forty kilometers from where you were supposed to be."

"Well, there's a simple explanation—"

"And you," he continued, turning to me. "A German paratrooper falls on your block and you don't notify the authorities. You decide to enrich yourself at the city's expense. Is there a simple explanation for that, too?"

I needed water. My mouth was so dry it felt scaly, like the skin of a lizard, and I had begun to see bright little sparks of light swimming in the peripheries of my vision.

"Well?"

"I'm sorry," I said.

"You're sorry?" He looked at me a moment longer and laughed. "Ah, well, you're sorry, all right then, that's fine. As long as you're sorry, that's the important thing. Listen, boy, do you know how many people I've executed? I don't mean on my orders, I mean done it myself, with this Tokarev—" Here he slapped the holstered pistol. "Do you want to guess? No? Good, because I don't know. I've lost count. And I'm the kind of man who likes to know. I keep track of things. I know exactly how many women I've fucked, and it's quite a few, believe me. You're a handsome boy," he said to Kolya, "but trust me, you won't catch up with me, even if you live to a hundred, and that seems doubtful."

I glanced at Kolya, expecting him to say something stupid and get us both killed, but Kolya, for once, had nothing to say.

"Sorry is what you say to the schoolmaster when you break a piece of chalk," the colonel continued. "Sorry doesn't work for looters and deserters."

"We thought he might have a little food on him."

The colonel stared at me for a long moment.

"Did he?"

"Just some cognac. Or brandy . . . schnapps, maybe."

"We shoot a dozen people every day for forging ration cards. You know what they tell us, before we put bullets in their brains? They were hungry. Of course they were hungry! Everyone is hungry. That won't stop us from shooting thieves."

"I wasn't stealing from Russians—"

"You stole state property. Did you take anything from the body?"

I hesitated as long as I dared.

"A knife."

"Ah. The honest thief."

I knelt, unstrapped the sheath from my ankle, and handed it to the colonel. He stared at the German leather.

"You had this on you all night? No one searched you?" He exhaled with a soft curse, weary of the incompetence. "No wonder we're losing the war." He pulled out the blade and studied the inscription. "BLOOD AND HONOR. Ha. May God fuck those whoresons in the ass. You know how to use it?"

"What?"

"The knife. Slashing," he said, slashing the air with the steel blade, "is better than stabbing. Harder to block. Go for the throat, and if that's not working, go for the eyes or the belly. Thigh's good, too, big veins in the thighs." All this instruction was accompanied by vigorous demonstration. "And never stop," he said, dancing closer, the steel flashing, "never let up; keep the knife moving, keep him on the defensive."

He sheathed the blade and tossed it to me.

"Keep it. You'll need it."

I stared at Kolya, who shrugged. All of this was too strange to understand so there was no point straining the mind, trying to sort out where we stood. I got back on one knee and strapped the knife to my ankle again.

The colonel had moved to the French windows,

where he watched yesterday's snow blowing across the frozen Neva.

"Your father was the poet."

"Yes," I admitted, standing straight and staring at the back of the colonel's head. No one outside my family had mentioned my father in four years. I mean this literally. Not a word.

"He could write. What happened was ... unfortunate."

What could I say to that? I stared at my boots and knew that Kolya was squinting at me, trying to figure out which unfortunate poet sired me.

"Neither of you has eaten today," said the colonel, not asking a question. "Black tea and toast, how does that sound? Maybe we can find some fish soup somewhere. Borya!"

An aide stepped into the sunroom, a pencil tucked behind his ear.

"Get these boys some breakfast."

Borya nodded and disappeared as quickly as he'd appeared.

Fish soup. I hadn't had fish soup since summer. The idea of it was wild and exotic, like a naked girl on a Pacific island.

"Come over here," said the colonel. He opened one of the French doors and stepped into the cold. Kolya and I followed him along a gravel path that led through a frost-blasted garden, down to the banks of the river.

A girl in a fox fur coat skated on the Neva. In a normal winter you'd see hundreds of girls skating on a weekend afternoon, but this wasn't a normal winter. The ice was solid and had been for weeks, but who had the strength for figure eights? Standing on the frozen mud at the river's edge, Kolya and I stared at her the way you'd stare at a monkey riding a unicycle down the street. She was freakishly lovely, her dark hair parted in the middle and tied up in a loose bun, her wind-whipped cheeks flushed and full and healthy. It took me a few seconds to realize why she looked so strange, and then it was obvious—even at a distance you could tell that the girl was well fed. There was nothing pinched and desperate about her face. She had an athlete's casual grace; her pirouettes were tight and fast; she never got winded. Her thighs must have been magnificent—long, pale, and strong—and I could feel my prick hardening for the first time in days.

"She's getting married next Friday," said the colonel. "A piece of meat she's marrying, I say, but all right. He's a Party man, he can afford her."

"That's your daughter?" asked Kolya.

The colonel grinned, his white teeth splitting his brawler's face.

"You don't think she looks like me? No, no, she got lucky there. She got her mother's face and her father's temper—this one will conquer the world."

Only then did I realize that the colonel's teeth were false, a bridge that seemed to encompass the entire upper row. And I knew, suddenly but surely, that the man had been tortured. They had brought him in during one purge or another, called him a Trotskyite or a White or a Fascist sympathizer, pried the teeth from his mouth, and beaten him till his eyes bled, till he pissed blood and shat blood, till the order came from whatever Moscow office: we have rehabilitated the man, let him alone now, he is one of us again.

I could picture it because I had pictured it often,

whenever I wondered about my father's last days. He had the misfortune of being a Jew and a poet and mildly famous, friends once with Mayakovsky and Mandelstam, bitter enemies with Obranovich and the others he considered tongues of the bureaucracy, the slingers of revolutionary verse who labeled my father an agitator and a parasite because he wrote about the Leningrad underworld, though—officially—there was no Leningrad underworld. More than this, he had the temerity to title his book *Piter*, the city's nickname, the name every native used, but banned from all Soviet text because "Saint Petersburg" was a czar's arrogance, named for the old tyrant's patron saint.

One summer afternoon in 1937 they took my father from the offices of the literary magazine where he worked. They never gave him back. The call from the Moscow office never came for him; rehabilitation was not an option. An intelligence officer might hold future value for the state, but a decadent poet did not. He might have died in the Crosses or in Siberia or somewhere in between, we never learned. If he was buried, there is no marker; if he was burned, there is no urn.

For a long time I was angry with my father for writing such dangerous words; it seemed stupid that a book was more important than sticking around and slapping the back of my head when I picked my nose. But later I decided he hadn't chosen to insult the Party, not consciously, not the way Mandelstam had (Mandelstam with his crazy bravery, writing that Stalin had fat fingers like slugs, a mustache like two cockroaches). My father didn't know that *Piter* was dangerous until the official reviews were written. He thought he was writing a book five hundred people would read, and maybe he was right, but at least one of those five hundred denounced him and that was that.

The colonel had survived, though, and looking at him I wondered if he found it strange that he had been so close to the shark's jaws and somehow fought his way back to shore, that he who had waited for another's mercy could now decide for himself whether to grant it. He didn't seem troubled at the moment; he watched his daughter skate, he clapped his busted-knuckled hands as she spun.

"So, the wedding is Friday. Even now, even in the middle of all of this—" said the colonel, gesturing with his hands to indicate Leningrad, the famine, the war, "—she wants a real wedding, a *proper* wedding. This is good, life must continue, we're fighting barbarians but we must remain human, *Russian*. So we will have music, dancing . . . a cake."

He looked at us each in turn as if there were something momentous about the word *cake* and he needed us both to understand.

"This is the tradition, says my wife, we need a cake. It is terrible luck, a wedding with no cake. Now, I've been fighting all my life against these peasant superstitions, the priests used them to keep people stupid and afraid, but my wife . . . she wants the cake. Fine, fine, make the cake. For months she's been hoarding her sugar, her honey, flour, all the rest."

I thought about this, the sacks of sugar, the jars of honey, the flour that must have been real flour, not moldy salvage from a torpedoed barge. Half the Kirov could probably survive two weeks on her batter alone.

"She has everything she needs, all except the

eggs." Again the portentous look. "Eggs," said the colonel, "are hard to find."

For several seconds we all stood silently, watching the colonel's daughter twirl.

"The fleet might have some," said Kolya.

"No. They don't."

"They have tinned beef. I traded a pack of playing cards for some tinned beef from one of the sailors—"

"They don't have eggs."

I don't think I'm stupid, but it was taking me a very long time to understand what the colonel was asking, and a longer time to fire up my courage to ask him.

"You want us to find eggs?"

"A dozen," he said. "She only needs ten, but I figure, one might break, a couple might be rotten." He saw our confusion and he smiled his wonderful smile, gripping our shoulders hard enough to make me stand straighter. "My men say there are no eggs in Leningrad, but I believe there is everything in Leningrad, even now, and I just need the right fellows to find it. A pair of thieves."

"We're not thieves," said Kolya, very righteous, staring into the colonel's eyes. I wanted to punch him. By all rights we should have been dead and frozen, piled onto a sledge with the rest of the day's corpses. We had our reprieve. Our lives had been returned in exchange for a simple task. A strange task, perhaps, but simple enough. And now he was going to ruin it—he was asking for his bullet, which was bad, but he was asking for my bullet, too, which was far worse.

"You're not thieves? You abandoned your unit—no, no, shut up, don't say anything. You abandoned

your unit and the moment you did that you for-
feited your rights as a soldier in the Red Army—
your right to carry your rifle, to wear that coat, those
boots. You're a thief. And you, Big Nose, you looted
a corpse. It was a German corpse so it doesn't per-
sonally offend me, but looting is theft. Let's not play
games. You're both thieves. Bad thieves, that's true,
incompetent thieves, absolutely, but you're in luck.
The good thieves haven't been caught."

He turned and walked back toward the house.
Kolya and I lingered, watching the colonel's daughter, her fox fur flashing in the sun. She must have
seen us by now, but she never acknowledged us,
never glanced our way. We were two of her father's
lackeys and therefore entirely boring. We watched
her as long as we could, trying to etch the image
into our brains for future masturbation, until the
colonel barked at us and we hurried after him.

"You have your ration cards?" he asked, taking
long strides, his respite finished, ready again for the
long day's work. "Hand them over."

I kept mine pinned to the inside pocket of my
coat. I unpinned it and saw Kolya pull his from his
folded sock. The colonel took them from us.

"You bring me the eggs by sunrise Thursday,
you get them back. You don't, well, you've got all of
January to eat snow, and there won't be any cards
waiting for you in February, either. That's assuming
one of my men doesn't find you and kill you before
then, and my men are very good at that."

"They just can't find eggs," said Kolya.

The colonel smiled. "I like you, boy. You won't
live a long life, but I like you."

We stepped inside the sunroom. The colonel sat
down at his desk and stared at the black telephone.

He raised his eyebrows, remembering something, opened the desk drawer, and pulled out a folded letter. He held it out for Kolya.

"That's a curfew waiver for the two of you. Anyone gives you trouble, show them that, you'll be on your way. And here, this, too. . . ."

He pulled four 100-ruble notes from his wallet and gave them to Kolya, who glanced at the letter and the rubles and slipped them into his pocket.

"That would have bought me a thousand eggs in June," said the colonel.

"And it will again next June," said Kolya. "Fritz won't last the winter."

"With soldiers like you," said the colonel, "we'll be paying for eggs with deutsche marks soon."

Kolya opened his mouth to defend himself, but the colonel shook his head.

"You understand this is a gift? You bring me a dozen eggs by Thursday, I give you your lives back. You understand the rareness of this gift?"

"What day is today?"

"Today is Saturday. You deserted your unit on a Friday. When the sun rises tomorrow it is Sunday. Can you keep track from this point forward? Yes? Good."

Borya returned with four slices of toast on a blue plate. The toast had been slathered with something oily, lard maybe, glistening and fatty and luscious. Another aide stepped into the sunroom behind him, carrying two cups of steaming tea. I waited for a third aide carrying bowls of fish soup, but he never came.

"Eat quick, boys," said the colonel. "You've got a lot of walking to do."

ig Nose. I like that. Who was your father, Big
Nose?"

"You wouldn't know him."

"If he was a published poet, I know him."

"Just leave it alone."

"You're a moody one, aren't you?"

We were crossing the Kamennoostrovsky Bridge
again, this time on foot. Kolya stopped at the mid-
point, gloved hands on the balustrade, looking
down the river toward the Dolgorukov mansion.
The colonel's daughter no longer skated her figures,
but Kolya watched for a moment anyway, hoping
for an encore.

"She smiled at me," he said.

"She didn't smile at you. What are you talking
about? She didn't even look at us."

"Perhaps you're jealous, my friend, but she definitely gave me a smile. I think I've seen her before,
at the university. I have a reputation."

"As a deserter?"

Kolya turned away from the balustrade and
glared at me. "I'll knock your teeth out if you call
me a deserter again."

"I'll shove my knife in your eye if you try it."

Kolya considered this and turned back to his river view.

"I'd get to you before you could pull the knife. I'm very quick when I need to be."

I thought about pulling the knife now, just to prove him wrong, but he didn't seem angry anymore and I wanted to keep moving.

We crossed the bridge, back to the mainland, and headed south on Pesochnaya, the river to our right, the rusted rails of the Finland line to the left. No trains had run since September, when the Germans encircled the city and cut the tracks of every line—Finland, Moscow, Vitebsk, Warsaw, Baltic—all severed and useless. The city's only connection now with the rest of Russia was by air, and few planes could make it through the Luftwaffe patrols.

"We could run for it, of course. Tough without ration cards, though." He considered the problem. "The NKVD boys don't worry me much. In the army they say the police can't find pussy in a whorehouse. But not having ration cards . . . tricky."

"We have to find the eggs," I told him. We were walking in the sunlight and breathing the air because of the colonel's command; if the payment for this reprieve was a dozen eggs, we would find a dozen fucking eggs. There was no room for negotiation or maneuvering.

"Finding the eggs is the best outcome, I agree. Doesn't mean I can't consider my options. Maybe there are no eggs in the city. Then what? You still have family in Piter?"

"No."

"Me neither. That's one good thing. Only have to worry about our own skins."

Signs were posted on the walls of fire-gutted

warehouses: HAVE YOU SIGNED UP YET FOR THE PEO-
PLE'S VOLUNTEERS? There were no residential buildings in this area and the street was empty, no one
else walking beneath the colorless sky. We could
have been the last two survivors of the war, the last
two defenders of the city, with only my stolen knife
and Kolya's purportedly quick fists to fight off the
Fascists.

"The Haymarket's our best chance," said Kolya.
"I was there a few months ago. They still had butter
and cheese, a little caviar, maybe."

"So how come the colonel's men couldn't find
any eggs?"

"It's the black market. Half that stuff is stolen.
You've got people trading their ration cards, all
sorts of lawbreaking. They're not going to sell to
anyone in a uniform. Especially not an NKVD
uniform."

It seemed like a reasonable argument. Kolya
whistled some tuneless song of his own invention
and we walked south toward the Haymarket.
Things were looking up. Execution was not imminent. I had more food in my stomach than I'd had
for weeks, and the strong black tea provided an extra spark. My legs felt strong enough to propel me
wherever I needed to go. Someone, somewhere,
had a dozen eggs, and we'd find them eventually.
In the meantime I enjoyed a vivid fantasy of the colonel's daughter skating naked on the Neva, her pale
ass shining in the sun.

Kolya slapped my back and gave me a lewd
grin, as if he had stared right through my glass
skull.

"Remarkable girl, wasn't she? You'd like to take
a shot at that?"

I said nothing, but Kolya seemed long practiced at carrying on one-sided conversations.

"The secret to winning a woman is calculated neglect."

"What?"

"Ushakovo. It's a line from *The Courtyard Hound*. Oh wait, you never read *The Courtyard Hound*." Kolya sighed, weary of my great ignorance. "Your father was a member of the literati and he left you illiterate. A little sad."

"Why don't you shut up about my father?"

"Radchenko, the protagonist, is a great lover. People come from all over Moscow to get his advice on wooing. He never leaves his bed, he just lies there, drinking tea—"

"Like Oblomov."

"Nothing like Oblomov! Why does everyone always say, 'Like Oblomov'?"

"Because it sounds exactly like Oblomov."

Kolya stopped walking and looked down at me. He was taller by a head and twice as broad in the shoulders, and he loomed over me now, threatening with his eyes.

"Every university fool knows Goncharov wasn't half the writer Ushakovo was. Oblomov is nothing. Oblomov is a morality lesson for the bourgeoisie, a little trifle you make your kids read so they don't grow up lazy. Now, Radchenko—Radchenko is one of the great heroes of the language. Him and Raskolnikov and Bezukhov and, I don't know, Chichikov, maybe."

"You're spitting on me."

"Well, you deserve to be spat on."

I continued walking south and Kolya, irritated as he was, soon fell into stride. Fate had shoved us together, that seemed beyond argument. Until Thursday, we were married.

Across the snow-dusted ice of the Neva the golden angel still sat atop the gilded spire of the Peter and Paul Cathedral even though people said the Wehrmacht had promised an Iron Cross to the artilleryman who knocked it down. Kolya gestured toward the Petrograd Side with his chin.

"I was stationed at the fortress when the zoo was bombed."

"I heard there were baboons running around the city, and a Siberian tiger—"

"That's a fairy tale," he said. "None of them got out."

"Maybe a few did. How do you know?"

"None of them got out. If you want to tell yourself something sweet to help you sleep, go ahead, but it's a lie." He spat on the ground. "Fritz burned the whole place to the ground. Betty the elephant . . . I loved that elephant. I'd go look at her all the time when I was a kid. The way she washed, sucking up water in her trunk and showering herself . . . She was graceful. You wouldn't think so, she was so damned big, but she was."

"She died?"

"What did I just tell you? They all died. Took Betty hours, though. The way she moaned . . . I was on guard duty and all I wanted to do was run over and shoot her in the heart. Just end it. You never want to hear an elephant dying."

It was a long walk to the Haymarket, six kilometers maybe, over the Liteiny Bridge, past the Summer Gardens where the elms and the oaks had been hacked down with hatchets, past the Church on Spilled Blood, with its glazed tile facade and soaring onion domes, built on the spot where Hrynie-wiecki splattered himself and the emperor. The farther south we walked, the more crowded the streets; everyone bundled in three layers, leaning into the wind as they walked, their faces pinched and wasted and pallid from lack of iron. On Nevsky Prospekt all the shops had been closed for months. We saw two women in their sixties walking very close together, their shoulders touching, eyes on the sidewalk looking for the patch of ice that could kill them. A man with a glorious walrus mustache carried a white bucket filled with black nails. A boy, no more than twelve, tugged a sled with a length of rope. A small body wrapped in blankets lay on the sled, a bloodless bare foot dragging along the hard-packed snow. Dragon's teeth studded the street, re-inforced concrete blocks arrayed in rows to hinder the movement of enemy tanks. A printed sign on the wall read WARNING! THIS SIDE OF THE STREET IS THE MOST DANGEROUS DURING THE BOMBING.

Nevsky before the war was the heart of the city, built to rival the grand promenades of London and Paris, sidewalk kiosks hawking cherry blossoms and chocolates, the aproned old men behind the counter in Eliseyev's slicing smoked sturgeon and sable, the clock tower of city hall rising above all the clamor, letting everyone know how late they were for whatever came next. Black Packards would whip past, horns blaring, carrying Party members from one meeting to another. Even if you had no money to buy anything and nowhere important to go, Nevsky was always a good place to walk. In June the sun didn't set till midnight and nobody wanted to waste the light. You could watch the pret-tiest girls in Piter staring through the bright windows of the fancy shops, their eyes appraising the newest dresses for sale, studying the cut so they could make the dress at home if they managed to snatch enough material from work. Even if you never said anything to these girls, even if you always watched from a distance—

"You're a virgin, aren't you," said Kolya, interrupting my thoughts with such eerie timing it startled me.

"Me?" I asked, stupidly. "What are you talking about?"

"I'm talking about the fact that you've never had sex."

Sometimes you know there's no point in lying; the game is over before it's begun.

"What do you care?"

"Listen, Lev, what if we try to be friends? What do you think about that? We're going to be together until we find these eggs, we might as well get along, right? Now, you seem like an interesting boy, a bit ornery, a bit moody in the Jewish way, but I like you. And if you weren't so fucking resistant all the time, I could probably teach you something."

"About girls?"

"About girls, yes. About literature. About chess."

"What are you, nineteen? How come you always talk like you're such an expert at everything?"

"I'm twenty. And I'm not an expert at everything. Just girls, literature, and chess."

"That's all."

"Mm. And dancing. I'm an excellent dancer."

"What do you want to bet on a game of chess?"

Kolya glanced at me and smiled. He exhaled, his breath rising in vapor above his head.

"I'll take that German knife of yours."

"And what do I get?"

"You won't get anything. You're not going to win."

"But let's say I do."

"I've got maybe another hundred grams of that sausage—"

"Hundred grams of sausage for a German pilot's knife? I don't think so."

"I have some pictures. . . ."

"What kind of pictures."

"Pictures of girls. French girls. You'd learn things you need to learn."

Pictures of French girls seemed like a prize worth playing for. I wasn't worried about losing the knife. There were plenty of people in Piter who could beat me at chess, but I knew all their names. My father had been city champion when he was still in university; he used to take me with him on Thursdays and Sundays to the Spartak Chess Club at the Palace of the Pioneers. When I was six, the club coach declared me a talent. For several years I was one of the top-ranked young players, winning little ribbons and medals at tournaments throughout Leningrad Oblast. This made my father proud, though he was too much of a bohemian to admit to caring about competitions and he never let me display my prizes in our apartment.

When I was fourteen, I quit the club. I had learned that I was a good player but would never be a great one. Friends of mine at Spartak, whom I had beaten consistently when we were younger, had left me far behind, advancing to a plane I could not access no matter how many games I played, how many books I read, how many endgame problems I worked on in bed at night. I was like a well-trained pianist who knows which notes to hit but can't make the music his own. A brilliant player understands the game in a way he can never quite articulate; he analyzes the board and knows how to improve his position before his brain can devise an explanation for the move. I didn't have the instincts. Quitting the club disappointed my father, but I wasn't sad about it. Chess became far more fun once I no longer had to worry about my citywide ranking.

Kolya stopped at the Kvissisana Café and stared through a plate glass window covered with taped crosses. The restaurant inside was empty, all the tables removed, nothing but a linoleum floor and a chalkboard on the wall still marked with August's specials.

"I took a girl here once. Best lamb cutlets in the city."

"And then you took her home and made love to her?" I said, deeply sarcastic but immediately fearing that he had done exactly that.

"No," said Kolya, checking his reflection in the window and brushing some stray blond hair back under his black fur cap. "We made love before dinner. After dinner we had a drink at the Europa. She was mad for me, but I liked a friend of hers better."

"So why didn't you take the friend to dinner?"

Kolya smiled, a superior's kind smile for his simple subordinate.

"Calculated neglect. You need an education."

We kept walking down Nevsky. It was one in the afternoon, but the winter sun was already drifting low in the western sky, our shadows elongating in front of us.

"So let's start slow," he said, "let's start with basics. Is there a girl you like?"

"No one special."

"Who said she needs to be special? You're a virgin, you need warm thighs and a heartbeat, not Tamara Karsavina."

"There's a girl named Vera who lives in my building. But she likes someone else."

"Fine. Step one, let's not worry about someone else. Let's worry about Vera. What's special about her? Why do you like her?"

"I don't know. She lives in my building."

"That's something. Anything else?"

"She plays the cello."

"Beautiful instrument. What color eyes does she have?"

"I don't know."

"You don't like the girl. You don't know what color eyes she has, you don't like her."

"I do like her, but all she cares about is Grisha Antokolsky, so what's the point?"

"Fine," said Kolya, very patient with his dull charge, "you think you like her because she doesn't like you. It's very understandable, but I'm telling you, you don't like her. Let's forget about Vera."

Forgetting about Vera didn't seem hard to do. I had spent the last three years trying to imagine what she looked like naked, but only because she lived two floors below me and once, at the youth center swimming pool, I had seen her nipples when her swimsuit straps slipped off. If it weren't for Vera's panicked tumble by the Kirov's gate, I wouldn't have been wandering the streets of Piter with a lunatic deserter, looking for eggs. She never looked back when the soldiers grabbed me. She was probably grubbing with Grisha in one of the Kirov's dark corridors while I was locked up in the Crosses.

"The colonel's daughter was pretty. I like her."

Kolya glanced at me, amused.

"Yes, the colonel's daughter is pretty. I like your optimism. But that one's not for you."

"She's not for you, either."

"You might be wrong about that. If you saw the look she gave me."

We walked past a group of young boys with stepladders and pails of whitewash who were busy painting over street signs and building numbers. Kolya stopped and stared at them.

"Hey!" he shouted at the closest boy, who wore so many layers of wool you would have thought he was fat, unless you saw the drawn skin of his face, his eyes shining and black above shadows as deep as an old man's. Very few children this young were left in the city; most had been evacuated back in September. The ones who remained tended to be very poor, many of them war orphans with no family in the east.

"What the devil are you doing?" asked Kolya. He turned to me, stunned by this disrespect. "Little bastards are vandalizing the Prospekt. Hey! Boy!"

"Suck my cock and make a wish," said the black-eyed boy, whiting out the number on the door of a watch repair shop.

Even Kolya seemed taken aback by this directive. He walked over to the boy, took him by the shoulders, and turned him around.

"You're talking to a soldier of the Red Army, boy—"

"Kolya," I started.

"You think this is the time for pranks? You and your little Gypsy friends want to run around—"

"You better take your hands off me," said the boy.

"Now you're threatening me? I've been shooting at Germans the last four months and now you want to threaten me?"

"Kolya," I repeated, louder this time. "They're on orders. If Fritz gets inside the city, he won't know where he's going."

Kolya looked from the black-eyed boy to the whitewashed street signs and over to me.

"How do you know that?"

"Because I was doing it two days ago."

Kolya released the boy, who glared up at him a moment longer before resuming his work.

"Well, it's damn clever," said Kolya, and we kept on toward Haymarket.

5

If you had something you wanted to buy, sell, or barter, you went to the Haymarket. Before the war the street stalls were considered the poor man's Nevsky Prospekt. After the blockade began, when the fancy shops closed one by one, when the restaurants chained shut their doors and the butchers had no more meat in their lockers, the Haymarket thrived. Generals' wives traded their amber necklaces for sacks of wheat flour. Party members haggled with peasants who had snuck in from the countryside, arguing over how many potatoes a set of antique silverware should purchase. If the negotiations lasted too long, the peasants would wave their hands dismissively and turn away from the city folk. "So eat your silverware," they would say with a shrug. They almost always got their asking price.

We walked from stall to stall, eyeing the stacks of leather boots, some still bloody from the feet of the previous owners. Tokarev rifles and pistols were cheap, easily bought with a few rubles or two hundred grams of bread. Lugers and grenades were more expensive, but available if you asked the right person. One stall sold glasses of dirt for one hundred rubles each—Badayev Mud, they called it, taken from the ground under the bombed food warehouse and packed with melted sugar.

Kolya stopped at a stall where a gaunt, stooped man with an eyepatch and an unlit pipe in his mouth sold unlabeled bottles of clear liquor.

"What's this?" asked Kolya.

"Vodka."

"Vodka? Made from what?"

"Wood."

"That's not vodka, friend. That's wood alcohol."

"You want it or not?"

"This isn't what we're here for," I told Kolya, who ignored me.

"Stuff makes a man blind," he said to the stall keeper.

The one-eyed man shook his head, bored with the ignorance but willing to exert some minimal effort to make a sale.

"You pour it through linen," he said. "Seven layers. After that, it's safe."

"Sounds like an elixir for the gods," said Kolya. "You should call it Seven-Layer Sin. That's a good name for a drink."

"You want it?"

"I'll take a bottle if you drink some with me."

"It's too early for me."

Kolya shrugged. "I see you take a nip, I'll buy the bottle. Otherwise, what can I tell you, the war's made me a cynic."

"Two hundred rubles a bottle."

"One hundred. Let's drink."

"What are you doing?" I asked him, but he didn't even glance at me.

The one-eyed man placed his cold pipe on the

table, found a tea glass, and searched around his stall for a bit of cloth.

"Here," said Kolya, handing over a white handkerchief. "It's clean. Relatively."

We watched the man fold the handkerchief three times and drape it over the mouth of the tea glass. He poured the liquor slowly. Even outdoors, with the wind gusting, the stuff smelled like poison, like a cleaning agent used on a factory floor. The one-eyed man set aside the handkerchief, which was now flecked with a soapy residue. He lifted the glass, sipped it, and set it back down on the table, his expression never changing.

Kolya inspected the level of the liquid in the cup, making sure the vendor had truly taken a sip. Satisfied, he picked up the glass and saluted us.

"For Mother Russia!" He downed the wood alcohol with a gulp, slammed the glass down on the table, wiped his mouth with the back of his hand, and gagged. He grabbed my shoulder, trying to support himself, his eyes wide open and tearing.

"You murdered me," he said, barely able to get the words out of his throat, pointing an accusing finger at the one-eyed man.

"I didn't tell you to drink it fast," he replied, unimpressed, putting the pipe back in his mouth. "One hundred rubles."

"Lev . . . Lev, are you there?" Kolya's face was turned toward mine, but his eyes were unfocused, looking straight through me.

"Very funny."

Kolya grinned and stood straight. "Can't trick a Jew, I should have known. Very good, pay the man."

"What?"

"Go ahead," he said, gesturing to the waiting vendor. "Give the man his money."

"I don't have any money."

"Don't try to cheat me, boy!" roared Kolya, grabbing the collar of my greatcoat and shaking me till I felt my bones rattling. "I am a soldier of the Red Army and I won't stand for any thievery!"

Abruptly he released me, shoving his hands into my coat pockets, pulling out scraps of paper, a bit of string and lint, nothing close to money. Kolya sighed and turned to the vendor.

"Apparently we have no money. I'm afraid I'll have to cancel the transaction."

"You think because you're a soldier," said the one-eyed man, opening his coat to show us the hilt of a Finnish dagger, "I won't carve you up?"

"I've got a glass of poison in my belly already. So why don't you try?"

Kolya smiled at the man and waited for a response. There was nothing behind Kolya's blue eyes, neither fear nor anger nor excitement about the prospect of a fight—nothing. This, I came to learn, was his gift: danger made him calm. Around him people would deal with their terror in the usual ways: stoicism, hysteria, false joviality, or some combination of the three. But Kolya, I think, never completely believed in any of it. Everything about the war was ridiculous: the Germans' barbarity, the Party's propaganda, the crossfire of incendiary bullets that lit the nighttime sky. It all seemed to him like someone else's story, an amazingly detailed story that he had stumbled into and now could not escape.

"Move on or I'll cut your lips off," said the one-eyed man, chewing the stem of his unlit pipe, hand on the hilt of his dagger. Kolya saluted and marched off to the next stall, relaxed and unworried as if the entire transaction had been clean and easy. I followed behind, heart thumping within my rib cage.

"Let's just find the eggs," I said. "Why do you have to go around provoking people?"

"I needed a sniff, I took a sniff, now I feel alive again." He took a deep breath and exhaled through pursed lips, watching the condensation rise into the air. "We both should have died last night. Do you understand that? Do you understand how lucky we are? So enjoy it."

I stopped at a stall where an old peasant woman wearing a headscarf sold patties of pale gray meat. Kolya and I stared at the meat. It looked fairly fresh, glistening with fat, but neither of us wanted to know what sort of animal it had been.

"Do you have any eggs?" I asked the old woman.

"Eggs?" she asked, leaning forward to hear. "Not since September."

"We need a dozen," said Kolya. "We can pay good money."

"You can pay a million rubles," she said, "there are no eggs. Not in Piter."

"Where?"

She shrugged, the lines creasing her face so deep they seemed carved. "I have meat. You want meat, it's three hundred for two patties. No eggs."

We went from stall to stall, asking everyone if they had eggs, but no one in the Haymarket had seen any since September. A few people had theories on where they could be found: high-ranking army officers had them flown in from Moscow;

farmers outside the city gave them to the Germans, along with butter and fresh milk, in exchange for their lives; an old man who lived near the Narva Gate kept chickens in a rooftop coop. This last rumor seemed obviously absurd, but the boy who told us insisted it was true.

"You kill a chicken, maybe it will last you a week. But you keep it alive, well, an egg a day, along with your rations, that will get you by till summer."

"You have to feed a chicken," said Kolya. "Who's got food for a chicken?"

The boy, his black curly hair spilling out from beneath an old Imperial Navy cap, shook his head as if it were a silly question.

"Chickens eat anything. A spoonful of sawdust, that's all they need."

The boy sold what people called library candy, made from tearing the covers off of books, peeling off the binding glue, boiling it down, and reforming it into bars you could wrap in paper. The stuff tasted like wax, but there was protein in the glue, protein kept you alive, and the city's books were disappearing like the pigeons.

"And you've seen these chickens?" asked Kolya.

"My brother has. The old man sleeps in the coop at night with a shotgun. Everyone in the building wants those chickens."

Kolya glanced at me and I shook my head. We all heard ten different siege myths a day, stories of secret meat lockers stocked with chilled haunches of beef, of larders crammed with caviar tins and veal sausages. It was always someone's brother or cousin who had seen the treasure. People believed in the stories because it matched their conviction that some-one, somewhere, was feasting while the rest of the city starved. And they were right, of course—the col-onel's daughter might not be eating roasted goose for dinner, but she was eating dinner.

"The old man can't stay in the coop all the time," I told the boy. "He has to get his rations. He has to get water and use the toilet. Someone would have grabbed the chickens months ago."

"He pisses off the roof. When it's coming out the other side, I don't know, maybe that's what he feeds the chickens."

Kolya nodded, impressed by the old man's clever means of keeping the birds alive, though I was convinced the kid was making this up as his lips moved.

"When was the last time you had a shit?" Kolya asked me, abruptly.

"I don't know. A week ago?"

"It's been nine days for me. I've been counting. Nine days! When it finally happens, I'll have a big party and invite the best-looking girls from the university."

"Invite the colonel's daughter."

"I will, absolutely. My shit party will be much better than this wedding she's planning."

"The new ration bread hurts coming out," said the curly-haired boy. "My father says it's all the cel-lulose they're putting in."

"Where do we find the old man with the chickens?"

"I don't know the address. If you walk toward Stachek Prospekt from the Narva Gate, you'll pass his building. There's a big poster of Zhdanov on the wall."

"There's a poster of Zhdanov on half the buildings in Piter," I said, getting a little irritated. "We're going to walk another three kilometers to find a bunch of chickens that don't exist?"

"The boy's not lying," said Kolya, patting the kid on his shoulder. "If he is, we'll come back here and break his fingers. He knows we're NKVD."

"You're not NKVD," said the boy.

Kolya pulled the colonel's letter from his coat pocket and slapped the boy's cheek with it.

"This is a letter from an NKVD colonel authorizing us to find eggs. What do you think about that?"

"You got another one from Stalin, authorizing you to wipe your ass?"

"He'll have to authorize me to shit first."

I didn't stay long enough to learn how the conversation ended. If Kolya wanted to tramp all over the city looking for the fabled chickens, that was his business, but nightfall was coming and I wanted to go home. I hadn't slept in thirty-some hours. I turned and walked toward the Kirov, trying to remember how much bread I had stashed under the loose tile in the kitchen. Maybe Vera had something for me. She owed me after the way she ran, never looking back even though I'd rescued her. It occurred to me that Vera and the others must have thought I was dead. I wondered how she had reacted, whether she had cried, hiding her face in Grisha's chest as he comforted her, or maybe pushing him away, angry, because Grisha had fled, abandoned her, while I stayed behind and saved her from certain execution. And Grisha would say, "I know, I know, I'm a coward, forgive me," and she would forgive him, because Vera forgave Grisha everything, and he would wipe away her tears, and tell her they would never forget me, my sacrifice. But of course they would—within a year they wouldn't be able to picture my face anymore.

"You there. You the one looking for eggs?"

Obsessed with my pitiful fantasy, it took me a moment to realize the question was meant for me. I turned and saw a bearded giant staring back at me, arms folded across his chest, rocking back and forth on his boot heels. He was the biggest man I'd ever seen, far taller than Kolya and broader in the chest. His bare hands looked big enough to crack my skull like a walnut shell. His beard was thick and black and shined as if oiled. I wondered how much food a man that big needed to eat every day, how he could possibly keep the meat on his titanic frame.

"You have eggs?" I asked, blinking up at him.

"What do you have for me?"

"Money. We have money. Wait, let me get my friend."

I ran back through the Haymarket. For the first time since I'd met him, I was happy to see Kolya's blond head. He was still joking with the curly-haired boy, probably describing his dream of a glorious shit.

"Hello, there he is!" he shouted when he saw me. "I thought you'd run off without me."

"There's a man who says he has eggs."

"Excellent!" Kolya turned to the boy. "Son, it has been a great pleasure."

We walked back the way I'd come, passing the stalls now shutting for the night. Kolya handed me a wrapped library candy.

"Here you are, my friend. Tonight we feast."

"The kid gave it to you?"

"Gave it to me? He sold it to me."

"How much?"

"One hundred for two."

"One hundred!" I glared up at Kolya as he unwrapped his bar and took a bite, grimacing at the flavor. "So we have three hundred left?"

"Correct. Impressive arithmetic."

"That money is for the eggs."

"Well, we can't go egg hunting without a little something to keep us going."

The bearded man waited for us at the edge of the Haymarket, arms still folded. He appraised Kolya as we came nearer, sizing him up the way a boxer takes the measure of his opponent.

"It's just the two of you?"

"How many of us do you need?" asked Kolya in return, smiling at the giant. "I hear you sell eggs."

"I sell everything. What do you have for me?"

"We have money," I said, fairly sure we had already gone over this.

"How much?"

"Enough," said Kolya. "We need a dozen eggs."

The bearded man whistled. "You're in luck. That's all I have."

"You see that?" said Kolya, gripping my shoulder. "This wasn't so hard."

"Follow me," said the giant, crossing the street.

"Where are we going?" I asked as we followed.

"I keep everything inside. It isn't safe out here. Soldiers come down every few days, steal everything they want, anyone says anything, they shoot him."

"Well, the soldiers are out there defending the city," said Kolya. "They can't fight if they're starving."

The giant glanced at Kolya's army coat, his regulation boots.

"Why aren't you defending the city?"

"I'm on a mission for a certain colonel. Nothing you need to worry about."

"This colonel sent you and the boy on a mission for some eggs, is that it?" The giant grinned down at us. His teeth gleamed like unmarked dice within his black beard. He didn't believe Kolya, of course. Who would?

We walked alongside the frozen Fontanka Canal, the ice littered with abandoned corpses, some covered with shrouds weighted down with stones, others stripped for their warm clothes, their white faces staring up at the darkening sky. The wind was beginning to wake for the night and I watched a dead woman's long blond hair blow across her face. She had taken pride in that hair once, washed it twice a week, brushed it out for twenty minutes before going to bed. Now it was trying to protect her, to shield her decay from the eyes of strangers.

The giant led us to a five-story brick building, all the windows boarded over with plywood. A massive poster, two stories high, portrayed a young mother carrying her dead child from a burning building. DEATH TO THE BABY KILLERS! read the text. After fishing in his coat pocket for his key, the giant unlocked the front door and held it open for us. I grabbed Kolya's sleeve before he could enter.

"Why don't you bring the eggs down here?" I asked the giant.

"I'm still alive because I know how to run my business. And I don't do business on the street."

I could feel my scrotum tightening, my timid

balls creeping closer to my body. But I was born and raised in Piter, I wasn't a fool, and I tried to keep my voice steady as I spoke.

"I don't do business in strangers' apartments."

"Gentlemen, gentlemen," said Kolya, smiling broadly. "No need for all the suspicion. A dozen eggs. Name your price."

"A thousand."

"A thousand rubles? For a dozen eggs?" I laughed. "Are they Fabergé?"

The black-bearded giant, still holding the door open, glowered down at me. I stopped laughing.

"They're selling glasses of dirt back there for a hundred rubles," he told me. "Which is better, an egg or a glass of dirt?"

"Listen," said Kolya, "you can stand here all day haggling with my little Jewish friend, or we can talk like honest men. We have three hundred. That's all we have. Is it a deal?"

The giant continued to stare at me. He hadn't liked me from the start; now that he knew I was a Jew I could tell he wanted to peel the skin from my face. He held out his massive palm to Kolya, beckoning for the cash.

"Ah, no, at this point I must side with my companion," Kolya said, shaking his head. "First the eggs, then the money."

"I'm not bringing them out here. Everyone's starving and everyone's got a gun."

"You're an awfully big man to be so afraid," teased Kolya.

The giant eyed Kolya with something like curiosity, as if he couldn't quite believe he was hearing the insult. Finally, he smiled, flashing those dice-white teeth.

"There's a man facedown out there," he said, gesturing with his chin to the Fontanka Canal. "Wasn't hunger that got him, wasn't the cold. His skull got smashed in with a brick. You want to ask me how I know?"

"I take your point," said Kolya, quite agreeable. He peered into the darkness of the building's vestibule. "Well, for what it's worth, a brick is quicker."

Kolya patted me on the back and stepped inside.

Everything I knew told me to run. This man was leading us into a trap. He had practically just confessed to being a murderer. Kolya had stupidly admitted exactly how much money we had on us. It wasn't much, but three hundred rubles and two ration cards—which the giant must have assumed we still had—were easily enough to get killed over these days.

But what was the other choice? Head down to the Narva Gate and find some fabled old man and his chicken coop? We were risking our lives walking into the building, but if we didn't find the eggs soon, we were dead anyway.

I followed Kolya. The front door closed behind us. It was gloomy inside, with no electricity for the bulbs and only the last of the daylight peeking in through gaps in the plywood covering the windows. I heard the giant moving behind me and I dropped to one knee, ready to unsheathe my knife. He passed by me and climbed the stairs, two at a time. Kolya and I glanced at each other. When Blackbeard was out of sight, I pulled out the German knife and slipped it into my coat pocket. Kolya raised his eyebrows, possibly impressed by the act, possibly mocking me. We headed up the stairs, taking them one by one but still panting by the time we reached the second floor.

"Where do you get the eggs?" asked Kolya, calling out to the giant who was already a flight above us. The big man was untroubled by the climb. He and the colonel's daughter were the two fittest people I'd seen in Piter in months. I wondered again where he got his energy.

"There's a peasant I know, he works on a farm near Mga."

"I thought the Germans took Mga."

"They did. The Germans like their eggs, too. They come every day and grab all they can find, but my friend hides a few. Can't hide too many or they'll figure it out."

The giant stopped on the fourth floor and rapped on an apartment door.

"Who is it?"

"It's me," he said. "With a couple of customers."

We heard a deadbolt slide back and the door opened. A woman wearing a man's fur hat and a bloodied butcher's apron blinked at Kolya and me, wiping her nose with the back of her gloved hand.

"What I was wondering," said Kolya, "is how you keep the eggs from freezing. Because frozen eggs won't do us much good, I'm afraid."

The woman stared at Kolya as if he were speaking Japanese.

"We keep them by the samovar," said the giant. "Come on, let's get it over with."

He gestured for us to enter the apartment. The silent woman stepped to the side to let us pass and Kolya walked right in, not a care in the world, looking around with a smile as if he'd just been invited into a new girlfriend's place. I waited by the door until the giant put his hand on my shoulder. He didn't shove me, exactly, but with a hand that big the effect was the same.

Wick lamps lit the small apartment and our long shadows crept across the walls, across the frayed rugs on the floor, the brass samovar in the corner, and a white sheet hanging on the far side of the room—partitioning off a sleeping area, I assumed. When the giant closed the door, the sheet billowed like a woman's dress in the wind. In the moment before it settled down I saw what lay behind it—not a bed, no furniture at all, just slabs of white meat hanging from hooks, suspended from a heating pipe by heavy chains, with plastic sheeting on the floor to collect the drippings. Maybe for half a second I thought it was pig, maybe my brain tried to convince my eyes that they weren't looking at what they were looking at: a flayed thigh that could only be a woman's thigh, a child's rib cage, a severed arm with the hand's ring finger missing.

The knife was in my hand before I realized I wanted it—something moved behind me and I wheeled and slashed, crying out, unable to form any words, throat constricted. The giant had pulled a foot-long section of steel pipe from his coat; he danced away from me, far quicker than a man that big should be, easily dodging the German steel.

The giant's wife drew a cleaver from her apron pouch. She was quick, too, but Kolya turned out to be quickest of all, pivoting on his back foot and hitting the woman with a right cross to the jaw. She crumpled to the floor.

"Run," said Kolya.

I ran. I thought the door would be locked, but it wasn't; I thought the giant's pipe would crush

my skull, but it didn't; and I was out in the hallway, hurtling down the staircase, jumping nearly
the entire flight to the landing below. I heard a
great shout of pure unworded fury and the thud of
the giant's hobnailed boots on the floorboards as
he charged across the room. I stopped there with
my hand on the banister, unable to catch my breath,
unwilling to run farther away, unable to climb the
dark stairs back to the cannibals' apartment. I
heard the terrible sound of steel slamming into
skull or plywood.

I was betraying Kolya, deserting him when he
was weaponless and I had a good knife. I tried to
will my feet to move, to carry me back to the battle,
but I was shaking so hard I couldn't keep my knife
hand steady. More shouts, more thuds of pipe on
what? Plaster flakes fell from the ceiling above me.
I cowered on the stairs, certain that Kolya was gone,
certain I could not run fast enough to escape the
giant—his wife would carve me with a few expert
chops of that heavy cleaver, and soon the parts of
me would be hanging from steel chains as the last of
my blood dripped onto the plastic sheeting.

The shouting continued, the walls shuddered,
Kolya was not dead yet. I held the knife with both
hands and put one foot on the step above me. I
could sneak into the apartment while the cannibal
was distracted, stick the knife in his back—but the
blade seemed flimsy to me now, far too small for
killing giants. It would prick him, draw a little
blood, and he would turn, grab my face, and squeeze
the eyeballs from my skull.

I took another step up and Kolya shot out of the
apartment, his boots skidding on the floor as he
nearly ran past the staircase. He made the turn,

hurling himself down the flight, grabbing my collar, and tugging me along with him.

"Run, you little fool! Run!"

We ran, and whenever I faltered or nearly tripped on a slick step, Kolya's hand was there to steady me. I heard the shouting above us, heard that monstrous heavy body thudding down the steps behind us, but I never looked back and I never ran faster. In the midst of all that terror, the shouts and the footfalls and the squeal of our heels on the wooden steps, there was something else, something strange. Kolya was laughing.

We made it out the front door of the building and into the dark street, the night sky already criss-crossed with roving searchlights. The sidewalks were empty; no one close by to help us. We ran into the middle of the street, sprinted three blocks, looking over our shoulders to see if the giant was still chasing us, never seeing him, never slowing down. Finally, we spotted an army car passing by and we ran into its path, arms raised, forcing the driver to hit the brakes, the tires skidding on the iced pavement.

"Get out of the road, you motherless shits!" shouted the driver.

"Comrade officers," said Kolya, palms raised, speaking calmly and with his perpetual, freakish confidence, "there are cannibals in that building back there. We've just escaped them."

"There are cannibals in every building," said the driver. "Welcome to Leningrad. Now step aside."

Another voice inside the car said, "Hold on a moment." An officer stepped out. He looked more like a professor of mathematics than a military man, with his trim gray mustache and his frail neck. He studied Kolya's uniform and then looked him in the eye.

"Why aren't you with your regiment?" he asked.

Kolya pulled the colonel's letter from his pocket and showed it to the officer. I could see the man's expression change. He nodded at Kolya and gestured for us to get in the car.

"Show us."

Five minutes later Kolya and I stepped back into the cannibals' apartment, this time escorted by four soldiers aiming their Tokarev rifles into the corners of the room. Even surrounded by armed men my fear nearly drowned me. When I saw the rib cage dangling from its steel chain, the skinned thigh and arm, I wanted to shut my eyes and never open them again. The soldiers, tough as they were, accustomed to carrying their comrades' mutilated corpses from the battlefield, even they turned away from the swaying chains.

The giant and his wife were gone. They'd left everything behind, the wick lamps still lit, the tea still hot in the samovar, but they had fled into the night. The officer shook his head, glancing around the apartment. Gaping holes yawned from the walls like open mouths where the steel pipe had struck.

"We'll put their names on the list, cancel their ration cards, all that, but it will be dumb luck if they get caught. There isn't much of a police force right now."

"Where's he going to hide?" asked Kolya. "He's the biggest fucker in Piter."

"Then you better hope you see him first," said one of the soldiers, running his finger along the ragged edge of a hole punched in the wall.

6

You really laid her out," I told Kolya as we trudged north past the clock tower of the Vitebsk Station, grandest of all Leningrad's train stations, even now, when no train had run in almost four months and the stained glass windows were boarded over.

"It was a solid shot, wasn't it? Never hit a woman before, but it seemed like the right move."

That is the way we decided to talk, free and easy, two young men discussing a boxing match. That was the only way to talk. You couldn't let too much truth seep into your conversation, you couldn't admit with your mouth what your eyes had seen. If you opened the door even a centimeter, you would smell the rot outside and hear the screams. You did not open the door. You kept your mind on the tasks of the day, the hunt for food and water and something to burn, and you saved the rest for the end of the war.

The curfew alarm hadn't sounded yet, but there wasn't much time left. We had decided to spend the night in the Kirov, where I knew I had enough scrap wood for a decent fire, and a full pot of river water for tea. It wasn't such a long walk, but now that my panic was gone I felt like an old man, the muscles of my legs aching from the running. Breakfast with the colonel had been beautiful at the time, but it also served to stretch out my stomach, and the hunger had returned. Now it was mixed with nausea, because I couldn't get the image of the child's rib cage out of my head. When I nibbled on the frozen library candy, I thought it tasted like dried skin, and I had to force myself to swallow the stuff.

Kolya limped along beside me, his legs as shot as mine, but in the moonlight he looked as worry free as ever, unburdened by any unpleasant thoughts. Maybe his mind was more peaceful because he had reacted bravely, with strength and decisiveness, while I cowered on the dark staircase, waiting to be saved.

"Look, I feel that I . . . I want to say I'm sorry. I ran away and I'm sorry. You saved my life."

"I told you to run."

"Yes, but . . . I should have come back. I had the knife."

"You had the knife, sure." Kolya laughed. "Lot of good it would have done you. You should have seen yourself, swinging at him. David and Goliath, ha. He was getting ready to eat you raw."

"I left you alone in there. I thought they were going to kill you."

"Well, they thought so, too. But I told you I had quick fists." He fired a few jabs into the air, grunting like a boxer: *huuunnh! huuunnh!*

"I'm not a coward. I know I looked like one back there, but I'm not."

"Listen to me, Lev," he said, draping his arm around my shoulders, forcing me to match his long strides. "You didn't want to go up to that apartment. I was the country fool who insisted on it. So you don't owe me an apology. And I don't think you're a coward. Anyone with a spoonful of sanity would have run."

"You didn't."

"*Quod erat demonstrandum*," he said, pleased with his simple Latin.

I felt a little better about everything. Kolya *had* told me to run. The giant could have poked a hole in my skull as easily as a child sticks his thumb through a cherry pie. Maybe I hadn't acted heroically, but I hadn't betrayed the nation, either.

"It really was a terrific punch."

"I don't think she'll be chewing on any children for a while."

Kolya grinned at the phrasing, but the grin didn't last for long. His words brought our minds back to that pale meat, the plastic sheeting wet with drippings. We were living in a city where witches roamed the streets, Baba Yaga and her sisters, snatching up children and hacking them to pieces.

A siren sounded, that long, lonely wail, and soon all the sirens in the city were echoing its cry.

"Here comes Fritz," said Kolya, and we increased our pace, forcing our tired bodies to move faster. We could hear the shells landing to the south, a distant beat of timpani, as the Germans began their nightly attack on the great Kirov Works, where half of Russia's tanks and airplane engines and heavy guns were built. Most of the men working there were out on the front lines now, but women had taken over on the lathes and presses and the Works never lost a step, coal always burning in the furnaces, smoke always rising from the redbrick smokestacks, the factories never shutting down, even when bombs fell through the roof, even when dead girls had to be carried from the assembly lines, cold hands still clutching their tools.

We hustled past the fine old buildings of Vitebsky Prospekt, with their white stone facades, ram-horned satyr heads grinning down at us from the pediments, carved in the days of the emperors. Each of these buildings would have a bomb shelter in its basement; citizens would be huddled down there, dozens of them clustered around a single flickering lamp, waiting for the all clear. The shells were landing close enough now that we could hear them whine in the air. The wind was louder, shrieking through the broken windows of abandoned apartments, as if God and the Germans were conspiring to blow down our city.

"On the front lines, you get good at judging where the shells will land," said Kolya, his hands jammed into the pockets of his greatcoat, as he walked into the wind that had been behind us a moment before. "You listen to them and you know: that one's falling a hundred meters to the left; that one's going in the river."

"I can tell a Junkers from a Heinkel the second I hear it."

"I should hope so. A Junkers sounds like a lion and a Heinkel is a mosquito."

"Well, a Heinkel from a Dornier, then. I captained the firefighting crew on the—"

Kolya held up his hand for me to shut up. He stopped walking and I stopped beside him.

"You hear that?"

I listened. I couldn't hear anything beyond the

winter wind that seemed to come from every direction at once, gathering its strength over the Gulf of Finland and howling down all the side streets. I thought Kolya heard a shell coming our way and I looked skyward, as if I could spot our death winging toward us, as if I could dodge it if I had. The wind finally calmed, gasping more quietly now, a child at the end of his tantrum. Shells exploded to the south, several kilometers away from the sound of it, but close enough to make the pavement shudder beneath us. But Kolya wasn't listening to the wind or the mortars. Someone inside the old building was playing the piano. I couldn't see any lights through the windows, no candles or lamps burning. The other residents must have gone down to the basement shelter (unless they were too weak from hunger or too old to care), leaving behind this stray genius to play in the darkness, impudent and precise, showing off with thundering double fortissimos immediately followed by fragile little pianissimos, as if he were having an argument with himself, the bullying husband and the meek wife all at once.

Music was an important part of my childhood, on the radio and in the concert halls. My parents were fanatic in their passion; we were a family with no talent for playing but great pride in our listening. I could identify any of Chopin's twenty-seven etudes after hearing a few bars; I knew all of Mahler, from *Lieder eines fahrenden Gesellen* to the unfinished Tenth. But the music we heard that night I had never heard before and have never heard since. The notes were muffled by window glass and distance and the unending wind, but the power came through. It was music for wartime.

We stood on the sidewalk, beneath a powerless streetlamp cobwebbed with hoarfrost, the great guns firing to the south, the moon veiled by muslin clouds, listening until the final note. When it ended, something seemed wrong: the performance was too good to go unacknowledged, the performer too skilled to accept no applause. For a long moment we were silent, staring up at the dark windows. Finally, when it seemed respectful to move again, we resumed our march.

"It's lucky no one's chopped up his piano for firewood," said Kolya.

"Whoever that is, nobody's chopping up his piano. Might have been Shostakovich himself. He probably lives around here."

Kolya glared at me and spat on the sidewalk.

"They evacuated Shostakovich three months ago."

"That's not true. He's on all the posters, wearing that fire warden's helmet."

"Yes, the great hero, except he's in Kuybishev, whistling those Mahler tunes he plagiarized."

"Shostakovich did not plagiarize Mahler."

"I thought you'd take Mahler's side," said Kolya, glancing down at me with that amused twist of his lips that meant, I now knew, he was about to say something irritating. "Don't you prefer the Jew over the Gentile?"

"They're not on different sides. Mahler wrote great music. Shostakovich writes great music—"

"Great? Ha. The man is a hack and a thief."

"You're an idiot. You don't know anything about music."

"I know that Shostakovich was on the radio in

September talking about our great patriotic duty to fight Fascism, and three weeks later he's in Kuybishev, eating porridge."

"It's not his fault. They don't want him dead so they made him go. Think how bad it would be for morale—"

"Oh, of course, think of the tragedy," said Kolya, adopting the professorial tone he used for high sarcasm. "We can't let the great ones die. If I were in charge, I'd push the other way. Put the famous on the front lines. Shostakovich takes a bullet to the head? Think of the outrage across the nation! Across the world! RENOWNED COMPOSER MURDERED BY NAZIS. Anna Akhmatova, she was on the radio, too. You remember? Telling all the women of Leningrad to be brave, to learn how to fire a rifle. Now where is she? Shooting at Germans? Hm, no, I believe not. At the Works, grinding shell casings? No, she's in fucking Tashkent, pumping out more of that narcissistic verse that made her famous."

"My mother and sister left, too. Doesn't make them traitors."

"Your mother and sister weren't on the radio telling us all to be brave. Look, I don't expect composers and poets to be heroes. I just don't like hypocrites."

He rubbed his nose with the back of his gloved hand and glanced back to the south, at the artillery bursts lighting the sky.

"Where is this goddamned building of yours, anyway?"

We had just turned the corner onto Voinova and I raised my hand to point out the Kirov. I was pointing at nothing, but for a long time I didn't even think to lower my hand. Where the Kirov had stood there was now rubble, a steep hill of broken concrete slabs, a scree of masonry and twisted steel rods and sprays of glass dust glittering in the moonlight.

If I had been alone, I would have stared at those ruins for hours without comprehension. The Kirov was my life. Vera and Oleg and Grisha. Lyuba Niko-laevna, the spinster on the fourth floor who read palms and mended dresses for all the women in the building, who saw me reading an H. G. Wells novel in the stairwell one summer night and the next day gave me a box filled with the works of Robert Louis Stevenson, Rudyard Kipling, and Charles Dickens. Anton Danilovich, the janitor, who lived in the base-ment and shouted at us whenever we threw stones in the courtyard or spat off the rooftop or built lewd snowmen and snowwomen with carrots for cocks and pencil erasers for nipples. Zavodilov, rumored to be a gangster, missing two fingers on his left hand and always whistling at the girls, even if they were homely, maybe whistling louder at the homely girls to keep their spirits up—Zavodilov who had par-ties that lasted till dawn, playing the latest jazz re-cords, Varlamov and his Hot Seven or Eddie Rozner; men and women with half-buttoned shirts laugh-ing and dancing out into the hallway, infuriating all the old folks, thrilling the kids who decided if we had to grow up, at least we could grow up to be like Zavodilov.

It was an ugly old building that always stank of disinfectant, but it was my home and I never thought it would fall. I waded into the tumble of debris, bending down to toss aside hunks of concrete. Kolya grabbed my arm.

"Lev . . . come with me. I know another place we can spend the night."

I pulled out of his grip and continued shoveling with my hands. He grabbed me again and this time he held my arm tight, so I couldn't pull away.

"There's no one alive down there."

"You don't know that."

"Look," he said quietly, pointing at a number of small red stakes that had been shoved into the rubble in various spots. "They've already been here digging. The building must have gone down last night."

"I was here last night."

"You were in the Crosses last night. Come. Come with me."

"People survive. I've read about it. People survive for days sometimes."

Kolya surveyed the wreckage. The wind whipped up miniature storms of concrete dust.

"If anyone's alive in there, you won't be able to pull them out with your bare hands. And if you stay here all night trying, you won't make it to morning. Come on. I have friends nearby. We need to get inside."

I shook my head. How could I abandon my home?

"Lev . . . I don't need you to think right now. I just need you to follow me. Understand? Follow me."

He tugged me down from the hill of rubble and I was too weak to resist, too tired for grief or anger or defiance. I wanted to be warm. I wanted to eat. We walked away from the Kirov's remnants and I could not hear my footsteps. I had become a phantom. There was no one left in the city who knew my full name. I felt no great misery for myself, just a kind of dull curiosity that I still seemed to be alive, my exhalations still visible in the moonlight, this son of Cossacks still marching beside me, looking at me from time to time to make sure I kept moving, checking the night sky for bombers.

ome in," she said, "come in. You're both frozen."
You could see that Kolya's friend had been
beautiful before the siege: her dirty blond hair
hung to the middle of her back; her lips were still full;
and she had a crescent-shaped dimple that creased
her left cheek every time she smiled. There was no
corresponding dimple on the right cheek, which
seemed odd, and I noticed that I kept waiting for her
to smile so I could see the solitary dimple again.

Kolya had kissed both her cheeks when she
opened the door and the blood had flooded her
face, making her look healthy for a second.

"They said you were dead!"

"Not yet," said Kolya. "This is my friend Lev.
He won't tell me his patronymic or his family name,
but maybe he'll tell you. I've got a feeling you're his
type. Lev, Sonya Ivanovna. One of my early con-
quests and still a dear friend."

"Ha! Bit of a short-lived conquest, wasn't it? Napoleon in Moscow?"

Kolya grinned at me. He still had an arm around
Sonya, holding her close to him. She had swaddled
herself in a man's greatcoat and three or four sweaters, but even beneath all that bulk I could see there
wasn't much left of her.

"This one was a classic seduction. Met her in art history class. Explained to her all the perversions of the masters, from Michelangelo's boys to Malevich's feet—did you know about this? He used to sketch his housekeeper's feet in the morning and jerk off to the drawings at night."

"Such a lie. No one else in the world has heard this story," she confided to me.

"She learned all about these lusty painters, got her juices flowing, couple of shots of vodka, that was it. I came, I saw, I conquered."

She leaned closer to me, touching the sleeve of my overcoat, and told me with a stage whisper: "He came, anyway. I'll give him that much."

I wasn't used to hearing women speak about sex. The boys I knew never shut up on the subject, though none of them seemed like great authorities, but the girls saved those talks for their own closed covens. I wondered if Grisha had laid Vera yet, before remembering that Grisha and Vera were both dead, buried beneath tombstones of broken concrete.

Sonya saw the miserable look on my face and assumed I was flustered by their brassy conversation. She gave me a warm smile, flashing that crescent dimple.

"Don't worry, darling. None of us are nearly as bohemian as we think we are." She turned to Kolya. "He's a sweet one. Where'd you find him?"

"He lived in the Kirov. Over on Voinova."

"The Kirov? That's the one that went down last night? I'm so sorry, sweet boy."

She gathered me in her arms. It was like being embraced by a scarecrow. I couldn't feel any body beneath her clothing, just layer after layer of smoky wool. Still, it felt good to have a woman showing concern. Even if she was just being polite, it felt good.

"Come," she said, taking my hand, leather glove on leather glove. "This is your home now. If you need to sleep here for a night, a week, this is where you sleep. Tomorrow you can help me carry some water up from the Neva."

"We've got work to do tomorrow," said Kolya, but she ignored him, ushering us into the sitting room. A band of six sat in a semicircle around a wood-burning stove. They looked like university students, the men still sporting elaborate sideburns and mustaches, the women wearing their hair cut short and Gypsy earrings. They shared several heavy blankets, sipped cups of tea, and watched us newcomers without saying a word of welcome. I understood their displeasure. Strangers were an irritation at best and fatal at worst—even if they meant no harm, they always wanted food.

Sonya introduced us all, naming everyone in the circle, but no one else spoke until Kolya made friends by unwrapping his library candy and passing it around. It was impossible to take much pleasure chewing the stuff, but it was something to eat, something to get the blood moving, and soon the conversation restarted.

Her friends, it turned out, were surgeons and nurses, not university students. They had just finished a twenty-four-hour shift, amputating arms and legs, plucking bullets from shattered bones, trying to patch together mutilated soldiers without the help of anesthetic or spare blood or electricity. They didn't even have enough hot water to properly sterilize their scalpels.

"Lev here lived in the Kirov," said Sonya, indicating me with a sympathetic tilt of her head. "That building on Voinova that was hit last night."

There were murmured apologies, small nods to indicate condolence.

"Were you inside when the bomb hit?"

I shook my head. I glanced at Kolya, who was scrawling notes with a stub of pencil in his journal, not paying any attention to us. I glanced back at the doctors and nurses, who waited for a reply. These people were strangers. Why burden them with the truth?

"I was staying with friends."

"A few of them got out," said one of the surgeons, Timofei, a painterly-looking fellow wearing rimless glasses. "I heard someone talking about it at the hospital."

"Really? How many?"

"Don't know. Wasn't listening too closely. Sorry, it's just . . . buildings go down every night."

The rumor of survivors lifted my spirits. The bomb shelter in the basement seemed sturdy—if people got there in time, they might have made it. Vera and the twins always rushed down to the shelter with their families when the sirens went off. Zavodilov the gangster, on the other hand—I don't remember ever seeing him in the shelter. He slept through the sirens as he slept through the mornings, with a cold washcloth draped over his forehead and a naked girl by his side. Or at least that's the way I imagined it. No, he wouldn't have made it to the shelter, but then again, Zavodilov spent many nights away from the Kirov, taking care of his mysterious business or drinking in some other criminal's apartment.

Sonya poured two more glasses of weak tea and handed one to me and one to Kolya. I took off my wool mittens for the first time since eating breakfast in the colonel's office. The warm glass felt like a living thing between my palms, a small animal with a heartbeat and a soul. I let the steam rise to my face and didn't realize for a moment that Sonya had asked me a question.

"Sorry?"

"I said, was your family in the building?"

"No, they got out of the city in September."

"That's good. So did mine. My little brothers went to Moscow."

"And now the Germans are at the gates of Moscow, too," said Pavel, a ferret-faced young man who stared at the iron stove and never made eye contact with anyone. "They'll take it in a few weeks."

"Let them take it," said Timofei. "We'll play a Rostopchin on them, burn everything down and retreat. Where will they find shelter? What will they eat? Let the winter take care of them."

"Play a Rostopchin . . . *ech*." Sonya made a face as if she smelled something nasty. "You make him sound like a hero."

"He *was* a hero. You shouldn't take your history from Tolstoy."

"Yes, yes, good Count Rostopchin, friend to the people."

"Don't put politics into it. This is about warfare, not the class struggle."

"Don't put politics into it? Who has to put politics into it? You think politics doesn't enter into warfare?"

Kolya silenced the bickering when he spoke up. He was looking into his cup of tea, holding it in both hands.

"The Germans won't take Moscow."

"According to which expert is this?" asked Pavel.

"According to me. Fritz was thirty kilometers from the city at the beginning of December. Now he's one hundred kilometers away. The Wehrmacht has never retreated before. They don't know how to do it. Everything they've trained for, everything they've studied in their books is attack. Attack, attack, attack. Now they're going backward and they won't stop till they're lying on their backs in Berlin."

No one said a word for a long count. The women in the group stared at Kolya, their eyes a little brighter in their gaunt faces. They were all a little in love with him.

"Forgive me for asking, comrade," said Pavel, putting an ironic lilt into *comrade*. "But if you're such an important figure in the army, privy to such critical conversations, why are you sitting here with us?"

"I can't discuss my orders," Kolya said, unruffled by the surgeon's insulting tone. He took a sip of tea and let the warm water sit in his mouth for a moment. He noticed that Sonya was still watching him and he smiled at her. The group was silent. Nobody had moved, but the dynamic had shifted, with Kolya and Sonya onstage in the spotlight and the rest of us silent spectators, wondering if we'd see a bit of skin. The foreplay had already begun, even though they sat apart from each other, even though both were wrapped within layer after layer of wool. I wished that someday some girl would stare at me that way, but I knew it would never happen. This narrow-shouldered frame, these eyes as watchful and fearful as a rodent's—I wasn't the type to in-spire lust. Worst of all was my nose, my hated nose, that beak of a thousand insults. It was bad enough to be a Jew in Russia, but to be a Jew with a nose from an anti-Semitic caricature, well, it inspired a good deal of self-loathing. Most of the time I was proud to be Jewish, but I didn't want to look Jewish. I wanted to look Aryan, blond haired and blue eyed, broad in the chest and strong jawed. I wanted to look like Kolya.

Kolya winked at Sonya and finished off his cup of tea. He sighed, staring at the dregs in the bottom of his cup.

"Do you know I haven't had a shit in nine days?"

That night all of us slept in the sitting room ex-cept for Kolya and Sonya, who jointly stood on some unseen signal and disappeared into the bed-room. The rest of us shared the blankets. We lay close together for warmth, so even though the stove ran out of fuel sometime in the night, I wasn't shiv-ering too badly. The cold actually bothered me less than Sonya's muffled little yelps. Her cries were im-possibly happy, as if Kolya were fucking away all the misery of the last six months, fucking away the hunger and the cold and the bombs and the Ger-mans. Sonya was lovely and kind, but her pleasure was awful to listen to—*I* wanted to be the one who could transport a pretty girl away from the siege with my cock. Instead I was lying on the floor of a stranger's apartment next to a man I didn't know, who twitched in his sleep and smelled like boiled cabbage.

I can't imagine the sex lasted very long—who had the energy for it?—but it seemed to go on half the night, Sonya yelping, Kolya speaking in low tones that I couldn't hear through the thin walls. He sounded very calm, as if he were reading to her from a newspaper article. I wondered what the hell he was telling her. What do you say to a girl you're fucking? It seemed like an important thing to know. Maybe he was quoting that writer he was always raving about. Maybe he was telling her about fighting the cannibal and the cannibal's wife, but that seemed unlikely. I lay in the darkness listening to them, as the wind shook the windows in their frames and the last embers popped in the stove. The loneliest sound in the world is other people making love.

8

The next morning we stood outside a building two blocks from the Narva Gate, staring up at a towering poster of Zhdanov.

"This must be it," said Kolya, stamping his feet to keep them warm—though it didn't seem possible, it was colder than it had been the day before. Only a single fish skeleton of cloud interrupted the endless blue sky. We headed for the front door of the building. It was locked, of course. Kolya banged on it, but no one came. We stood there like idiots, slapping our gloved hands together, our chins buried beneath the folds of our scarves.

"So now what do we do?"

"Someone will go in or out, eventually. What's wrong with you today? You seem a little grumpy."

"Nothing's wrong with me," I said, but even I could hear the grumpiness in my tone. "Took us an hour to get here, we're going to wait another hour to get inside, and there won't be any old man with a coop full of chickens."

"No, no, something is bothering you. You're thinking about the Kirov?"

"Of course I'm thinking about the Kirov," I snapped back, angry with him for asking because I had not been thinking about the Kirov.

"We had a lieutenant named Belak back in the fall. Army man to the bone, wore the uniform his whole life, fought against the Whites, all that. So one night he sees this kid Levin crying over a letter he just got. This was in a trench outside of Zelenogorsk, right before the Finns took it back. Levin couldn't talk, he was bawling so hard. Someone was dead, killed by the Germans. I don't remember if it was his mother, his father, maybe the whole family, I don't know. Anyway, Belak took the letter, folded it very neatly, slipped it into Levin's coat pocket, and said, 'All right, get it out. But after this I don't want to see you crying until Hitler's hanging from a rope.'"

Kolya stared into the distance, contemplating the lieutenant's words. He must have thought they were profound. To me they sounded manufactured, the kind of line my father always hated, fake dialogue invented by some Party-approved journalist for one of those buoyant "Heroes at the Front!" articles *Truth for Young Pioneers* always ran.

"So he stopped crying?"

"Well, he stopped right then. Just sniffled for a bit. But that night he was at it again. That's not really the point."

"What's the point?"

"There's no time for grieving. The Nazis want us dead. We can cry about it as much as we want, but that won't help us fight them."

"Who's crying? I'm not crying."

Kolya wasn't listening to me. Something was caught between his two front teeth and he tried to pry it out with his fingernail.

"Belak stepped on a land mine a few days later. Nasty business, land mines. What they do to a man's body. . . ."

His voice trailed off, contemplating his old officer's mangled body, and I felt bad that I had insulted the lieutenant in my mind. Maybe his words were clichéd, but he was trying to help the young soldier, to distract him from the tragedy at home, and that mattered more than original phrasing.

Kolya banged on the building door again. He waited for a moment, sighed, stared at the solitary cloud drifting across the sky.

"I'd like to live in Argentina for a year or two. I've never seen the ocean. Have you?"

"No."

"You are grumpy, my Israelite. Tell me why."

"Go fuck a pig."

"Ah! There it is!" He gave me a little shove, danced away, moving his hands like a boxer, pretending to spar with me.

I sat down on the doorstep. Even that small movement caused a swarm of sparks to fly across my vision. We had drunk more tea at Sonya's when we woke up, but there was no food, and I was saving the rest of my library candy. I looked up at Kolya, who was now watching me with some concern.

"What were you saying last night?" I asked him. "When you were, you know, when you were with her."

Kolya squinted, confused at the question.

"With whom? With Sonya? What did I say?"

"You were talking to her the whole time."

"When we made love?"

The phrase itself was embarrassing. I nodded. Kolya frowned.

"I didn't know I said anything."

"You were talking the whole time!"

"The usual stuff, I suppose." A sudden smile lit his face. He sat beside me on the lintel step. "But of course, if you've never visited a country, you probably don't know the customs. You want to know what to say."

"I was just asking a question."

"Yes, but you're curious. Why are you curious? Because you're a little bit nervous. You want to do things properly when you get the chance. This is very smart of you. I'm serious! Quit your scowling. You take compliments worse than anyone I know. Now, listen: women don't like silent lovers. They're giving you something precious and they want to know you appreciate it. Give me a little nod to show you're listening."

"I'm listening."

"Every woman has a dream lover and a nightmare lover. The nightmare lover, he just lies on top of her, crushing her with his belly, jabbing his little tool in and out till he's finished. He's got his eyes clenched shut, he doesn't say a word; essentially he's just jerking off in the poor girl's pussy. Now the dream lover—"

We heard the *shush* of sled runners on hard-packed snow and turned to see two girls dragging a sled loaded down with buckets of ice from the river. They were heading straight toward us and I stood, brushing off my coat, relieved that Kolya's lecture had been interrupted. Kolya stood beside me.

"Ladies! Do you need a hand carrying that ice?"

The girls exchanged a glance. They were both about my age, sisters or cousins, with the same broad faces and downy upper lips. They were Piter girls, untrusting of strangers, but at the same time, climbing the stairs to their apartment with four pails of ice . . .

"Who are you here to see?" asked one of them, with a librarian's prim correctitude.

"We'd like to speak to a certain gentleman about his chickens," said Kolya, choosing honesty for unknown reasons. I expected the girls to laugh at us, but they didn't.

"He'll shoot you if you go up there," said the second girl. "He doesn't let anyone get near those chickens."

Kolya and I stared at each other. He licked his lips and turned back to the girls, flashing his most seductive smile.

"Why don't you let us carry the pails. We'll worry about the old man."

By the fifth floor, sweating through all my layers of wool, my seagull legs trembling with the effort, I was starting to regret the decision. There must have been an easier way into the building. We took long breaks at each landing, where I panted and flexed my hands, pulling off my mittens to inspect the deep grooves the pail handles were sawing into my palms. Kolya quizzed the girls about their reading habits and their ability to recite the opening stanzas of *Eugene Onegin*. To me the girls seemed spiritless, cud chewers, with no mischief in their eyes and no spark in their speech, but nobody bored Kolya. He chatted with them as if they were the most delightful creatures ever to grace a ball, looking one in the eye and then the other, never allowing silence. By the fifth floor it was clear that both girls were taken with him, and I got the sense they were now trying to determine which of them held the upper hand.

A surge of envy rose in me again, that sense of injustice compounded with anger and self-loathing—why did they like him? The long-winded braggart! And why did I begrudge him their attention? I didn't care about these girls, after all. Neither was remotely attractive to me. This man saved my life yesterday and today I cursed him because girls grew awkward in his presence, blood rushing to their faces, staring at the floor and playing with the buttons on their coats?

But Sonya I liked. Sonya with her crescent dimple and her warmth, welcoming me into her home, offering me a place to stay whenever I needed it, even though one more week without food would kill her—the shape of her skull was too easy to read beneath her near-translucent skin. Perhaps I liked her so much because I met her thirty minutes after seeing the tombstones of the Kirov. Maybe the sight of her kept me from dwelling too much on all my neighbors, trapped beneath the slabs of fallen concrete.

Even when those images slipped through my mind, they lacked barbs, passing cleanly through, and I would find myself thinking again about the colonel's daughter, or the colonel himself, or the giant chasing us down the steps with his steel pipe, or the woman at the Haymarket selling glasses of Badayev dirt. If I thought about the Kirov at all, it was the building itself that I remembered, my childhood playground, with its long corridors so well designed for footraces, its stairwells with the lead glass windows so layered with dust you could draw your self-portrait with your fingertip, the courtyard where all the kids gathered after the first big snowfall of every year for the annual snowball fight, floors one through three against floors four through six.

My friends and neighbors—Vera and Oleg and Grisha and Lyuba Nikolaevna and Zavodilov—seemed unreal already, as if their deaths had erased their lives. Perhaps I had always known they would disappear one day, and so I had kept them at a distance, laughed at their jokes and listened to their plans but never really trusted their existence. I had learned how to protect myself. When the police took my father, I had been a dumb boy, unable to understand how a man—that willful, brilliant man—could cease to exist at the snap of an unseen bureaucrat's fingers, as if he were nothing but cigarette smoke exhaled by a bored sentry in a watchtower in Siberia, a sentry who wondered if his girlfriend back home was cheating on him, who stared over the wintry woods, unaware of the great blue maw of sky above him that waited to swallow the curling smoke and the sentry and everything growing on the ground below.

Kolya was saying good-bye to the girls, dropping his pails inside their apartment door and motioning for me to do the same.

"Be careful up there," said one of the girls, the bolder one, I suppose. "He's eighty years old, but he'll shoot you in a second."

"I've been on the lines fighting Fritz," said Kolya, reassuring her with a smile and a wink. "I think I can handle a cranky grandfather."

"If you want something to eat on your way down, we're making soup," said the second girl. The bold one shot her a look and I wondered, with little real curiosity, if she was peeved at the offer of free food or at the flirtatious gesture.

Kolya and I climbed the final flight of stairs to the roof door.

"Here's the plan," he told me. "Let me do the talking. I'm good with old people."

I pushed open the door and the wind came at us, blowing bits of ice and dust into our faces, the grit of the city. We lowered our heads and pressed forward, two Bedouins in a sandstorm. Ahead of us was a mirage, what could only be a mirage—a shed nailed together with wood planks and roofing felt, the gaps stuffed with scraps of wool and old newspapers. I was a city boy to the bone; I had never been to a farm or even seen a cow; but I knew this was a chicken coop. Kolya looked at me. Our eyes were watering from the wind, but we were both grinning like madmen.

There was a crooked door on one end of the coop with an unfastened hook-and-eye latch on the outside. Kolya knocked softly on the door. No one answered.

"Hello? Don't shoot us! Ha, ha! Ah, we just wanted to visit with you. . . . Hello? All right, I'm going to open the door. If that's a bad idea, if you're thinking of shooting, just say something now."

Kolya stepped to one side of the door frame, motioned for me to do the same, and prodded open the door with the toe of his boot. We waited for a shouted curse or a shotgun blast, but neither came. When it seemed safe, we peeked into the coop. It was dark inside, lit by a single wick lamp hanging from a hook on the wall. The floor was covered with old straw that stank of bird shit. One wall was lined with empty nesting boxes, each big enough for a single chicken. A boy sat at the far end of the coop, his back against the wall, his knees drawn to his chest. He wore a woman's rabbit fur coat. He looked ridiculous but warm.

A dead man sat in the straw beneath the nesting boxes, back against the wall, limbs stiff and splayed like an abandoned marionette. He had a long white beard, the beard of a nineteenth-century anarchist, and skin like melted candle wax. An antique shotgun still lay across his lap. From the looks of him he'd been dead for days.

Kolya and I stared at this grim tableau. We had entered into someone else's private misery and we felt the guilt of interlopers. I did, at least. Shame didn't afflict Kolya the way it did me. He walked inside the coop, knelt beside the boy, and gripped his knee.

"Are you all right, little soldier? You need some water?"

The boy didn't look at him. His blue eyes seemed enormous in his starved face. I broke off a square of the library candy, stepped into the coop, and held out my hand. The boy's eyes shifted slowly in my direction. He seemed to register my presence and the food in my hand before he looked away again. He was very far gone.

"Is this your grandfather?" asked Kolya. "We should bring him out to the street. Not good for you to be sitting here alone with him."

The boy opened his mouth and even that effort seemed to cost him. His lips were crusty, as if they had been glued together.

"He doesn't want to leave the birds."

Kolya glanced at the empty nesting boxes.

"I think it's all right now. Come on, there are some nice girls downstairs, they'll give you some soup, some water to drink."

"I'm not hungry," said the boy, and I knew he was doomed.

"Come with us anyway," I said. "It's too cold in here. We'll warm you up, get you a little water."

"I have to watch the birds."

"The birds are gone," said Kolya.

"Not all of them."

I doubted the boy would last until tomorrow, but I didn't want him to die here, alone with the bearded corpse and the empty nesting boxes. The dead were everywhere in Piter: stacked in great heaps behind the city morgue; burned in the fire pits outside the Piskarevsky Cemetery; scattered across the ice of Lake Ladoga, something for the seagulls to pick at, if there were still seagulls. But this was a lonelier place to quit than anywhere else I'd seen.

"Look," said Kolya, shaking one of the empty nesting boxes. "Nobody home. You were a good watchman, you protected the birds, but they're gone now. Come with us."

He extended his gloved hand, but the boy ignored it.

"Ruslan would have shot you."

"Ruslan?" Kolya glanced at the old man's body. "Ruslan was a fierce old fellow, eh? I can tell. I'm glad you're the peaceful sort."

"He told me everyone in the building wanted our birds."

"He was right."

"He said they'd come up here and slit our throats if we let them. Steal our birds and boil them for soup. So one of us always had to stay awake, hold the shotgun."

The boy spoke in a monotone, never looking at us, his eyes vague and unfocused. I could see now that he was trembling, his teeth clacking together when he wasn't speaking. Patches of light brown down spread across his cheeks and neck, his body's last effort to insulate itself.

"He told me they'd keep us alive till the siege was over. Couple of eggs a day, that and the rations would do us. But we couldn't keep them warm enough."

"You need to forget about the damn chickens. Come on, give me your hand."

The boy continued to ignore Kolya's out-stretched hand and finally Kolya motioned for me to help him. But I had seen something, a movement where there shouldn't be movement, a stirring beneath the boy's fur coat, as if his giant heart were beating so loud its thump was visible.

"What do you have there?" I asked.

The boy stroked the front of his fur coat, calming whatever lay beneath. For the first time the boy's eyes met mine. Weak as he was, millimeters from the finish line, I could see the toughness in him, the stubborn will he inherited from the old man.

"Ruslan would have shot you."

"Yes, yes, you keep saying that. You saved one of the birds, didn't you? That's the last one." Kolya looked at me. "How many eggs can a chicken lay in a day?"

"What the hell do I know?"

"Listen, boy, I'll give you three hundred rubles for that bird."

"People used to offer us a thousand. He always said no. The birds can keep us alive all winter, he said. What are we going to do with rubles?"

"Buy yourself some food? That bird's going to die like all the others if you keep it here."

The boy shook his head. All the talking had wearied him and his eyelids drifted lower.

"All right, how about this? Here, give me that," Kolya said to me, snatching the library candy from my hand. He added it to his last sliver of sausage and the three hundred rubles and placed them all in the boy's lap.

"That's everything we have. Now, listen to me. You're going to die here tonight if you don't move. You need to eat and you need to get off the roof. We're going to bring you down to those girls on the fifth floor—"

"I don't like them."

"You don't have to marry them. We're going to give them this money and they'll feed you some soup and let you stay a few nights, get your strength back."

The boy didn't have the energy for more than the slightest of head shakes, but his meaning was clear. He wasn't leaving.

"You're staying here to protect the bird? What the hell are you going to feed it?"

"I'm staying for Ruslan."

"Let the dead bury the dead. You're coming with us."

The boy began to unbutton his coat. He held the brown-feathered bird against his chest like a suckling newborn. It was the saddest little chicken I've ever seen, bedraggled and dazed. A healthy sparrow would have torn it apart in a street fight.

He held the chicken out to Kolya, who stared at it, unsure what to do or say.

"Take it," said the boy.

Kolya looked at me and then back to the boy. I had never seen him so confused.

"I couldn't keep them alive," said the boy. "We had sixteen in October. And this is all that's left."

We had wanted the chicken so badly, but now that the boy was offering it for free something seemed wrong.

"Take it," said the boy. "I'm tired of them."

Kolya took the chicken from the boy's hands, holding the bird away from his face, worried she might claw at his eyes with her hook-nailed feet. But the chicken had no violence in her. She sat limp in Kolya's palms, trembling in the cold, staring dully at nothing at all.

"Keep it warm," said the boy.

Kolya opened his coat and slipped the bird inside, where she could bundle between layers of wool and still find space to breathe.

"Now go away," said the boy.

"Come with us," I said, one last effort though I knew it was useless. "You shouldn't be alone right now."

"I'm not alone. Go away."

I looked at Kolya and he nodded. We headed for the crooked door. On the way out, I turned and glanced back at the boy, sitting there silently in his woman's coat.

"What's your name?"

"Vadim."

"Thank you, Vadim."

The boy nodded, his eyes too blue, too large for his pale, gaunt face.

We left him alone in the chicken coop with the dead old man and the empty nesting boxes, the wick burning low in the lamp, three hundred rubles and the unwanted food on his rabbit fur lap.

9

Sonya had collected a basket of wood chips from the splintered roof beams of a bomb-blasted nursing school on Vasilevsky Island; her stove burned hot as we sat in front of it, drinking weak tea and staring at the feeble chicken. We had fashioned a makeshift nesting box from an old cookie tin and a bed of shredded newspaper. The chicken huddled there, head against her chest, ignoring the teaspoonful of ground millet we'd sprinkled on the scraps of editorial, Muscovites imploring us to stand strong. Fucking Moscow. The general feeling around Piter was that if the siege had to happen, better it happen to us, because we could survive anything, while the porcine bureaucrats in the capital would probably surrender to the nearest Oberstleutnant if they couldn't get their weekly ration of sturgeon. "They're as bad as the French," Oleg used to say, though even Oleg knew that was going too far.

Kolya had nicknamed the chicken Darling, but there was no affection in her eyes as she stared back at us, stupid and suspicious.

"Doesn't she have to have sex before she lays eggs?" I asked.

"I don't think so," said Sonya, picking at a crust

of dried skin on her lip. "I think the males fertilize the eggs, but she lays them on her own. My uncle manages a poultry collective in Mga."

"So you know about chickens?"

She shook her head. "I've never even been to Mga."

We were all children of the city. I had never milked a cow or shoveled manure or baled hay. Back in the Kirov we always made fun of the peasants from the collectives, their bad haircuts and freckled necks. Now the country folk were having their laugh, feasting on fresh-killed rabbit and boar while we tried to survive on moldy ration bread.

"She won't lay twelve eggs by Thursday," I said. "She won't even live till Thursday."

Kolya sat on a backless steel stool, his long legs spread out in front of him, scrawling notes in his notebook with his ever-smaller stub of pencil.

"Don't give up on her yet," he said, not looking up from his writing. "She's a Leningrad chicken—she's tougher than she looks. The Germans thought they'd celebrate Christmas in the Astoria, didn't they?"

The Nazis had printed thousands of invitation cards to a grand victory party Hitler intended to throw at the Astoria Hotel after conquering what he had called, in a speech to his torch-bearing storm troopers, "the birthplace of Bolshevism, that city of thieves and maggots." Our soldiers had found a few of the invitations on the bodies of fallen Wehrmacht officers. They had been reprinted in the newspapers, copied by the thousands, and nailed to walls all over the city. The Politburo hacks could not have devised better propaganda. We hated the Nazis for their stupidity as much as anything else—if the city fell, we wouldn't leave any hotels where the Germans could sip schnapps in the piano bar and bed down in deluxe suites. If the city fell, we'd bring her down with us.

"Maybe she's shy," said Sonya. "Maybe she doesn't want to lay eggs with all of us watching."

"Maybe she needs to drink something."

"Mm, that's smart. Let's get her some water."

No one moved. We were all hungry and tired and hoping someone else would stand and fill a cup with water. Outside the light was already fading from the sky. We could hear the drone of search-lights warming up, their massive filaments slowly brightening. A lone Sukhoi circled above the city, the hum of its propeller steady and reassuring.

"She's an ugly little turd, isn't she?"

"I think she's sweet," said Sonya. "She looks like my grandmother."

"Maybe we should shake her, see if they fall out."

"She needs water."

"Yes, get her some water."

Another hour passed. Finally, Sonya lit the oil lamps, turned on the radio, and spilled a little river water from a jug onto a saucer, which she placed in Darling's box. Darling glared at her but made no ef-fort to sip the water.

Sonya retook her seat and sighed. After a mo-ment to gather her energy, she turned to the knit-ting stand beside her chair, picked up a torn sock, her needle and thread, and a porcelain darning egg that she tucked into the sock's heel to pull the fabric taut. I watched her bony fingers at work. She was a pretty girl, but her hands were like the

Reaper's, fleshless and pale. She knew how to mend a sock, though. The needle flashed in the lamplight as it dipped in and out, in and out, lulling me close to sleep.

"You know who's a vile little cunt?" asked Kolya out of nowhere. "Natasha Rostov."

The name was familiar, but I couldn't place it right away.

Sonya frowned but did not look up from her knitting. "The girl in *War and Peace*?"

"I can't stand that bitch. Everyone falls in love with her—all of them, even her brothers—and she's nothing but a vapid twit."

"Maybe that's the point," said Sonya.

I was half asleep but I smiled. In spite of all his irritating qualities, I couldn't help liking a man who despised a fictional character with such passion.

Sonya closed the holes in the sock with her deft, skeletal hands. Kolya drummed his pants legs with his fingers, scowling at the thought of Natasha Rostov and the unfairness of it all. Darling shivered in the warm room, trying to retract her beaked head into her body, as if she dreamed she were a turtle.

The playwright Gerasimov spoke on the radio: "Death to cowards! Death to panic mongers! Death to rumor spreaders! To the tribunal with them. Discipline. Courage. Firmness. And remember this: Leningrad is not afraid of death. Death is afraid of Leningrad."

I snorted and Kolya looked over at me.

"What's wrong? You don't like old Gerasimov?"

"What's to like?"

"He's a patriot, anyway. He's right here in Piter, not safe somewhere with Akhmatova and her lot."

"I'm with Lev," said Sonya, tossing another handful of wood chips into the oven. The embers shone on her blond hair and for a second her little ears were crimson and translucent. "He's a salesman for the Party, that's all."

"He's worse than that," I said, and I could hear the anger entering my voice. "He calls himself a writer, but he hates writers—he just reads them to see if they wrote anything dangerous, anything insulting. And if he decides they did, well, that's it; he denounces them in the Litburo, he attacks them in the newspaper, on the radio. Somebody on some committee somewhere says, 'Well, Gerasimov says the man's a threat, and Gerasimov's one of us, so the man must be a threat . . .'"

I stopped talking in the middle of the sentence. My embittered voice seemed to echo in the small apartment, though I think it was my imagination, my embarrassment at revealing too much, too soon. Sonya and Kolya stared at me—she seemed worried for me, while he seemed impressed, as if all this time he had thought I was a deaf-mute and just now realized I could form words.

"Your father was Abraham Beniov."

I said nothing, but Kolya hadn't been asking a question. He nodded as if everything was suddenly clear to him.

"I should have figured it out quicker. I don't know why you'd want to hide something like that. The man was a poet, a real poet, there aren't many of them. You ought to be proud."

"You don't have to tell me to be proud of him," I snapped back. "If you're asking me a bunch of stupid questions and I don't want to answer them, that's my business. I don't talk about my family with strangers. But don't ever tell me to be proud of my father."

"All right," said Kolya, holding up his hands, "all right, I'm sorry. I didn't mean it like that. I just meant we're not strangers anymore."

"I feel like an idiot," said Sonya. "Forgive me, Lev—I haven't heard of your father. He was a poet?"

"A great one," said Kolya.

"Fair to middling, he always said. He told me for his generation there was Mayakovsky and everyone else, and he was right there in the center section with everyone else."

"No, no, don't listen to him. He was a fine writer. Truly, Lev, I'm not saying this to be kind. 'An Old Poet, Once Famous, Seen at a Café.' Wonderful poem."

That was the poem in all the anthologies, at least all the anthologies printed before 1937. I had read it dozens of times since they took my father, but it had been years since I'd heard another voice speak the title.

"And he was . . . he was . . ." Here Sonya made a motion with her chin, an *over there* motion. It could mean anything: sent to Siberia, shot in the back of the head, silenced on orders of the Central Committee. The specifics were never known. *He was removed?* she was asking, and I nodded.

"I have that poem memorized," said Kolya, but he did me a favor and didn't recite it.

The apartment door opened and Timofei, one of the surgeons I'd met the previous night, walked over to warm his hands by the stove. When he noticed Darling sitting in her nesting box, he crouched and inspected her, his hands on his knees.

"Where did this come from?"

"Kolya and Lev got him from a boy near the Narva Gate."

Timofei stood and grinned at us. He pulled two large onions from the pockets of his overcoat.

"Got these at the hospital. Wasn't planning on sharing, but seems to me we've got the possibility of a beautiful soup tonight."

"Darling's not for the pot," said Kolya. "We need her for the eggs."

"The eggs?" Timofei looked at us, at Darling, back to us. He seemed to think we were joking.

"Everyone's quitting on Darling," Kolya continued, "but I think she's got it in her. Do you know anything about chickens? You think she can lay a dozen by Thursday?"

"What the hell are you talking about?"

The surgeon seemed more and more irritated. Kolya glared back at him, insulted by the man's tone.

"Don't you speak Russian? We're waiting for the eggs!"

For a moment I thought the conversation would turn violent, which would have been a bad thing for the Red Army; we needed our surgeons and Kolya would have splattered the man with a single punch. But Timofei finally laughed, shaking his head, waiting for us to laugh with him.

"Laugh all you want," I told him. "You're not touching the chicken."

"It's not a chicken, you idiot. It's a rooster."

Kolya hesitated, not sure if this was a joke the surgeon was playing or a trick to get us to throw

Darling into the soup. I leaned forward in my chair and peered at the bird. I don't know why I thought peering would help. What was I looking for, little balls?

"You're saying she won't lay eggs?" asked Kolya, watching Timofei carefully.

The surgeon spoke slowly, as if he were conferring with morons.

"It's a he. And the odds aren't good."

10

That night the soup tasted like June, like the dinners we remembered from before the siege. An admirer of Sonya's, a pilot in the VVS, had given her an unspoiled potato. Kolya protested that he didn't want to eat the gift of another lover, but his complaints were ignored, as he had hoped, and the Darling soup was thick with potato and onion and plenty of salt. Happily for us, the other surgeons were spending the night somewhere else. Sonya traded a wing and a cup of the broth to her neighbor for a bottle of drinkable vodka; the Germans lobbed only a few lazy shells at the city, as if to remind us they were still there but had better things to do on this particular evening; by midnight we were drunk, our bellies full, Kolya and Sonya fucking in the bedroom while I played speed chess with Timofei by the light of the stove.

Halfway through the second game I moved my knight; Timofei stared at the board, burped, and said, "Oh. You're good."

"You just figured it out? I mated you in sixteen moves last game."

"Thought it was the drink. . . . I'm fucked, aren't I?"

"You're still alive. Won't be long, though."

He tipped over his king and burped again, pleased with his burping, pleased there was food in his stomach.

"Not much point in that. Ah, well. You can't tell a chicken from a rooster, but you know chess."

"I used to be better." I right-sided his king and played his move for him, trying to see how long I could extend the endgame.

"You used to be better? When you were an embryo? What are you, fourteen?"

"Seventeen!"

"Are you shaving yet?"

"Yes."

Timofei looked skeptical.

"I shaved my mustache. . . . It grows slower in the winter."

Sonya gasped in the other room and began to laugh, forcing me to picture her, her head tilted back, her throat exposed, her nipples hard on her small breasts.

"I don't know where they get the energy," said Timofei, lying back on the layered blankets and stretching his arms. "Give me chicken soup every night and I'll never need another woman as long as I live."

He closed his eyes and soon he was asleep, another of the fast sleepers, leaving me alone to listen to the lovers.

Kolya woke me before dawn, handing me a cup of tea as he studied the abandoned chessboard. Timofei still slept on his back, his mouth open, his arms stretched above his head as if he were surrendering to the enemy.

"Who was playing black?"

"Me."

"You had him in six."

"I had him in five. Unless he made a mistake, and then I had him in three."

Kolya frowned, looking at the pieces until he figured it out.

"You know how to play."

"You still want to make that bet? What was it, nude pictures of French girls?"

He smiled, rubbing the sleep from his eyes.

"I should just give them to you as a favor. Show you where all the parts are. Come on, get your boots on."

"Where are we going?"

"Mga."

Kolya might have been a deserter, but he had enough natural authority in his voice that my boots were half laced before I thought to question his directive. He had already slipped on his greatcoat and leather gloves; he looped his scarf twice around his neck and checked his teeth in a small mirror hanging over the samovar.

"Mga's fifty kilometers away."

"Good day's walk. We had a big dinner last night, we can make it."

Slowly I awakened to the insanity of this proposition.

"That's behind German lines. Why do we have to go to Mga?"

"It's Monday, Lev. We need the eggs by Thursday and we're not going to find any in Piter. Sonya's uncle runs that poultry collective out there, right? I'm betting the Germans kept it going. They like their eggs, too."

"That's our plan? We're going to walk fifty kilometers, right past the Germans, to a poultry collective that maybe didn't get burned down, grab a dozen eggs, and come home?"

"Well, anything would sound ridiculous if you said it with that tone of voice."

"Tone of ... I'm asking you a question! That's our plan? Sonya's never even been there! How are we supposed to find it?"

"It's in Mga! How hard can it be to find anything in Mga!"

"I don't even know how to find fucking Mga!"

"Ah," said Kolya, grinning now as he put on his Astrakhan fur hat. "That one's easy. It's on the Moscow line. We just follow the tracks."

Timofei grunted in his dreams and rolled onto his side. I'd learned that doctors and soldiers could sleep through any non-life-threatening ruckus; my argument with Kolya might have been a softly sung lullaby, judging from the look of peaceful contentment on Timofei's face. I looked at him and I hated him, hated him for getting to sleep on his bed of wool blankets, warm and comfortable and well fed, with no grandson of Cossacks to harass him, no NKVD colonel sending him out to the wilderness to find ingredients for a wedding cake.

I turned back to Kolya, who was adjusting his hat to a properly heroic angle with the help of the mirror. I hated him even more, the cheerful swaggering brute, happy and fresh at six in the morning as if he'd just returned from a two-week holiday at the Black Sea. I imagined that he still stank of sex, though the truth was I couldn't smell anything at all so early in the day, with the apartment so cold. My mighty nose was all show, a good target for bullies' taunts but strangely bad at picking up scents.

"You think it's so crazy," he said, "but every one
of those peasant swindlers selling potatoes for two
hundred rubles in the Haymarket brought them in
from outside the city. People make it past the lines
every day. Why can't we?"

"Are you drunk?"

"Off a quarter a bottle of vodka? I don't think
so."

"There has to be somewhere closer than Mga."

"So tell me."

He was swaddled now for the weather, his jaw
bristling with four days' worth of blond beard. He
waited for me to propose my alternative to his stupid plan, but as the seconds ticked past I realized I
didn't have one.

He smiled at me, a smile fine enough for a Red
Fleet recruitment poster.

"The whole thing's a fucking joke, I agree. But
it's a pretty good joke."

"Yes, it's a wonderful joke. And the funniest part
is that we're going to die out there and the colonel's
daughter won't get her cake and nobody will ever
know what we were doing in Mga."

"Calm yourself, my morbid little Israelite. I
won't let the bad men get you—"

"You can eat shit."

"—but we have to move now. If we want to
make it there with any daylight left."

I could have ignored him and gone back to sleep.
The stove had gone cold in the night, the last of the
wood chips burned through, but it was still warm
enough under all the piled blankets. Sleeping made
more sense than marching out to Mga—where the
Germans waited in their thousands—in search of
chickens. Anything made more sense than that.

Still, no matter how much I protested the idea, I knew from the first that I would follow. He was right: there were no eggs in Leningrad. But that wasn't the only reason for following. Kolya was a braggart, a know-it-all, a Jew-baiting Cossack, but his confidence was so pure and complete it no longer seemed like arrogance, just the mark of a man who had accepted his own heroic destiny. This wasn't the way I had imagined my adventures, but reality ignored my wishes from the get-go, giving me a body best suited for stacking books in the library, injecting so much fear into my veins that I could only cower in the stairwell when the violence came. Maybe someday my arms and legs would thicken with muscle and the fear would drain away like dirty bathwater. I wish I believed these things would happen, but I didn't. I was cursed with the pessimism of both the Russians and the Jews, two of the gloomiest tribes in the world. Still, if there wasn't greatness in me, maybe I had the talent to recognize it in others, even in the most irritating others.

I stood, grabbed my coat off the floor, slipped it on, and followed Kolya to the front door, which he held open for me with grave courtesy.

"Wait," he said, before I could cross the threshold. "We're going on a journey. We should sit."

"I didn't know you were superstitious."

"I like the traditions."

There were no chairs so we sat on the floor beside the open door. The apartment was quiet. Timofei snored from his spot near the stove; the windows shuddered in their frames; the radio broadcast its endless metronome, signaling that Leningrad remained unconquered. Outside someone nailed

11

The Moscow line had been cut only four months before, but the rails were already beginning to rust. Most of the ties had been pried from the ground and split for firewood, though they were impregnated with creosote and dangerous to burn. Kolya walked atop of one rail, a gymnast on the balance beam, hands held out to the side. I trudged along behind him, in the center of the tracks, unwilling to play his game, partly because I was angry with him, partly because I knew I'd lose.

The rails ran east past redbrick apartment blocks and three-story department stores, past the Kotlyarov streetcar barns, past abandoned factories that had built things nobody could use or afford during wartime. A crew of young women wearing overalls below their winter coats, under the supervision of an army engineer, labored to convert a post office into a defensive position. The corner of the sturdy old building had been demolished to make way for a machine-gun nest.

"Great body on that one," said Kolya, indicating a woman wearing a blue headscarf lugging sandbags from an idling truck.

"How can you tell?"

It was a ludicrous claim. The woman was at least

fifty meters away; her jacket was heavily padded and she wore several layers beneath it.

"I can tell. She has a dancer's posture."

"Ah."

"Don't give me your *ah*. I know ballerinas. Believe me. I'll bring you to the Mariinsky Theater some night, take you backstage. Let's just say I have a reputation."

"You never shut up about your reputation."

"There is very little in this world that makes me happier than a ballerina's thighs. Galina Ulanova—"

"Oh, stop."

"What? She's a national treasure. Her legs should be bronzed."

"You never slept with Galina Ulanova."

He gave me a small, secretive smile, a smile that said he knew many things but couldn't share them all at once.

"I'm being cruel," he admitted. "Talking to you about things of this nature . . . it's sadistic. Like talking about Velázquez with a blind man. Let's change the subject."

"You don't want to talk about ballerinas you didn't sleep with for the next thirty-nine kilometers?"

"Three boys go to a farm to steal chickens," he began in his joke-telling voice. He used a different accent for jokes, though I couldn't tell what kind of accent it was supposed to be or why he thought it made things funnier.

"The farmer hears them and rushes over to the farmhouse. So the boys jump into three potato sacks and hide."

"Is this going to be a long joke?"

"The farmer kicks the first sack and the boy inside says, 'Meow!' pretending to be a cat."

"Oh, he was pretending to be a cat?"

"I just said that," said Kolya, looking back at me to see if I was starting trouble.

"I know he's pretending to be a cat. Once he says, 'Meow,' it's obvious he's pretending to be a cat."

"You're surly again because I slept with Sonya? Are you in love with her? Didn't you have a nice time with what's his name? The surgeon? You looked so cute curled up together by the stove."

"And what's that accent you're doing? Is it supposed to be Ukrainian?"

"What accent?"

"Every time you tell a joke you use some stupid accent!"

"Listen, Lev, my little lion, I'm sorry. I know it's not easy for you, lying there all night, your meat in your hand, listening to her happiness—"

"Just tell your dumb joke."

"—but I promise you, before you hit eighteen—when's your birthday?"

"Oh, shut up."

"I'm going to find you a girl. Calculated neglect! Don't forget."

All this time he continued to walk atop the steel rail, one foot in front of the other, never losing his balance, never looking down, going faster than I could walk in the usual way.

"Where was I? Ah, the farmer, he kicks the first sack, 'Meow,' and so on. He kicks the second sack, and the boy inside says, 'Woof!' Pretending to be—"

Kolya pointed at me to finish the sentence.

"A cow."

"A dog. When he kicks the third sack, the boy inside says, 'Potatoes!'"

We walked in silence.

"Well," said Kolya at last, "other people think it's funny."

On the outskirts of the city, the apartment blocks were no longer stacked one on top of the other. The concrete and brick was now broken by stretches of frozen marsh and snow-covered lots where future buildings were meant to rise before the war ended all construction. The farther we walked from the city center, the fewer civilians we saw. Army trucks with chains on their tires rattled past, the weary soldiers in the flatbeds staring at us with no interest as they motored toward the front.

"Do you know why it's called Mga?" Kolya asked.

"Somebody's initials?"

"Maria Gregorevna Apraksin. One of the characters in *The Courtyard Hound* is based on her. Heiress to a long line of field marshals, peculators, and royal toilet lickers. She's convinced her husband is trying to murder her so he can marry her sister."

"Is he?"

"Not at first, no. She's completely paranoid. But she never shuts up about it and then he does start to fall in love with the sister. And he realizes life really would be better without his wife around. So he goes to Radchenko for advice, but he doesn't know that Radchenko's been fucking the little sister for years."

"What else did he write?"

"Hm?"

"Ushakovo," I said. "What other books did he write?"

"*The Courtyard Hound*, that's it. It's a famous story. The book came out, it was a failure. There was only one review and the critic absolutely blasted it. Called it vulgar and despicable. Nobody read it. Ushakovo worked on that book for eleven years. Eleven years, can you imagine that? And it disappears like it was dropped into the ocean. But he starts all over again, a new novel; his friends who see pieces of it say it's his masterpiece. Except Ushakovo's getting more and more religious, spending time with this church elder who convinces him that fiction is Satan's work. And one night Ushakovo becomes convinced that he's going to hell; he's in a complete panic; he tosses the manuscript in the fire. Poof, gone."

This sounded strangely familiar.

"But that's exactly what happened to Gogol."

"Well, no, not exactly. Very different in the particulars. But an interesting parallel, I agree."

The rails veered away from the road, past stands of birch saplings too slender for firewood. Five white bodies lay facedown in the white snow. A family of winter dead, the dead father still clutching his dead wife's hand, their dead children sprawled a short distance away. Two battered leather suitcases lay open beside the corpses, emptied of everything but a few cracked picture frames.

The family's clothes and boots had been stripped away. Their buttocks had been hacked off, the softest meat, easiest for making patties and sausages. I couldn't tell if the family had been murdered by gunfire, or knives, or an exploding shell, by German artillerymen or Russian cannibals. I didn't want to know. They had been dead a long time, at least a week, and their bodies had started to become part of the landscape.

Kolya and I continued east along the Vologda line. He didn't tell any more jokes that morning.

A little before noon we reached the edge of the Leningrad defenses: thickets of barbed wire, trenches three meters deep, dragon's teeth, machine-gun nests, antiaircraft batteries, and KV-1 tanks covered with white camouflage netting. The soldiers we had seen earlier had ignored us, but now we were too far east to be civilians, and too strange of a pair to be Army. As we walked along the tracks a band of young privates, hauling the tarpaulin off a 6x6 truck, turned to stare at us.

Their sergeant walked toward us, not pointing his carbine at us, precisely, but not pointing it away, either. He had the posture of a lifelong Army man and the high cheekbones and narrow eyes of a Tartar.

"You two have papers?"

"We do," said Kolya, reaching inside his jacket. "We have excellent papers."

He handed over the colonel's letter and nodded toward the truck.

"That the new-model Katyusha?"

The tarpaulin had been flung to the ground, revealing racks of parallel rails jutting skyward, waiting to be loaded with rockets. According to what we heard on the radio, the Germans feared the Katyusha more than any other Soviet weapon—they called it Stalin's organ, after the rockets' low and mournful howls.

The sergeant glanced at the rocket launcher and back to Kolya.

"Never mind about that. Which Army are you with?"

"The Fifty-fourth."

"The Fifty-fourth? You're supposed to be in Kirishi."

"Yes," said Kolya, giving the sergeant an enigmatic smile and nodding at the letter in the man's hand. "But orders are orders."

The sergeant unfolded the letter and read. Kolya and I watched the privates position the finned-tail rockets on the Katyusha's rails.

"Give them hell tonight!" shouted Kolya. The soldiers on the truck glanced at us and said nothing. They looked like they hadn't slept in days; it took all their concentration to load the rockets without dropping them, there was no energy to waste on madmen.

Unwilling to be ignored, Kolya began to sing. He was a baritone with a strong, confident voice.

"On the bank Katyusha starts singing, of a proud gray eagle of the steppe, of the one Katyusha loves deeply, of the one whose letters she's kept."

The sergeant finished the letter and refolded it. The colonel's message had clearly impressed him; he looked at Kolya now with genuine respect, nodding his head in time with the old song.

"That's the stuff. I heard Ruslanova herself sing it during the Winter War. Gave her a hand when she was coming offstage, think she had one glass too many. You know what she said to me? 'Thank you, Sergeant,' she said. 'You look like a man who knows how to use his hands.' What do you think of that? Always the hell-raiser, Ruslanova. But it's a beautiful song."

He slapped Kolya on the chest with the letter, giving it back, smiling at both of us.

"Sorry I had to stop you boys. You know how it

is. . . . They say there's three hundred saboteurs inside Leningrad and more coming every day. But
now I know what you're up to, working for the
colonel. . . ."

He gave Kolya a wink.

"I know all about it, organizing the partisans,
that's the stuff. You let us regulars take 'em from the
front, you boys plug 'em from the back, we'll be
leaving hot turds in the Reichstag come summer."

Kolya had read the colonel's letter aloud the day
we got it and it didn't mention partisans—it said
only that we should not be detained or harassed as
we were operating under the discretion of the colonel himself—but the newspapers were full of stories
about simple country folk who had been trained to
fight as deadly guerrillas by NKVD specialists.

"You keep 'em dancing with the organ here,"
said Kolya—I didn't know if he was mimicking the
sergeant's speech intentionally or not—"and we'll
make sure they can't get any more strudel from the
Vaterland."

"There you go, there you go! Cut off the supply
lines, let 'em starve in the woods, it'll be 1812 all
over again."

"But no Elba for Hitler."

"No, no, not for him, no Elba for Hitler!"

I wasn't entirely sure the sergeant knew what
Elba was, but he was adamant that Hitler wouldn't
get it.

"We'll give him a bayonet in the balls, but no
Elba!"

"We should keep moving," said Kolya. "We
have to make Mga by nightfall."

The sergeant whistled. "That's a long way. Stay
to the woods, you hear? Fritz owns the roads, but

a Russian doesn't need a road to walk on, does he? Ha! You have enough bread? No? We can spare some. Ivan!"

The sergeant shouted at a scruffy young private standing beside the truck.

"Find some bread for these boys. They're going behind lines."

12

Outside of Leningrad the trees still grew, crows muttered on birch branches, squirrels raced between the firs. The squirrels looked fat and innocent, easy targets for a man with a pistol. They were lucky to live in occupied Russia.

We marched through the woods, through open fields of cold sunshine, keeping the train tracks visible to our left. The snow was hard packed, scattered with pine needles, decent for walking. We were in German-controlled territory, but there was no indication of a German presence, no sign at all of war. I was strangely happy. Piter was my home, but Piter was a graveyard now, a city of ghosts and cannibals. Walking in the countryside I felt a physical change, as if I were breathing pure oxygen after months at the bottom of a coal mine. The tangles in my gut uncoiled, my ears unclogged, I had strength in my legs I hadn't felt for months.

Kolya seemed affected in the same way. He squinted in the glare off the snow, pursing his lips to blow great gusts of vapor, as delighted by this trick as a five-year-old.

Spotting a green scrap of paper near the trunk of a grand old birch, he bent down to pick it up. It looked normal enough, a ten-ruble banknote, Lenin's eyes glaring at us from beneath his broad bald head—except that ten-ruble notes were gray, not green.

"Counterfeit?" I asked.

Kolya nodded, pointing to the sky with one finger as he scrutinized the bill.

"Fritz drops them by the bushel. The more counterfeit notes floating around, the less the real ones are worth."

"But it's not even the right color."

Kolya flipped the note around and read aloud the printed text on the other side.

"*The prices for food items and the necessities of daily life have increased enormously and the black market in the Soviet Union is florishing.* 'Flourishing' is spelled wrong, by the way. *Party functionaries and Jews are working dark deals at home while you at the front have to sacrifice your life for these criminal.* 'These criminal,' that's nice. They occupy half the country and they can't even find someone who speaks the language? *Soon you will see the reason, so keep this ten-ruble note. It will guarantee your safe return to a free Russian after the war.*"

Kolya grinned and glanced up at me. "You working some dark deals, Lev Abramovich?"

"I wish."

"They think these things will turn us? Don't they understand? We invented propaganda! All this is bad tactics; they're irritating the people they're trying to convert. Young man thinks he's found a ten-ruble note, he's happy, maybe he can buy an extra slice of sausage. But no, it's not money, it's a poorly spelled surrender coupon."

He speared the note to a tree branch and set it on fire with his lighter.

"You're burning your chance to come back to a free Russian after the war," I told him.

Kolya smiled as he watched the note blacken and curl. "Come on. We have a long way to go."

After another hour slogging through the snow, Kolya prodded me in the shoulder with his gloved fingers.

"Do Jews believe in the afterlife?"

The day before the question would have annoyed me, but right then it seemed funny, so perfectly Kolya, asked with genuine curiosity and apropos of nothing.

"It depends on the Jew. My father was an atheist."

"And your mother?"

"My mother's not Jewish."

"Ah, you're a half-breed. No shame in that. I've always thought I had Gypsy blood in me from somewhere up the stream."

I looked up at him, his eyes as blue as a husky's, a smattering of blond hair showing from beneath the black fur cap.

"You don't have Gypsy blood."

"What, the eyes? Plenty of blue-eyed Gypsies in the world, my friend. Anyway, the New Testament's very clear about the whole thing. You follow Jesus, you go to heaven; you don't, you're off to hell. But the Old Testament . . . I don't even remember if there is a hell in the Old Testament."

"Sheol."

"What?"

"The underworld is called Sheol. One of my father's poems is called 'The Bars of Sheol.'"

It was very odd to speak openly about my father and his work. The words themselves seemed unsafe, as if I were confessing a crime and the authorities might hear. Even here where the Litburo had no sway, I worried about getting caught, worried about spies lurking in the larches. If my mother were around, she would have silenced me with a look. Still, it was good to talk about him. It made me happy that poems are referred to in the present tense even when the poet is in the past tense.

"What happens in Sheol? They punish you for your sins?"

"I don't think so. Everybody goes there, doesn't matter if you were good or bad. It's just dark and cold and nothing's left of us but our shadows."

"Sounds about right." He scooped up a handful of clean snow and took a bite, let it melt in his mouth. "A few weeks ago I saw a soldier with no eyelids. He was a tank commander, his tank broke down somewhere in the worst of it, and by the time they found him, the other boys in the tank were dead from the cold and he had frostbite over half his body. Lost some toes and fingers, a bit of his nose, his eyelids. I saw him sleeping in the infirmary, thought he was dead, his eyes wide open. . . . I don't know if you call them 'open' if there's no way to shut them. How do you stay sane with no eyelids? You have to go the rest of your life without ever once closing your eyes? I'd rather be blind."

I had not seen Kolya morose before; the sudden shift in his mood made me anxious. Both of us heard the howling at the same time; we turned and looked through the crooked avenues of birch trees.

"Is that a dog?"

He nodded. "Sounds like it."

A few seconds later we heard the howl again. There was something terribly human in its loneliness. We needed to keep walking east, we needed to reach Mga by nightfall, but Kolya headed off toward the crying dog and I followed without arguing.

The snow was deeper here and soon we were wading through thigh-high drifts. The energy I had felt ten minutes before began to seep away. I was tired again, battling for each step forward. Kolya slowed his pace so that I could keep up. If he was impatient with me, he didn't show it.

I had my head down so I could choose each footfall—a twisted ankle was certain death now—and I saw the tread marks before Kolya. I grabbed his sleeve to stop him. We were at the edge of a vast clearing in the woods. The glare of sunlight off the hectares of snow was bright enough that I had to shield my eyes with my hand. The snow had been corrugated by dozens of tank treads, as if an entire Panzer brigade had passed through. I didn't know treads the way I knew airplane engines, couldn't tell a German Sturmtiger's from a Russian T-34's, but I knew these weren't our tanks. We would have already broken the blockade if we had this much armor in the woods.

Gray and brown heaps lay scattered across the snow. At first I thought they were discarded coats, but I saw a tail on one, an outstretched paw on another, and I realized they were dead dogs, at least a dozen of them. We heard another howl and finally we saw the howler, a black-and-white sheepdog dragging itself off the field, its front legs doing the work its hind legs could not. Behind the wounded animal was a blood-smeared trail more than a hundred meters long, a red brushstroke slapped across a white canvas.

"Come on," said Kolya, stepping into the field before I could stop him. The tanks were gone, but they had been here recently; the tracks were still cleanly defined in the snow, unblurred by wind. The Germans were near, in force, but Kolya didn't care. He was already in the middle of the clearing, marching toward the sheepdog, and as usual I hurried to catch up.

"Don't get too close to any of them," he told me. I didn't know why he told me that. Was he worried about disease? Did he think a dying dog might bite me?

When we got closer to the sheepdog, I could see that a wood box was strapped to its back, held in place with a leather harness. A wood post extended straight up from the box. I glanced around the field and saw that all the other dogs wore the same contraptions.

The sheepdog did not look at us. He was intent on reaching the fringe of trees on the far side of the field, where he thought he could find safety, or comfort, or a quiet place to die. Blood dribbled from two bullet holes near his hip and another must have pierced his belly, for something wet and coiled was dragged along beneath him, innards never meant to see daylight. He panted, his long pink tongue dangling from the side of his mouth, his black lips curling back from his yellowing teeth.

"They're mines," said Kolya. "They teach them

to find food underneath a tank's armor, and then they starve them, and when the Panzers come they let them loose. Boom."

Except none of the dogs had gone boom. The Germans clearly knew all about it; they'd warned their gunners and their gunners were good shots. Dead dogs littered the field, but there were no tank carcasses, no upended armored cars, no explosions at all. It was another ingenious Russian ploy that had failed completely, as all of the Russian ploys had failed, and I pictured the hungry dogs sprinting toward the Panzers, their paws kicking up fantails of snow, their eyes bright and happy as they raced for their first meal in weeks.

"Give me your knife," said Kolya.

"Be careful."

"Give it to me."

I pulled the German dagger from its sheath and handed it to him. The sheepdog kept trying to drag his gutted self toward the woods, but he was losing strength in his front legs. He finally quit when he saw Kolya approaching, as if he had decided that this was far enough. He lay in the blood-wet snow, staring up at Kolya with weary brown eyes. The wood post stuck straight up from the box on his back like the mast of a sailboat. It seemed a flimsy thing, no thicker than a drumstick.

"You're my good boy," said Kolya, kneeling beside the sheepdog, holding the back of the dog's head steady with his left hand. "You're my good boy."

Kolya cut the dog's throat with one quick motion. The dog shuddered, the blood pouring from him, steaming in the cold air. Kolya lowered the dog's head gently to the ground, where he continued to twitch for a few seconds, pawing at nothing, like a dreaming puppy, and then he was dead.

We were silent for a moment, giving our respect to the fallen dog. Kolya wiped both sides of the bloody blade on the snow, dried it on the sleeve of his overcoat, and handed it back to me.

"We just lost forty minutes. Walk fast."

13

We marched at double time through the birch forest, the railroad tracks to our left, the sun tumbling fast from the sky. Kolya hadn't spoken since the field of dead dogs. I could tell he was worried about the time; he had miscalculated our speed, how fast we could walk across snow-covered terrain, and our detour had ruined any chances of making Mga by nightfall. The cold was a greater danger than the Germans now and the temperature was already dropping fast. Without shelter we would die.

We hadn't seen a human being since saying farewell to the Tartar sergeant and we kept our distance from the abandoned railway stations at Koloniya Yanino and Dubrovka. Even from two hundred meters away we could see the toppled statue of Lenin outside the Dubrovka station, the black graffiti spray painted on the concrete wall: STALIN IST TOT! RUSSLAND IST TOT! SIE SIND TOT!

At three in the afternoon the sun dipped below the western hills and the brooding gray clouds above us flared orange. I heard the whine of airplane engines and looked up to see four Messerschmitts racing toward Leningrad, so high above us they seemed harmless as fruit flies. I wondered what buildings they would flatten, or if they would be shot down by our boys on the ground, or our pilots in the air. It seemed wonderfully abstract to me, somebody else's war. Wherever they dropped their bombs, it wouldn't be on me. When I realized that thought was my own, I felt a surge of guilt. What a selfish shit I had become.

We were walking past Berezovka, a name I'd first heard in September when the Red Army and the Wehrmacht clashed outside the village. According to the newspapers, our boys fought with great valor and tactical brilliance, outfoxing the German commanders and frustrating Hitler himself, who followed each development from his war room in Berlin. But everyone in Leningrad knew how to read a newspaper article. The Russian forces were always "calm and determined," the Germans were always "stunned by the fury of our resistance"—these phrases were mandatory. The key information came near the bottom of each article, tucked away inside a closing paragraph. If our men "withdrew to reserve our fighting strength," we had lost the battle; if the troops "gladly sacrificed themselves to repel the enemy invaders," we had been massacred.

Berezovka was a massacre. According to the papers, the village was famous for its church, built on the direct order of Peter himself, and a bridge where Pushkin challenged a rival to a duel. These landmarks were gone. Berezovka was gone. A few fire-blackened walls still stood above the snow; if not for that, there would be no sign that the village had ever existed.

"They're fools," said Kolya, as we skirted around the hamlet's torched remnants. I looked up at him, not sure whom he meant.

"The Germans. They think they're so efficient, the greatest war machine ever built. But you look at history, you read the books, and the best conquerors always gave their enemies a way out. You could fight Genghis Khan and get your heads lopped off or you could submit and pay him taxes. That's an easy choice. With the Germans, you can fight them and get killed or you can surrender and get killed. They could have turned half this country against the other half, but they don't have subtlety; they don't understand the Russian mind; they just burn everything."

What Kolya said was true enough, as far as it went, but it seemed to me that the Nazis had no interest in a subtle invasion. They didn't want to change anyone's mind, at least no one among the inferior races. The Russians were a mongrel people, spawned by hordes of Vikings and Huns, raped by generations of Avars and Khazars, Kipchaks and Pechenegs, Mongols and Swedes, infested by Gypsies and Jews and far-roaming Turks. We were the children of a thousand lost battles and defeat was heavy in us. We no longer deserved to exist. The Germans believed in the lesson of Darwin's mockingbirds—life must adapt or die. They had adapted to brute reality; we mixed-race drunks on the Russian steppes had not. We were doomed, and the Germans were only playing their mandated role in human evolution.

I didn't say any of that, though. All I said was, "They gave the French a way out."

"All the Frenchmen with balls died on the way home from Moscow in 1812. You think I'm joking? Listen, one hundred and thirty years ago they had the best army in the world. Now they're the whores of Europe, just waiting to be fucked by whomever comes along with a hard cock. Am I wrong? So what happened to them? Borodino, Leipzig, Waterloo. Think about it. Courage got blasted out of their gene pool. Their little genius Napoleon castrated the whole country."

"We're losing the light."

He glanced up at the sky and nodded. "If it comes to it, we can build a dugout and make it through till morning."

He walked faster, accelerating our already-quick pace, and I knew that I couldn't keep up for much longer. Last night's soup was a delicious memory; the sergeant's gift of ration bread had been devoured before noon. Each footstep was an effort now, as if my boots had been lined with lead.

It was already so cold I could feel it in my teeth; the cheap fillings plugging my cavities shrunk when the temperature dipped low. But I couldn't feel my fingertips even though I wore thick wool mittens and had shoved my hands into the pockets of my overcoat. Nor could I feel the tip of my nose. What a good joke that would be—I spent most of my adolescence wishing for a smaller nose; a few more hours in the woods and I wouldn't have a nose.

"We're going to build a dugout? With what? You brought a shovel?"

"You still have hands, don't you? And the knife."

"We need to get inside somewhere."

Kolya made a great show of looking around the darkening woods, as if a doorway might be hidden in one of the tall pines.

"There is no inside," he said. "You're a soldier now, I've drafted you, and soldiers sleep wherever they close their eyes."

"That's very beautiful. But we need to get inside."

He placed his gloved hand on my chest and for a second I thought he was angry with me, insulted by my unwillingness to brave the winter night outdoors. But he wasn't admonishing me; he was making me stand still. He gestured with his chin to an access road that ran parallel to the train tracks. It was a few hundred meters away, and the shadows were growing deeper, but there was still enough light to see a Russian soldier standing with his back to us, his rifle slung over his shoulder.

"Partisan?" I whispered.

"No, he's regular Army."

"Maybe we've taken Berezovka back. A counterattack?"

"Maybe," whispered Kolya. We crept closer to the sentry, treading carefully. We didn't know any passwords and no one with a rifle would wait to see if we were truly Russian.

"Comrade!" shouted Kolya when we were fifty meters away, his hands raised above his head. I raised mine, too. "Don't shoot! We're here on special orders!"

The sentry did not turn. Many soldiers had lost their hearing in the last few months; exploding shells had ruptured thousands of eardrums. Kolya and I exchanged a glance and walked closer. The soldier stood knee-deep in the snow. He was far too still. No living man could pose like a statue in cold this severe. I turned a full circle, scanning the woods, convinced this was a trap. Nothing moved but the birch branches in the wind.

We walked up to the soldier. He must have been a brute in his day, with his bulging brow and his wrists thick as ax handles. But he'd been dead for days, his paper-white skin wrapped too tightly around his skull, ready to split. A neat little bullet hole, crusted with frozen blood, punched through his cheek just below his left eye. A wood sign hung from his neck on a wire loop, the phrase PROLETARIER ALLER LÄNDER, VEREINIGT EUCH! spelled out with a black marker. I didn't speak German, but I knew the phrase, as did every boy and girl in Russia who had suffered through endless lectures on dialectical materialism: Workers of all lands unite!

I pulled the sign off the dead soldier's neck, careful not to let the ice-cold wire brush against his face, and tossed it away. Kolya unfastened the strap of the rifle and inspected the weapon: a Mosin-Nagant with a crooked bolt. He tried it a few times, shook his head, and let it drop to the ground. The soldier wore a hip holster with a Tokarev pistol; a leather lanyard ran through a loophole in the hilt of the gun, securing it to the holster. The dead man was an officer, a pistol waver—the Tokarev wasn't meant for Germans, it was for Russians who refused to advance.

Kolya drew the automatic, untied the lanyard, checked the pistol's butt, and saw that the magazine had been taken. The ammo loops in the officer's belt were empty, too. Kolya unbuttoned the man's coat and found what he was looking for, a burlap pouch with a steel-buckled leather strap.

"Sometimes we put them under our coats at night," he said, opening the pouch and grabbing three pistol magazines. "The buckle's too shiny, reflects the moonlight."

He slammed one of the magazines home and tried the action. Satisfied the pistol was sound, he

stuffed it and the extra ammunition into his overcoat pocket.

We tried to pull the dead man out of the snow,
but he was frozen into the ground, as rooted as a
tree. Dusk was leeching all the colors from the forest; the night was almost on us; there was no more
time to spare for corpses.

We hurried east, walking close to the tracks now,
hoping that any Germans moving through the frozen woods would be in vehicles and easy to hear
from a distance. The crows had quit cawing and the
wind had stopped blowing. The only sounds were
our boots sinking through the snow and the distant,
arrhythmic drumbeat of mortar shells falling around
Piter. I tried to hide my face behind the wool of my
scarf and the collar of my overcoat, tried to use the
warmth of my breath to heat my cheeks. Kolya
stamped his gloved hands together and pulled his
black fur cap down so low it almost covered his
eyes.

A few kilometers east of Berezovka we walked
along the perimeter of a large farm, the undulating
fields of snow demarcated with low stone walls.
Hay bales big as igloos sat abandoned in the fields,
the harvest interrupted, the farmers fled to the east
or dead. An old stone farmhouse stood at the far
edge of the farm, protected from the northern wind
by a copse of larch trees fifty meters high. Firelight
shone through the mullioned windows, warm and
buttery, spilling onto the snow in front of the house.
Black smoke plumed from the chimney, barely visible as a curling smudge against the dark blue sky. It
looked like the most inviting house ever built, the
country residence of the emperor's favorite general,

heated and well stocked for Christmas with everyone's favorite smoked meats and pastries.

I looked up at Kolya as we trudged through the snow. He shook his head but never took his eyes off the farmhouse, and I could see the longing in his expression.

"It's a bad idea," he said.

"It's a better idea than freezing to death on the way to Mga."

"Who do you think is in there? A country gentleman, sitting by the fire, petting his dog? You think we're in a fucking Turgenev story? Every house in town was burned down, this one's still standing. What happened, they got lucky? It's Germans in there, the officers, probably. We're going to storm the house with a pistol and a knife?"

"If we keep walking, we're dead. If we go to the house and the Germans are there, we're dead. But if it's not Germans—"

"So let's say they're Russians," he said. "That means the Germans let them stay there, which means they're working with the Germans, which means they're the enemy."

"So we can appropriate food from the enemy, can't we? And a bed?"

"Listen, Lev, I know you're tired. I know you're cold. But trust me, trust a soldier, this won't work."

"I'm not going any farther. I'd rather take a chance on the farmhouse."

"There might be a place in the next town—"

"How do you know there *is* a next town? The last one is ashes. How much farther to Mga, another fifteen kilometers? Maybe you can make it. I can't."

Kolya sighed, rubbing his face with the back of

his leather glove, trying to get some circulation going.

"I concede that we're not going to make it to Mga. That's no longer an issue. I've known for hours."

"You didn't want to tell me about it? How far away are we?"

"Far. The bad news is, I don't think we're going the right way."

"What do you mean?"

Kolya was still looking at the farmhouse and I had to shove him to get his attention. "What do you mean we're not going the right way?"

"We should have crossed the Neva hours ago. And I don't think Berezovka is on the Mga line."

"You don't think . . . Why didn't you say something?"

"I didn't want you to panic."

It was too dark to see the expression on his stupid Cossack face.

"You told me Mga is on the Moscow line."

"It is."

"You told me all we have to do is follow the Moscow tracks and they'll take us to Mga."

"Yes, all true."

"So where the fuck are we?"

"Berezovka."

I took a deep breath. I longed for powerful fists so I could pulp his skull.

"What's the good news?"

"Pardon?"

"You said the bad news is we're going the wrong way."

"There isn't any good news. Just because there's bad news doesn't mean there's good news, too."

There was nothing left to say so I started walking to the farmhouse. The moon rose above the tree-tops, the ice-skinned snow snapped beneath my boots, and if a German sniper was targeting my head, I wished him good aim. I was hungry, but I knew how to deal with my hunger; we were all experts now at dealing with hunger. The cold was brutal, but I was used to the cold, too. But my legs were quitting on me. Before the war they were weak, poorly suited for running and jumping and whatever else legs are meant for. The siege had whittled them down to broomsticks. Even if we had been on the right path to Mga, I never could have made it. I couldn't have walked another five minutes.

Halfway to the farmhouse Kolya caught up with me. He had pulled out the Tokarev pistol and held it in his gloved hand.

"If we're going to do this," he said, "we don't have to be stupid about it."

He led me behind the house and made me wait on the back porch under the eave, where the firewood was stacked safe and dry. A three-kilo tin of Beluga caviar would not have seemed more luxurious at that moment than the neatly stacked firewood, rising in crisscross formations higher than my head.

Kolya crept over to a frosted window and peeked inside, the sleek black fur of his Astrakhan cap shimmering in the firelight. Inside the house music played on a phonograph—jazz piano, something American.

"Who's in there?" I whispered. He held up his palm to silence me. He seemed transfixed by whatever he saw, and I wondered if we had stumbled across more cannibals out in the snowy depths of the country or, more likely, the mutilated remains of the family who once lived here.

But Kolya had dealt with cannibals before and he had seen plenty of corpses. This was something new, something unexpected, and after another thirty seconds I disobeyed his order and joined him at the window, careful not to brush off any of the icicles hanging from the lintel. I crouched beside him and peered over the bottom edge of the glass.

Two girls in nightshirts danced to the jazz recording. They were lovely and young, no older than me, the blonde leading the brunet. She was very pale, her throat and cheeks washed with freckles, her eyebrows and eyelashes so light they disappeared when seen edgewise. The dark-haired girl was smaller, clumsy, unable to find the rhythm in the syncopation. Her teeth were too big for her mouth and her arms were chubby, creased at the wrists like a baby's. You wouldn't have noticed her in peacetime, strolling down the Nevsky, but there was something wildly exotic now about a plump girl. Somebody with power loved her and kept her fed.

I was so dazzled by the sight of the dancing girls that I didn't realize for a moment they were not alone. Two more girls lay on their bellies on a black bearskin rug in front of the fireplace. Both had their chins propped on their hands, their elbows on the rug, watching the dance with serious expressions on their faces. One looked Chechen, her black eyebrows nearly meeting above her nose, her lips painted bright red, her hair piled up in a wet towel above her head, as if she had just bathed. The other girl had the long, elegant neck of a ballerina, her nose a perfect right angle in profile, her brown hair tied back in tight pigtails.

The interior of the farmhouse looked more like a hunting lodge. The heads of dead animals festooned the walls of the great room: brown bear, wild boar, an ibex with massive curling horns and a scruffy chin beard. A stuffed wolf and lynx flanked the fireplace, posed in mid prowl, their mouths open and fangs glistening white. Candles burned in wall sconces.

Kolya and I crouched outside the window and stared at the scene until the song ended and the Chechen-looking girl got up to change the record.

"Play that one again," said the blonde. Her voice was muffled by the glass, but it was still easy to hear her.

"Not again! Please," said her partner, "something I know. Put on the Eddie Rozner."

I turned to look at Kolya. I expected him to be grinning, ecstatic about this surreal vision we'd stumbled across in the middle of the snowy wasteland. But he looked grim, his lips pressed together, something angry in his eyes.

"Come on," he said, standing and leading me back around to the front of the house. A new record had started playing, more jazz, a trumpeter leading his band in a merry charge.

"We're going in? I think they had food in there. I thought I saw some—"

"I'm sure they have plenty of food."

He knocked on the front door of the farmhouse. The music stopped playing. A few seconds later the blond girl appeared behind the mullioned window next to the doorway. She stared at us for a long time without saying anything or making any move toward the door.

"We're Russian," said Kolya. "Open the door."

She shook her head. "You shouldn't be here."

"I know," he said, holding up the pistol so the girl could see it. "But we are, so open the door, goddamn your mother."

The blonde looked back toward the great room. She whispered something to someone standing out of sight and listened to the response. Nodding, she turned to look at us again, took a deep breath, and opened the door.

Stepping inside the farmhouse felt like entering the belly of the whale, the warmest place I'd been in months. We followed the blonde into the great room, where her three friends stood in an uneasy line, fingers fidgeting with the hems of their nightshirts. The little brunet with the chubby arms looked ready to cry; her lower lip quivered as she stared at Kolya's pistol.

"Is anyone else here?" he asked.

The blonde shook her head.

"When are they coming?" he asked.

The girls exchanged glances.

"Who?" asked the one who looked Chechen.

"Don't play with me, ladies. I'm an officer in the Red Army, I'm on special orders—"

"Is he an officer, too?" asked the blonde, looking at me. She wasn't smiling, quite, but I could see the amusement in her eyes.

"No, he's not an officer, he's an enlisted man—"

"An enlisted man? Really? How old are you, sweetness?"

All the girls were looking at me now. In the

warmth of the room, under the weight of their stares, I could feel the blood rushing to my face.

"Nineteen," I said, standing very straight. "Twenty in April."

"Tssk, you're little for nineteen," said the Chechen girl.

"Fifteen at best," said the blonde.

Kolya racked the pistol's slide, chambering a bullet—a dramatic sound in the quiet room. The gesture seemed overly theatrical to me, but Kolya had a way of pulling off theatrical gestures. He kept the pistol pointed at the floor and looked into each girl's face, taking his time with each one.

"We've come a long way," he said. "My friend here is tired. I'm tired. So I'll ask you again, one last time, when are they coming?"

"They usually come around midnight," said the chubby brunet. The other girls watched her closely but said nothing. "After they're finished with the shelling."

"Is that right? So after the Germans get bored firing their artillery at all of us in Piter, they come here for the night and you take care of them?"

In certain ways I am deeply stupid. I don't say this out of modesty. I believe that I'm more intelligent than the average human being, though perhaps intelligence should not be looked at as a single gauge, like a speedometer, but as a full array of tachometers, odometers, altimeters, and the rest. My father taught me how to read when I was four, which he always bragged about to his friends, but my inability to learn French or remember the dates of Suvorov's victories must have troubled him. He was a true polymath, able to recite any stanza of *Eugene Onegin* at command, fluent in French and English, good enough at theoretical physics that his professors at the university considered his abdication to poetry a minor tragedy. I wish they had been more charismatic, his professors. I wish they had taught him the consolation of physics, explained to their star student why the shape of the universe and the weight of light were more important than unrhymed verses on the swindlers and abortionists of Leningrad.

My father would have known what was happening in that farmhouse the moment he looked through the window, even at seventeen. So I felt like an idiot when I finally realized why these girls were here, who was feeding them and making sure they had enough firewood stacked beneath the eaves.

The blond girl glared at Kolya, her nostrils flaring, her skin flushing beneath her freckles.

"You . . . ," she said, and for a moment she couldn't say anything else, her anger was too intense to articulate. "You walk in here and condemn us? The Red Army hero? Where have you been, you and your army? The Germans came and burned everything, and where was your army? They shot my little brothers, my father, my grandfather, every man in my town, while you and your friends cowered somewhere else. . . . You come here and point your gun at me?"

"I'm not pointing my gun at anybody," said Kolya. It was a strangely meek comment coming from him, and I knew he had already lost the fight.

"I would do anything to protect my sister," she continued, nodding at the chubby brunet. "Anything at all. You were supposed to protect us. The glorious Red Army, Defenders of the People! Where were you?"

"We've been fighting them—"

"You can't protect anybody. You abandoned us. If we don't live in the city, we can't be important, is that it? Let them have the peasants! Is that it?"

"Half the men in my unit died fighting for—"

"Half? If I was the general, all of my soldiers would die before we let a single Nazi into our country!"

"Well," said Kolya, and for several seconds he said nothing else. Finally he pocketed his automatic. "I'm glad you're not the general."

14

Despite the rough start, it didn't take us long to make peace with the girls. We needed one another. They hadn't spoken to another Russian in two months, they didn't have a radio, and they were desperate to hear news about the war. When they heard about the victories outside of Moscow, Galina, the young brunet, smiled at her sister, Nina, and nodded, as if she had predicted such a thing. The girls asked about Leningrad, but they weren't interested in how many people died in December or how much ration bread was now allotted per month. The little country villages they were from had suffered even more than Piter, and stories of the unconquered city's misery only bored them. Instead they wanted to know if the Winter Palace still stood (it did), if the Bronze Horseman had been moved (it had not), and whether a certain shop on the Nevsky Prospekt, apparently famous for selling the finest shoes in Russia, had survived the attacks (neither Kolya nor I knew or cared).

We didn't ask the girls too many questions. We knew the story well enough without the details. The men from their towns had been slaughtered. Many of the young women had been sent west, to work as slaves in German factories. Others fled to the east, walking hundreds of kilometers with their babies and their family icons, hoping they could move faster than the Wehrmacht. The prettiest girls were not allowed to follow their sisters east or west. They were reserved for the invaders' pleasure.

We all sat on the floor near the fireplace. Our socks and gloves rested on the mantel, getting warm and dry. In exchange for information, the girls gave us cups of scalding hot tea, slices of black bread, and two baked potatoes. The potatoes had already been split open for us. Kolya took a bite and looked at me. I took a bite and looked at Galina, sweet faced and plump armed. She sat with her back against the stone ledge of the fireplace, her hands tucked under her bare legs.

"Is that butter?" I asked her.

She nodded. The potatoes tasted like real potatoes, not the sprouted, shriveled, bitter lumps we ate in Piter. A good potato with butter and salt could buy you three hand grenades or a pair of leather-and-felt boots in the Haymarket.

"Do they ever bring eggs?" asked Kolya.

"One time," said Galina. "We made an omelet."

Kolya tried to make eye contact with me, but I only cared about my buttered potato.

"They have a base near here?"

"The officers are in a house near the lake," said Lara, the girl who looked Chechen but was actually half Spanish. "In Novoye Koshkino."

"That's a town?"

"Yes. That is my town."

"And the officers definitely have eggs?"

Now I looked up at him. I had decided to chew the potato very slowly, to make the experience last. We had been lucky for dinner two nights in a row, the Darling soup and now these potatoes. I didn't expect our luck to last for three nights. I chewed with precision and watched Kolya's face for any sign of stupid intentions.

"I don't know if they have them right now," said Lara, laughing a little bit. "You're really hungry for eggs?"

"Yes," he said, smiling back at her, dimples creasing his cheeks. Kolya knew which smile flaunted his dimples best. "I've been craving eggs since June. Why do you think we're out here? We're looking for eggs!"

The girls laughed at this strange joke.

"Are you organizing the partisans?" asked Lara.

"We can't discuss our orders," said Kolya. "But let's just say it's going to be a long winter for Fritz."

The girls glanced at one another, unimpressed by the swaggering talk. They had seen the Wehrmacht at closer range than Kolya had; they had formed their own opinions about who was going to win the war.

"How far is Novoye Koshkino?" he asked.

Lara shrugged. "Not far. Six, seven kilometers."

"Might be a good target," he said to me, chewing a slice of black bread, self-consciously nonchalant. "Pick off a bunch of Wehrmacht officers, leave them with a headless brigade."

"They're not Wehrmacht," said Nina. Something about the way she spoke made me look up at her. She was not a fearful girl, but what she was saying frightened her. Her sister, Galina, stared into the fire, chewing on her lower lip. "They're Einsatzgruppen."

Russians had gotten a crash course in German since June. Dozens of words had entered our everyday vocabulary overnight: *Panzers* and *Junkers*, *Wehrmacht* and *Luftwaffe*, *Blitzkrieg* and *Gestapo*, and all the other capitalized nouns. *Einsatzgruppen*, when I first heard it, didn't have the same sinister tang as some of the others. It sounded like the name of a finicky accountant in a bad nineteenth-century stage comedy. But the name no longer seemed funny, not after all the articles I'd read, the radio reports, and the overheard conversations. The Einsatzgruppen were Nazi death squads, killers handpicked from the ranks of the regular army, the Waffen-SS, and the Gestapo, chosen for their brutal efficiency and their pure Aryan blood. When the Germans invaded a country, the Einsatzgruppen would follow behind the combat divisions, waiting until the territory was secured before hunting down their chosen targets: Communists, Gypsies, intellectuals, and, of course, Jews. Every week *Truth* and *Red Star* printed new photographs of ditches piled high with murdered Russians, the men all shot in the back of the head after they had dug their own communal graves. There must have been high-level debates in the newspapers' editorial offices on whether or not to run such potentially demoralizing pictures. But as morbid as the images were, they crystallized matters: this was our fate if we lost the war. These were the stakes.

"It's the Einsatzgruppen officers who come here at night?" Kolya asked.

"Yes," said Nina.

"I didn't know they bothered with artillery," I said.

"They don't, not usually. It's a game they play.

They make bets. They aim for different buildings in the city and the bomber pilots tell them what they hit. That's why we asked about the Winter Palace. That's the one they all want to hit."

I thought about the fallen Kirov, about Vera Osipovna and the Antokolsky twins, whether they had been crushed by tumbling masonry or had survived the building's collapse, trapped beneath great slabs of reinforced concrete, only to die slowly, begging for help, as smoke and gas choked them in the rubble. Maybe they were dead because a German in the forest, sipping from a passed flask of schnapps and joking with his fellow officers, gave a young gunner the wrong coordinates, and the seventeen-centimeter shells meant for the Winter Palace fell on my ugly gray apartment building instead.

"How many come?"

Nina glanced at the other girls, but none of them returned her gaze. Galina picked at some unseen scab on the back of her hand. One of the burning logs tumbled off the andirons and Lara shoved it to the back of the fireplace with a poker. Olesya, the girl with the pigtails, hadn't said a word since we entered the farmhouse. I never learned if she was shy, or born mute, or if the Einsatzgruppen had sliced her tongue from her mouth. She picked up our empty plates and teacups and carried them out of the room.

"It depends on the night," Nina finally said. She spoke casually, as if we were discussing a game of cards. "Sometimes nobody comes. Sometimes two, or four. Sometimes more."

"They drive?"

"Yes, yes, of course."

"And they stay the night?"

"Sometimes. Not usually."

"And they never come during the day?"

"Once or twice."

"So, forgive me for asking, but what keeps you from walking away?"

"You think this is so easy to do?" asked Nina, annoyed by the question, by the implication.

"Not easy," said Kolya. "But Lev and I, we left Piter at dawn and here we are."

"These Germans you're fighting, the ones who have taken half our country, you think they're stupid? You think they would leave us here alone if we could just open the door and walk to Piter?"

"But why not? Why can't you?"

I could see the affect of his questions on the girls, the anger in Nina's eyes, the shame in Galina's as she stared at her soft white hands. Knowing Kolya even for a few days, I believed he was genuinely curious, not trying to batter the girls with his interrogation—but still, I wished he would shut up.

"Tell them about Zoya," Lara said.

Nina seemed annoyed by the advice. She shrugged and said nothing.

"They think we're cowards," Lara added.

"I don't care what they think," said Nina.

"Fine, I'll tell them. There was another girl, Zoya."

Galina stood, brushed off her nightshirt, and walked out of the great room. Lara ignored her.

"The Germans loved her. For every man who came here for me, six came for her."

Lara's blunt telling made all of us uncomfortable. Nina clearly wanted to follow the other girls out of the room, but she stayed where she was, her eyes darting around, looking at everything except Kolya and me.

"She was fourteen. Her mother and father were both in the Party. I don't know what they did, but I guess it was something important. The Einsatzgruppen found them and shot them in the street. They hanged the bodies from a lamppost so everyone in the town could see what happened to Communists. They brought Zoya here the same time they brought us, the end of November. Before that there were other girls. After a few months they get bored of us, you see. But Zoya was the favorite. She was so little and she was so afraid of them. I think they liked that. They would tell her, 'Don't worry, I won't hurt you, I won't let them hurt you,' things like that. But she'd seen her parents hanging from the lamppost. Any one of them who touched her, he could be the man who shot her mother and father, or ordered them shot."

"We all have stories," said Nina. "She panicked."

"Yes, she panicked. She was fourteen; she panicked. It's different for you; you have your sister. You're not alone."

"She had us."

"No," said Lara, "it's different. Every night, after they left, she cried. For hours, I mean, until she fell asleep, and sometimes she didn't sleep. The first week we tried to help her. We'd sit with her and hold her hand, tell her stories, anything to get her to stop crying. But it was impossible. Have you ever tried to comfort a baby with a fever? You try everything: you hold her in your arms, you rock her, you sing to her, you give her something cool to drink; doesn't matter, nothing works. She never stopped crying. And after a week of this, we stopped feeling sorry for her. We got angry. What Nina says is true: all of us have stories. All of us lost family. None of us could sleep with Zoya crying. The second week she was here, we ignored her. If she was in one room, we went to another. She knew we were angry—she didn't say anything, but she knew. And the crying stopped. All at once, as if she had decided that was enough. For three days she was very quiet, no more crying, just keeping to herself. And on the fourth morning she was gone. We didn't even know until later, when the officers came. They waltzed in here drunk, singing her name. I think they used to make bets, and the winner got Zoya first. They would bring friends from other units to see her, they would take pictures of her. But she was gone and, of course, they didn't believe us. We told them we had no idea but I would have called me a liar, too. I hope we would have lied, if we'd known. I hope we would have done that for her. I don't know that we would have."

"Of course we would have," said Nina.

"I don't know. It doesn't matter. They went out looking for her, Abendroth and the others. He's their, well, I don't know the ranks. Major?" She looked at Nina, who shrugged. "The major, I think. He's not the oldest, but he gives the orders. He must be good at what he does. And he always had her first, every time he came, didn't matter if they brought a colonel from somewhere, he'd take her for himself. When he was done with her, he'd come sit by the fire and drink his plum schnapps. Always plum schnapps for him. His Russian is perfect. And his French— He lived in Paris for two years."

"Hunting down the Resistance leaders," said Nina. "One of the others told me. He was so good at it they made him the youngest major in the Einsatzgruppen."

"He likes to play chess with me," said Lara. "I can play a decent game. Abendroth spots me a queen, sometimes a queen and a pawn, and I never last more than twenty moves, even when he's drunk, and he's usually drunk. If I'm . . . if I'm busy, he sets up the board and plays both sides himself."

"He's the worst of them," said Nina.

"Yes. I didn't think so at first. But after Zoya, yes, he's the worst of them. So they got their dogs and they followed her tracks and they went into the woods to find her. It only took them a few hours. She hadn't gotten far. She was so weak. . . . She'd been little to begin with, and she'd barely eaten a thing since she'd been here. They brought her back. They'd torn all the clothes off her. She looked like a wild animal, filthy, dead leaves in her hair, bruised all over her body where they'd hit her. They'd tied her wrists together and her ankles. Abendroth made me get the saw from out by the woodpile. When Zoya ran, she took my coat and my boots, so they figured I was the one helping her. He told me to get the saw. I don't know what I thought, but I wasn't thinking that . . . maybe I thought they'd use it for the rope. Maybe they wouldn't hurt her because they liked her so much."

I heard a muffled cry and looked over to see Nina scratching her forehead, her palm covering her eyes, her lips pressed together as she willed herself silent.

"Four of them held her down by her hands and her feet. She wasn't fighting them, not then. How could she fight them? All forty kilograms of her. . . . She thought they were going to kill her and she didn't care; she wanted it, she was waiting for it. But they didn't kill her. Abendroth made me give him the saw. He didn't take it from me; he made me put it in his hands. He wanted me to know that . . . that I gave it to him. We were all in this room, Nina and Galina and Olesya and me. They made us stay. They wanted us to watch, that was our punishment. We helped this girl try to escape and now we had to watch. All the Germans were smoking—they'd been out in the cold looking for her and now they were smoking their cigarettes—the room was full of their smoke. Zoya looked peaceful, like she might even smile. She was so far beyond them now, they couldn't touch her. But she was wrong about that. Abendroth got down next to her and whispered something in her ear. I don't know what he said. He took the wood saw and he put the teeth of it against her ankle and he began sawing. Zoya . . . Maybe I'll live a long time, I doubt it, but maybe I will, and I'll never get that scream out of my brain. Those were four strong men holding her down, and she was nothing but bones, but she fought them, now she fought them, and you could see them straining to keep her down. He sawed off her one foot and he moved to the next. One of the Germans ran out of the room . . . do you remember that, Nina? I forget his name. He never came back here. Abendroth sawed off the other foot and Zoya never stopped screaming. I thought that's it, I can't be sane again after seeing this, this is too much now, this is too much. And when he stood up, his uniform was covered with her blood—her blood was on his hands, on his face—and he gave us a little bow. Do you remember that? Like he'd just performed for us. He said, 'This is what happens to little girls who walk

15

Lara brought us to a small bedroom in the back of the house, where I imagined the valets slept in the time of the emperors. She carried a brass candelabrum with two lit candles, which she rested on the little writing desk. The pine-paneled walls were unadorned, the bunk bed had no sheets on the mattresses, and I almost tripped on the warped floorboards, but the room was warm enough. The narrow windows offered a view of a moonlit toolshed and a wheelbarrow lying on its side in the snow.

I sat on the lower mattress and ran my finger over a name carved in the wall. ARKADIY. I wondered how long ago Arkadiy stayed in this room, and where he was now, an old man shivering somewhere in the cold night or just bones in the churchyard. He had been good with the knife, his ARKADIY was a delicate filigree in the dark wood, slants and curlicues, a strong slash underlining the name.

Lara and Kolya came up with a code—banging pots with serving spoons—that would allow her to signal to us how many Germans showed up for their late-night entertainment. When she left, Kolya pulled out his pistol and began taking it apart, neatly arranging the various parts on the writing desk, checking them for damage and wiping them off with the sleeve of his shirt before reassembling the weapon.

"Have you ever shot anybody?" I asked.

"Not that I know about."

"What does that mean?"

"It means I shot my rifle a hundred times, maybe a bullet hit someone, I don't know." He slapped the magazine back into the butt of the automatic. "When I shoot Abendroth, I'll know it."

"Maybe we should just leave now."

"You're the one who wanted to come in here."

"We needed to rest. We needed food. I feel a lot better now."

He turned and looked at me. I was sitting on the bed with my hands under my legs, my overcoat spread out behind me.

"There could be eight of them coming," I said. "We've got one gun."

"And one knife."

"I can't stop thinking about Zoya."

"Good," he said. "Keep thinking about her when you stick the knife in his gut."

He threw his overcoat onto the top mattress and clambered up there, sitting cross-legged with his pistol beside him. He pulled his journal from the pocket of his overcoat. His stub of pencil had shrunk to the size of a thumbnail, but he jotted down notes with his usual speed.

"I don't think I can do it," I said, after a long silence. "I don't think I can stick a knife in anyone."

"Then I'll have to shoot them all. What's it been now, eleven days since I had a shit? What do you think the record is?"

"Probably a lot longer than that."

"I wonder what it's going to look like when it finally comes out."

"Kolya . . . why don't we just go now? Take the girls and go back to the city. We'd make it. They've got plenty of food we could bring. We've got our blood flowing again. Bring some extra blankets—"

"Listen to me. I know you're afraid. You're right to be afraid. Only an idiot would be calm sitting in a house knowing the Einsatzgruppen are coming. But this is what you've been waiting for. This is the night. They're trying to burn down our city; they're trying to starve us to death. But we're like two of Piter's bricks. You can't burn a brick. You can't starve a brick."

I watched the candles gutter in the candelabrum, watched the shadows dance across the ceiling.

"Where'd you hear that?" I finally asked him.

"Which part, the bricks? My lieutenant. Why? You're not inspired?"

"It was going along all right until then."

"I like the bricks. 'You can't burn a brick. You can't starve a brick.' It's nice. It has nice rhythm."

"This is the same lieutenant who stepped on a land mine?"

"Yes. Poor man. Well, forget about the bricks. I promise you, little lion, we're not dying out here. We're going to kill a few Nazis and we're going to find those eggs. I have a little Gypsy blood in me; I can read the future."

"You don't have any Gypsy blood."

"And I'll insist the colonel invites us to his daughter's wedding."

"Ha. You love her."

"I do. I believe I am truly in love with that girl. She is quite possibly an idiot bitch, but I love her. I want to marry her and she never has to say a word. She doesn't have to cook for me; she doesn't have to carry my babies. Just skate naked on the Neva, that's all I want. Do a little spin above my open mouth."

For a few seconds he helped me forget the fear, but it never left for long. I could not remember when I was not afraid, but that night it came on stronger than ever before. So many possibilities terrified me. There was the possibility of shame, of cowering again on the fringe of the action while Kolya fought the Germans—except this time, I knew he would die. There was the possibility of pain, suffering through the kind of torture Zoya suffered through, the saw teeth biting through my skin, muscles, and bone. And there was the excellent possibility of death. I never understood people who said their greatest fear was public speaking, or spiders, or any of the other minor terrors. How could you fear anything more than death? Everything else offered moments of escape: a paralyzed man could still read Dickens; a man in the grips of dementia might have flashes of the most absurd beauty.

I heard the bedsprings creaking and looked up to see Kolya leaning over the side of the top mattress, his upside-down face peering at me, his blond hair hanging in filthy clumps. He looked like he was worried about me, and all at once I felt like crying. The only one left who knew how frightened I was, the only one who knew I was still alive and that I might die tonight, was a boastful deserter I'd met three nights before, a stranger, a child of Cossacks, my last friend.

"This will cheer you up," he said, dropping a deck of cards in my lap.

They seemed like ordinary playing cards until I flipped them over. Each presented a different photographed woman, some naked, some wearing garter belts and lace corsets, their heavy breasts tumbling from their cupped hands, their lips slightly parted for the camera.

"I thought I had to beat you at chess to get these."

"Easy with that, easy. Don't crease the corners. Those came all the way from Marseille."

He watched me shuffle through the nudes, smiling when he saw me give certain models closer looks.

"What about the girls here, eh? Four beauties. We're going to be heroes after tonight, you realize this, yes? They'll be falling all over us. So which one do you want?"

"We're going to be dead after tonight."

"Truly, my friend, truly you have to stop speaking like this."

"I guess I like the little one with the chubby arms."

"Galina? All right. She looks like a veal calf, but all right, I understand."

He was quiet for a moment while I studied a picture of a shirtless woman wearing jodhpurs, cracking a bullwhip.

"Listen, Lev, after this is over tonight, promise me you'll talk to your little calf. Don't run away like the shy boy you are. I'm very serious about this. She likes you. I saw her looking at you."

I knew for a fact that Galina had not been looking at me. She had been looking at Kolya, as they all had, as he knew very well.

"What happened to calculated neglect? You said that according to *The Courtyard Hound*, the secret to winning a woman—"

"There's a difference between ignoring a woman and enticing her. You entice her with mystery. She wants you to come after her, but you keep circling. It's the same with sex. Amateurs yank down their pants and shove it in there like they're trying to spear a fish. But the man with talent knows it's all about teasing, circling, coming close, and moving away."

"This one's nice," I said, holding up a card featuring a woman posed as a bullfighter, holding a red cape and wearing nothing but a montera.

"That's my favorite one. When I was your age, I must have filled twenty socks staring at her."

"*Truth for Young Pioneers* says that masturbation defeats the revolutionary spirit."

"Without a doubt. But as Proudhon said—"

I never found out what Proudhon said. The double clang of a copper spoon against a copper pot interrupted Kolya. We both sat up in our beds.

"They came early," he whispered.

"Only two of them."

"They picked the wrong night to travel light." The moment those words were in the air the spoon struck the pot again—once, twice, three times, four.

"Six," I whispered.

Kolya swung his legs over the side of the mattress and quietly lowered himself to the floor, pistol in his hand. He blew out the candles and squinted out the window, but we were on the wrong side of the house and there was nothing to see. We heard car doors slamming shut.

"This is what we do," he told me, his voice low

and calm. "We wait. Let them relax, warm up, have a few drinks. They'll take their clothes off, with any luck they won't be near their guns. Remember, they're not here to fight. They're here to have a good time, enjoy the girls. You hear? We have the advantage."

I nodded. Despite what he said, the arithmetic seemed very bad to me. Six Germans and two of us. Would the girls try to help us? They hadn't lifted a hand for Zoya, but what could they have done for Zoya? Six Germans and eight bullets in the Tokarev. I hoped Kolya was a good shot. Fear coursed through me, electric, forcing my muscles to twitch and my mouth to go dry. I felt more awake than I ever had before, as if this moment, in the farmhouse outside of Berezovka, was the first true moment of my life and everything that came before was a fitful sleep. My senses seemed amplified, extraordinary, responding to the crisis by giving me all the information I needed. I could hear the crunch of jackboots on packed snow. I could smell pine needles burning in the fireplace, that old trick to perfume the house.

The rifle shot startled us. We stood quietly in the darkness, trying to understand what was happening. After a few seconds, several more rifles echoed the first. We heard the Germans shouting to each other, panicked, their voices overlapping.

Kolya ran for the door. I wanted to tell him to wait, that we had a plan and the plan called for waiting, but I didn't want to be alone in there while the rifles fired outside and the Germans screamed their ugly words.

We ran to the great room and threw ourselves onto the floor when a bullet smashed through one of the mullioned windows. All four girls were already lying belly-down on the floor, their arms up by their faces to protect themselves from flying glass.

I had been living in a war for half a year, but I had never been this close to a gunfight and I had no idea who was fighting. I could hear the chuffing cough of machine guns fired just outside the house. The rifle cracks seemed to come from farther away, the edge of the woods, possibly. Bullets hammered the stone walls of the farmhouse.

Kolya crawled up to Lara and jostled her.

"Who's shooting at them?"

"I don't know."

Outside we heard a car engine igniting. Doors slammed and the car accelerated, tires spinning in the snow. The rifles fired even faster now, one on top of the other, bullets ripping through sheet metal, a very different sound from bullet on stone.

Kolya rose to a crouch and crept to the front door, keeping his head below the window line. I followed. We kneeled with our backs against the door. Kolya checked his pistol one last time. I pulled the German knife from my ankle sheath. I knew I looked silly holding it, the way a young boy looks holding his father's shaving razor. Kolya grinned at me as though he was about to start laughing. This is all very strange, I thought. I am in the middle of a battle and I am aware of my own thoughts, I am worried about how stupid I look with a knife in my hand while everyone else came to fight with rifles and machine guns. I am aware that I am aware. Even now, with bullets buzzing through the air like angry hornets, I cannot escape the chatter of my brain.

Kolya put his hand on the doorknob and turned it slowly.

"Wait," I said. We stayed very still for a few seconds. "It's quiet."

The gunfire had ended abruptly. The car engine still hummed, but I couldn't hear the wheels turning. The German voices had gone silent as suddenly as the bullets. Kolya glanced at me and slowly pulled the door open, just enough to peer through. The moon was high and bright, lighting the brutal landscape: Einsatzkommandos in white anoraks sprawled facedown in the snow and a Kübelwagen rolling slowly down the unshoveled driveway, windows shot out, engine block smoking. The dead man in the passenger seat sagged halfway out of the side window, his fingers still wrapped around his machine pistol. A second Kübel, parked at a jaunty angle beside the farmhouse, had never moved. Two Germans lay halfway between it and the house, their skulls pouring dark junk onto the snow. I had just enough time to register the precision of the shots, the superb accuracy of the sniper, when a bullet flew through the gap between Kolya's head and mine, twanging in the air like a plucked string.

Both of us tumbled backward and Kolya kicked the door shut with his boot. He cupped his hands around his mouth and yelled toward the shattered window beside the front door.

"We're Russians! Hey! Hey! We're Russians!"

For a few seconds there was silence, before a distant voice responded: "You look like a fucking Fritz to me!"

Kolya laughed, punching me in the shoulder in his happiness.

"My name is Nikolai Alexandrovich Vlasov!" he shouted toward the window. "From Engels Prospekt!"

"There's an original name! Any Nazi with a few years of Russian could come up with that!"

"Engels Prospekt!" shouted another voice. "There's an Engels Prospekt in every fucking town in the country!"

Still laughing, Kolya grabbed hold of my coat and shook me, for no other reason than his blood was spiked with adrenaline, he was alive and happy and he needed to shake something. He crawled closer to the broken window, skirting the shards of broken glass lying on the floor.

"Your mother's cunt has a peculiar tubular shape!" he yelled. "Nonetheless I tolerate its effluvium and enthusiastically lick its inner folds whenever she demands!"

A very long silence followed this sentence, but Kolya did not seem concerned. He was chuckling at his own joke, winking at me like an old veteran of the Turkish war exchanging insults with his buddies at the bathhouse.

"How about that?" he added at the top of his lungs. "You think anyone with a few years of Russian could come up with that?"

"Which one of our mothers are you describing?" The voice sounded closer now.

"Not the one who shoots so well. One of you is a genius with the rifle."

"You have a gun on you?" asked the voice outside.

"A Tokarev pistol."

"And your little friend?"

"Just a knife."

"Both of you step outside. Keep your hands up high or my friend will shoot your tiny balls off."

Lara and Nina had crawled into the front hall-way during this conversation, their nightshirts sequined with bits of glass from the blown-out windows.

"Did they kill them?" whispered Nina.

"All six," I told her. I thought the girls would be pleased, but when they heard the news they exchanged worried looks. Their life of the past few months was over now. They would have to run without knowing where their next meal would come from or where they would sleep. Millions of Russians could say the same, but things were worse for the girls. If the Germans caught them again, they would suffer a harsher punishment than Zoya had.

As Kolya reached for the doorknob, Lara put her hand on his leg, making him wait for a moment.

"Don't," she said. "They won't trust you."

"Why wouldn't they trust me? I'm a soldier of the Red Army."

"Yes, and they're not. There isn't a Red Army unit within thirty kilometers of here. They'll think you're a deserter."

He smiled and covered her hand with his own.

"Do I look like a deserter to you? Don't worry. I have papers."

Papers did not impress Lara. As Kolya reached again for the doorknob, she crawled closer to the broken window.

"Thank you for rescuing us, comrades!" she shouted. "These two in here are our friends! Please don't shoot them!"

"You think I would have missed his fat blond

head if I wanted to hit it? Tell the joker to come outside."

Kolya opened the door and stepped outside, his hands held high in the air. He squinted across the snow, but the fighters were still out of sight.

"Tell the little one to come out here, too."

Lara and Nina looked frightened for me, but Lara nodded, telling me with an encouraging nod that it would be all right. I felt a brief surge of anger for the girl: why couldn't she step outside? Why did they have to be here at all? If the farmhouse had been empty, Kolya and I could have slept through the night and left in the morning, rested and dry. The thought passed through my head, immediately followed by guilt for its absurdity.

Nina squeezed my hand and smiled at me. She was easily the finest-looking girl who had ever smiled at me. I imagined describing the scene for Oleg Antokolsky: Nina's little white hand gripping mine, her pale eyelashes fluttering as she stared at me, worried for my safety. Even as the moment passed I was narrating it for my friend, forgetting for the moment that Oleg would probably never hear the story, that the odds were strong he lay buried beneath the rubble on Voinova Street.

I tried to smile back at Nina, failed, and walked out the door with my hands in the air. Since the war began I had read hundreds of accounts of the country's heroes in action. All of them refused to acknowledge they were heroes. They were honest citizens of the Motherland, protecting her from the Fascist rapists. When asked in interviews why they had rushed the pillbox, or clambered onto a tank to drop a grenade down the hatch, all responded that they hadn't even thought about it, they were just doing what any other good Russian would have done.

Heroes and fast sleepers, then, can switch off their thoughts when necessary. Cowards and insomniacs, my people, are plagued by babble on the brain. When I stepped out of the door, I thought, *I am standing in the front yard of a farmhouse outside Berezovka and partisans are pointing their rifles at my head.*

Judging from the broad smile on Kolya's face, he thought nothing at all. We stood side by side while our unseen interrogators looked us over. Our overcoats were back in the farmhouse and we shivered in the night air, the cold reaching down to our bones.

"Prove you're one of us." The voice seemed to come from beside one of the snow-covered hay bales, and as my eyes adjusted to the light I could see a man kneeling in the shadows, a rifle raised to his shoulder. "Shoot each of the Germans in the head."

"That's not much of a test," said Kolya. "They're already dead."

The man's ability to make a bad situation worse no longer surprised me. Perhaps a hero is someone who doesn't register his own vulnerability. Is it courage, then, if you're too daft to know you're mortal?

"We're still alive," said the partisan in the shadows, "because we shoot them even when we think they're dead."

Kolya nodded. He walked over to the idling Kübel, which had finally rolled to a stop, its tires buried in a meter of snow.

"We're watching you," advised the partisan. "A bullet in every head."

Kolya shot the dead driver and the dead passenger, the muzzle flashing in the night like a photographer's camera. He turned and walked through the snow, stopping to shoot the Germans lying in their awkward poses.

At the sixth man, as he stooped to press the pistol to the fallen Einsatzkommando's skull, he heard something. He got down on his knees and listened for a moment before standing up and calling out.

"This one's still alive."

"That's why you're going to shoot him."

"Maybe he has something useful to tell us."

"Does he look like he's able to talk?"

Kolya turned the German onto his back. The man moaned softly. Pink foam bubbled from his mouth.

"No," said Kolya.

"That's because we shot his lungs out. Now do him a favor and end him."

Kolya stood, aimed his pistol, and shot the dying man in the forehead.

"Holster your gun."

Kolya did as he was told and the partisans emerged from their hiding places, stepping out from behind the hay bales, climbing over the low stone walls separating the farm fields, trudging through the snow at the edge of the woods. A dozen men in long coats, their rifles in their hands, their breath rising above their heads as they closed in on the farmhouse.

Most of them looked like farmers, fur-lined hats pulled down to their eyebrows, faces broad and flat and unfriendly. There was no common uniform. Some wore Red Army leather boots, others walked in gray felt; some wore tan overcoats, others gray. One man was dressed in what looked like a Finnish ski troop's winter whites. Walking in front was the man I took to be their leader, a week's worth of beard darkening his jaw, an old hunting rifle strapped to his shoulder. Later that night we learned his name was Korsakov. If he had a first name and a patronymic, we never heard them. Korsakov probably wasn't his real name, anyway—the partisans were notoriously paranoid about their identities, with good reason. The Einsatzkommandos responded to local resistance by publicly executing the families of known resisters.

Korsakov and two of his comrades approached us while the other partisans searched the dead Germans, taking their machine pistols and ammunition, their letters and flasks and wristwatches. The man in the ski outfit knelt beside one of the bodies and tried to tug a gold wedding band from the corpse's ring finger. When it wouldn't come off, the partisan stuck the finger in his mouth. He saw me staring at him and winked, pulling the wet finger from his lips and sliding the ring free.

"Don't worry about them," said Korsakov, when he saw what I was watching. "Worry about me. Why are you two here?"

"They're here to organize the partisans," said Nina. She and Lara had stepped out of the farmhouse in their bare feet, their arms wrapped around themselves, the wind blowing their hair.

"Is that right? Do we seem unorganized?"

"They're friends. They were going to kill the Germans if you didn't show up."

"Were they? How kind." He turned away from

her and called out to the partisans searching the dead men in the car. "What do we have?"

"Small fish," a bearded partisan shouted back, holding up the insignia he'd torn from the officer's collars. "Leutnants and Oberleutnants."

Korsakov shrugged and shifted his gaze back to Nina, appraising her pale calves and the shape of her hips below her nightshirt.

"Get back inside," he told her. "Put some clothes on. The Germans are dead; you can quit being a whore."

"Don't you call me that."

"I'll call you whatever I want. Get back inside."

Lara took Nina's hand and dragged her back to the farmhouse. Kolya watched them go and turned to the partisan leader.

"You're unkind, comrade."

"I'm not your comrade. And if it weren't for me, they'd have German cocks halfway up them right now."

"All the same—"

"Shut your mouth. You're wearing an Army uniform, but you're not with the Army. You're a deserter?"

"We're here on orders. I have papers in my coat, inside the house."

"Every collaborator I ever met had papers."

"I have a letter from Colonel Grechko of the NKVD, authorizing us to come here."

Korsakov grinned and turned to his men.

"And Colonel Grechko, he has authority out here? I love these policemen in the city, giving us orders."

One of the men standing beside him, a rangy fellow with close-set eyes, laughed loudly, showing us his bad teeth. The other man did not laugh. He wore winter camouflage coveralls patterned with brown and white swirls, a trompe l'oeil of dead leaves. His eyes peeked out below the fringe of his rabbit fur cap. He was small, smaller than me, and young, with no trace of stubble on his pink cheeks. His features were very fine, the bones of his face precisely defined, his lips full, twisted into a smirk now as he stared back at me.

"You see something strange?" he asked, and I realized it wasn't a man speaking at all.

"You're a girl," Kolya blurted out, staring at her. I felt stupid for both of us.

"Don't look so shocked," said Korsakov. "She's our best shot. Those Fritzes over there with half their heads? That's because of her."

Kolya whistled, glancing from her to the dead Germans to the fringe of woods at the edge of the farm fields.

"From over there? What is that, four hundred meters? On moving targets?"

The girl shrugged. "You don't have to lead them so much when they're running through snow."

"Vika's after Lyudmila Pavlichenko's record," said the man with the under bite. "She wants to be the number-one woman sniper."

"How many is Mila up to now?" asked Kolya.

"*Red Star* says two hundred," Vika replied with a little roll of her eyes. "The Army gives her a confirmed kill every time she blows her nose."

"That's a German rifle, isn't it?"

"K ninety-eight," she said, slapping the barrel with her palm. "Best rifle in the world."

Kolya nudged me with his elbow and whispered under his breath. "I've got a little bit of a hard-on."

"What's that?" asked Korsakov.

"I said my cock's going to fall off if we stand out here much longer—pardon my language." He gave Vika an old-fashioned bow before turning back to Korsakov. "You want to see my papers, let's go inside and see the papers. You want to shoot your countrymen here in the snow, all right, shoot us. But enough of this standing in the cold."

The partisan clearly preferred the idea of shooting Kolya to looking at his papers, but killing an Army man was no small matter, especially with so many witnesses. He didn't want to give in too quickly, either, and lose face in front of his men. So the two of them stood there glaring at each other for another ten seconds while I bit my lip to keep my teeth from chattering.

Vika broke the stalemate. "These two are falling in love," she said. "Look at them! They can't decide if they want to fight each other or roll naked in the snow."

The other partisans laughed and Vika walked toward the farmhouse, ignoring Korsakov's glare.

"I'm hungry," she said. "Those girls in there look like they've been eating pork chops all winter."

The men followed her, carrying their loot, eager to get out of the cold and into the house. I watched Vika stomping her boots in front of the door, ridding her soles of snow, and I wondered what her body looked like beneath those winter camouflage coveralls, beneath the layers of wool and felt.

"Is she yours?" Kolya asked Korsakov, after Vika had stepped inside the farmhouse.

"Are you joking? That one's more boy than girl."

"Good," said Kolya, punching me in the arm. "Because I think my friend here has a crush."

Korsakov glanced at me and began to laugh. I always hated when people laughed at me, but this time I welcomed his amusement. I knew he wasn't going to kill us.

"Best of luck to you, boy. Just remember, she can shoot your eyes out from half a kilometer."

16

Korsakov had given his men an hour to warm up and feed themselves, and now they were sprawled across the great room, their socks hanging from the fireplace screen, their overcoats spread out on the floor. Vika lay on her back on a horsehair sofa beneath the mounted ibex head, her ankles crossed, her fingers playing with the rabbit fur cap resting on her chest. Her dark red hair was cut short as a boy's, so dirty it clumped together in spikes and whorls. She stared into the ibex's glass eyes, fascinated by the murdered animal—wondering about the hunt, I imagined, about the hunter's shot, if it was a clean kill or if the wounded beast ran for miles, not understanding that death had already burrowed into his muscle and bone, a tumbling slug that could not be outrun.

I was sitting on a window ledge watching her and trying to make sure she didn't know I was watching her. She had stripped off her coveralls to let them dry. She wore a heavy wool woodcutter's shirt that once belonged to a man twice her size and two pairs of long underwear. Unlike most redheads, she didn't have a single freckle. She worried at her upper lip with the bottom row of her crooked little teeth. I couldn't stop looking at her. She was no man's idea of a pinup girl—underfed as she was, looking like she'd spent the last week sleeping in the forest—but I wanted to see her naked. I wanted to unbutton the woodcutter's shirt, toss it aside, and lick her pale belly, strip off the long underwear and kiss her thin thighs.

This graphic daydream was a departure for me. Had Kolya's pornographic playing cards riled my imagination? Usually my fantasies were chaste, anachronistic—I'd envision Vera Osipovna, fully clothed, giving me a cello recital in the loneliness of her bedroom, and afterward I would praise her playing, impressing her with my eloquence and mastery of the musicians' vocabulary. The fantasy would end with some strong kissing, Vera's out-flung leg knocking over the music stand, her face hot and flushed as I flashed a mysterious smile and left her standing, her collar askew, one button of her shirt undone.

My fantasies generally ended before getting to the sex because I was afraid of sex. I didn't know how to do it. I didn't even know enough to fake knowing how to do it. I understood the basic anatomy, but the geometry of the act confused me, and without a father or an older brother or any close friends with experience, there was no one around to ask.

But there was nothing chaste in my hunger for Vika. I wanted to jump on her, my pants around my ankles. She could show me where everything went and once we were sorted, her fingers with their dirty, bitten nails would rake my shoulders; her head would tilt back, exposing her long white throat and the tremor of pulse below her jaw; her heavy eyelids would open wide, pupils constricting in the blue of her eyes until they were the size of the dot above the *i*.

All of the women of the house—Nina and Galina, Lara and Olesya—were prettier than Vika at first glance. Their hair was long and brushed; they had no dried mud on the backs of their hands; they even wore a bit of lipstick. They hurried in and out of the great room, carrying bowls of shelled walnuts and salted radishes. There was a new group of armed men to please—countrymen, yes, but still dangerous and unpredictable. One of them, sitting cross-legged on the floor by the fire, grabbed Galina's chubby wrist as she leaned down to refill his glass of vodka.

"You take a look outside yet? Is your boyfriend one of them lying on his face?"

His friend beside him laughed and the partisan, encouraged, yanked Galina into his lap. She was used to rough treatment; she didn't cry out or spill a drop of the vodka.

"Did they bring you lots of tasty things to eat? They must have, eh, feel these cheeks!" He brushed a callused thumb across her soft pink cheek. "And what did you do for them? Anything they wanted, was that it? Danced naked while they sang the 'Horst Wessel Song'? Sucked them off while they drank their schnapps?"

"Get off her," said Vika. She was lying on her back just as she had been, still looking up at the ibex head while her feet in their thick wool socks swayed to the beat of an unheard song. Her voice was uninflected—if she was angry, it was impossible to tell. As soon as the words were in the air I wished I had said them instead. It would have been a brave gesture, possibly suicidal, but Galina had been kind

to me and I should have defended her—not because
of my noble nature, but because it might have impressed Vika. But in the moment when I might have
acted I froze, another act of cowardice to dwell on
through the years. Kolya would have intervened
without hesitation, but Kolya was in the back bedroom with Korsakov, looking over the colonel's letter of safe transit.

The partisan gripping Galina's wrist hesitated
before responding to Vika. I knew he was afraid.
I've been afraid for so long I can spot the fear in
other people before they know it's there. But I also
knew he would say something back, something cutting to prove to his comrades that he wasn't afraid,
even though they all knew he was.

"What's the matter?" he finally asked. "You
want her for yourself?"

It was a weak effort and none of his friends gave
him a laugh. Vika didn't bother responding. She
never looked his way. The only sign that she had
heard him at all was a slow smile that spread across
her face, and it wasn't clear if that was in response
to his taunt or the ibex's glass-eyed glare. After a
few more seconds the partisan grunted, let go of
Galina, and gave her a weak push.

"Go on, serve the others. You've been a slave so
long that's all you're good for."

If the partisan's insults wounded her, Galina hid
it well. She poured glasses of vodka for the other
men in the room and all of them were polite, nodding their heads in thanks.

After a minute to consider the odds of severe
embarrassment, I walked over to the horsehair sofa
and sat on the end of it, close to Vika's feet in their
gray wool socks. The ibex's chin beard dangled

above my head. I glanced up at it and then over to Vika. She was staring right at me, waiting to hear whatever ludicrous thing I was planning to say.

"Was your father a hunter?" I asked. This was the question I had formulated while standing on the other side of the room. As soon as I said it I wondered why I had thought it was a good way to start a conversation. Some article I had read about snipers, something about Sidorenko shooting squirrels when he was a boy.

"What?"

"Your father . . . I thought maybe that's how you learned to shoot."

I couldn't tell if it was boredom or disgust in her blue eyes. Up close, by the light of the oil lamps and the fireplace, I could see a spray of small red pimples across her forehead.

"No. He wasn't a hunter."

"I guess a lot of snipers started out as hunters. . . . Anyway, I read something about it."

She wasn't looking at me anymore, she was back to studying the ibex. I was less interesting than a stuffed animal. The other partisans watched me, elbowing each other and grinning, leaning close to whisper and laugh quietly.

"Where'd you get that German rifle?" I asked her, a little desperate, a gambler who keeps on betting even as his hands get worse and worse.

"Off a German."

"I have a German knife." I pulled up my pants leg, unsheathed the knife, and turned it in my hand, letting the fine steel catch the light. The knife got her attention. She held out her hand and I passed it to her. She tested the edge of the blade against her forearm.

"Sharp enough to shave with," I said. "Not that you need to . . . I mean . . ."

"Where'd you find it?"

"On a German."

She smiled and I was very proud of the line, as if I'd said something massively clever, responding to her taciturnity with my own.

"And where'd you find the German?"

"Dead paratrooper in Leningrad." I hoped that was vague enough to leave open the possibility that I had killed the paratrooper.

"They're dropping into Leningrad? It's started?"

"Just a commando raid, I guess. Only a few got through. Didn't go so well for the Fritzes." I thought that sounded right, offhand, as if I were the sort of killer who spoke casually of the enemies I'd dispatched.

"You killed him yourself?"

I opened my mouth, fully prepared to lie, but the way she looked at me, her lips curled into that smirk that both angered me with its condescension and made me want to kiss her . . .

"The cold killed him. I just saw him falling."

She nodded and handed back the knife, stretching her arms behind her head and giving a tremendous yawn, not bothering to cover her mouth. Her teeth were like children's teeth, very small and not quite matching. She looked content, as if she'd just eaten a nine-course meal served with the best wines, though all I'd seen her nibble on was a black radish.

"The cold is Mother Russia's oldest weapon," I added, some line I'd heard a general spout on the radio. Immediately I wished I could retract it.

Maybe it was true, but it had been a propaganda cliché for months now. Even mouthing the phrase *Mother Russia* made me feel like one of those stupid smiling Young Pioneers, marching in the parks in their white shirts and red ties, singing "The Little Joyful Drummer."

"I have a knife, too," she said, slipping a birch-handled dagger out of a sheath tucked into her belt and offering it to me hilt first.

I turned the slender blade in my hand. There was a pattern of fine lines on the steel, like ripples in disturbed water.

"It seems a little flimsy."

"It's not." She leaned forward to run the tip of her index finger along the textured blade. "That's Damascus steel."

She was close enough now that I could study the curling ridges of her ear or the creases that interrupted the smooth span of her forehead when she raised her eyebrows. A few stray pine needles were lodged in the thickets of her hair and I resisted the impulse to pluck them out.

"It's called a puukko," she told me. "All the Finnish boys get them when they come of age."

She took the knife back from me and tilted it so she could admire the play of firelight on metal.

"The best sniper in the world is a Finn. Simo Häyhä. The White Death. Five hundred and five confirmed kills in the Winter War."

"So you took that off some Finn you shot?"

"Bought it for eighty rubles in Terijoki." She slipped the dagger back into the sheath on her belt and surveyed the room, looking for something more interesting to occupy her attention.

"Maybe you can be the Red Death," I said, trying to keep talking because I knew if I stopped, I would never regain the courage to start again. "That was some fine sniping out there. I guess the Einsatz-kommandos aren't used to people shooting back at them."

Vika regarded me with her cold blue eyes. There was something not entirely human about her gaze, something predatory, lupine. She made a circle of her lips before shaking her head.

"Why do you think those were Einsatzkomman-dos?"

"The girls told us that's who comes here."

"What are you, fifteen? You're not a soldier—"

"Seventeen."

"—but you're traveling with a soldier who's not with his unit."

"Well, as he was saying, we have special orders from Colonel Grechko."

"Special orders to do what? Organize the parti-sans? Do I look so very stupid to you?"

"No."

"You came here to visit the girls? Is that it? One of these is your girlfriend?"

I was strangely proud that she thought one of the lovely girls in the house might be my girlfriend, even though I could hear the insulting tone in her phras-ing, *one of these.* She was curious about me, that was a start. And she was right to be curious. Why should a Piter boy be all the way out here, twenty ki-lometers behind enemy lines, resting in a comfort house maintained for officers of the invaders?

I remembered what Kolya had told me about enticing a woman with mystery.

"We have our orders, I'm sure you have yours, let's keep it at that."

Vika stared at me in silence for a few seconds. She might have been enticed, but it was hard to tell.

"Those Germans out there with their brains in the snow? That's regular Army. You'd think a man—sorry, a *boy*—working with the NKVD would know the difference."

"I didn't get a chance to inspect their insignia because you people were pointing your rifles at us."

"We're looking for Einsatz, though. That's big game. We've been hunting this corpse-fucker Abendroth the last six weeks. Thought he might be here tonight."

I had never heard the curse "corpse-fucker" before. The phrase sounded brutally vulgar coming from her lips. I smiled for some reason, a smile that must have seemed odd and unprovoked. In my mind I pictured her with her pants off; the image was sharp and detailed, far more convincing than my imagined nudes usually were. Maybe Kolya's pornographic playing cards really had helped.

"Abendroth's in a house in Novoye Koshkino," I told her. "By the lake."

The information seemed to entice her more than anything else I had said. My inappropriate smile matched with my knowledge of the Nazi's whereabouts made me momentarily intriguing.

"Who told you that?"

A more mysterious man would have known how to deflect the question, how to sidestep like a boxer, bobbing and weaving, never getting tagged. I knew something she wanted to know. For the first time I had a slight advantage over her. The words *Novoye Koshkino* gave my NKVD credentials a touch of credence, offered me some leverage I could exploit.

"Lara," I said, giving it all away with a word.

"Which one is Lara?"

I pointed her out. As Vika's unblinking gaze shifted, I felt that I had somehow betrayed Lara. She had been generous—given us shelter from the cold, fed us warm food, ventured into the brutal winter night in her bare feet to help defend us from the suspicious partisans—and I had surrendered her name to this smirking blue-eyed killer. Vika slid her feet off the sofa, her toes in their wool socks grazing against my pants leg. She stood and walked over to Lara, who was crouched by the fire, adding another log to the blaze. With her boots off I saw how small Vika really was, but she moved with the kind of lazy grace you see in athletes when they're relaxing away from the playing field. *This is modern warfare*, I thought, *where muscle means nothing and a slender girl can halve a German's head at four hundred meters.*

Lara seemed nervous when she saw the sniper smiling down at her. She rubbed the soot off her hands as she listened to Vika. I couldn't hear the conversation, but I saw Lara nod, and from the way she gestured with her hands I figured she was giving Vika directions.

Kolya walked into the room with Korsakov. Each had a glass of vodka in hand and they were laughing at some joke, best of chums now, the earlier hostility forgotten. I had expected nothing less—Kolya was a great salesman, especially when he was selling himself. He ambled over to the horsehair sofa and sat down with a sigh, slapping my knee and downing the last of his vodka.

"You get enough to eat?" he asked me. "We're ready to move."

"We're leaving? I thought we'd sleep here tonight."

The gunfight had riled my system, but now that some time had passed since the bullets were flying, I felt the fatigue seeping back into my bones. We had walked all day through the snow and I hadn't slept since Sonya's apartment.

"Come on, you're smarter than that. What do you think is going to happen when those Fritzes out there don't come back from their little party tonight? How long before they send a platoon to find out where their Oberleutnants disappeared to?"

Vika had gotten what she needed from Lara. Now she spoke in low tones to Korsakov, the two of them standing in the corner of the room—the broad-shouldered, stubble-jawed partisan commander and his little assassin, lit by the flickering fire.

The other partisans began to get ready, pulling on their dry socks and their felt boots, swallowing one more glass of vodka for the long march ahead of them. The girls of the house had disappeared to the back rooms where, I guessed, they would grab whatever they could carry and decide where to go next.

"We could take the German cars," I said, inspired by the idea. "Drop off the girls in Piter . . ." Like most ideas I considered inspired, the brilliance of it faded before I reached the end of the second sentence.

"Drive a Kübel toward the Leningrad line," said Kolya. "Hm, yes, that's a thought. And when our own people blow us off the road and some Don Cossack country idiot pulls our smoking bodies from the wreckage, he'll say, 'Huh! These German boys look just like us!' No, little lion, we're not going back to Piter yet. We've got business in Novoye Koshkino."

Twenty minutes later we were trudging through the snow again, the warmth of the farmhouse already slipping from memory. Flanked by mighty pines, we walked in single file with nine paces between each man, on Korsakov's explicit orders. I didn't understand the tactical significance of the formation, but trusted that these men were masters of the ambush and knew what they were doing. Kolya walked in front of me and with my head hanging low I was aware only of the hem of his greatcoat and his black leather boots. The rest of the bodies in our little caravan were phantoms, unseen and unheard except for the occasional crack of a stepped-on twig or the rasp of a canteen cap unscrewed for a sip of still-hot tea.

I had never really believed that truism that soldiers learned how to sleep while they marched, but as we continued east, lulled by the rhythm of our boots rising and falling in the snow, I lurched in and out of wakefulness. Even the cold could not keep me alert. Novoye Koshkino was only a few kilometers from the farmhouse by road, but we were far from any road, circling around German encampments that Kolya and I would have stumbled into if we were unescorted. Korsakov had said the march would take four hours; before the first one was over I felt that someone had poured thick syrup into a hole in my skull. Everything I did I did slowly. If I wanted to rub my nose, I was aware of the brain's command and the hand's grudging obedience, the long journey the hand took on the way to the face, the search for the nose (usually an easy target), and the hand's grateful return to its cozy little cave in the depths of my father's navy coat.

The more tired I got the more doubtful the whole scenario seemed. How could this be real? We were a band of enchanted mice, marching beneath the chalked moon on the blackboard sky. A sorcerer lived in Novoye Koshkino, a man who knew the ancient words that could transform us back into the men we once were. But there would be perils on the way, giant black cats scrambling over the ice, lunging for us as we scurried for cover, our long tails twitching with fear.

My boot sank deep into a mound of soft snow and I nearly turned my ankle. Kolya stopped and looked back when he heard me stagger, but I managed to right myself, give him a quick nod, and keep walking without any help.

The girls who lived in the farmhouse had left at the same time we did. They did not have any overcoats or winter boots; the Germans had taken those items away after Zoya made her run. Without proper clothing the girls resorted to layering, throwing on every shirt they had, every sweater and pair of leggings, until they teetered beneath the weight, wobbling through the great room like drunk, obese peasants. Galina had brought up the idea of taking the Nazis' overcoats, but she was quickly shushed—their chances were bad enough, if they were captured, but getting captured while wearing a dead officer's coat was the end.

Kolya and I had kissed their cheeks at the doorway. They had decided not to go to Leningrad; a few of them had family there, but the uncles and cousins might have died already or fled to the east. More important, there was no food in Leningrad for the residents and certainly no food for four girls from the villages with no ration cards. Leningrad didn't make sense, so they were heading south. They had brought whatever provisions were left after the partisans took what they wanted. Korsakov let them keep two of the Germans' Lugers for protection. Their odds were not good, but they seemed in high spirits as they walked out the farmhouse door. They had been prisoners there for months, had suffered their own tortures night after night, and now they were free. I kissed all eight cheeks, waved good-bye, and never saw them again or heard anything about them.

Something jolted my shoulder, my eyes popped open, and I realized I'd been walking in a semiconscious trance. Kolya marched beside me now, his gloved hand gripping me through my coat.

"You still with us?" he asked quietly, watching me with real concern.

"I'm here."

"I'll walk with you. Keep you awake."

"Korsakov told us to—"

"I don't take orders from that motherless pig. You saw how he treated the girls."

"You're the one who was getting so chummy with him."

"We need him right now. And his little friend . . . I saw you staring at her back there by the fireplace. You'd like to take a shot at the sniper, eh? Eh? Ha!"

I shook my head, too tired even to groan at his miserable joke.

"Have you ever been with a redhead? Oh wait, what am I saying, you've never been with anyone. The good news is they're demons between the sheets. Two of the three best fucks of my life were redheads. Two of four, anyway. But the other side of the coin, they hate men. A lot of anger there, my friend. Beware."

"All redheads hate men?"

"Makes a lot of sense when you think about it. Any redhead you meet out here, chances are she's descended from some Viking who ran around hacking people's arms off before raping her ancestral grandmother. She's got the blood of the pillagers in her."

"That's a good theory. You should tell her about it."

On every stride I tried to step into the boot prints of the partisan who walked eighteen strides ahead of us. Stepping into crushed snow took less energy than stepping into fresh powder, but the man in front had long legs, and I was having a hard time matching him.

"And just so I'm clear," I began, panting a little and ducking beneath an out-flung branch laden with pine needles, "we're marching to Novoye Koshkino to find the house where the Einsatzgruppe is headquartered because they might have some eggs there?"

"That's what we're doing for the colonel. But for us, and for Russia, we're marching to Novoye Koshkino to kill the Einsatz because they need to be killed."

I lowered my head so that most of my face was shielded from the wind by the upturned collar of my father's greatcoat. What was the point of further discussion? Kolya considered himself a bit of a bohemian, a free thinker, but in his own way he was as much a true believer as any Young Pioneer. The worst part about it was that I didn't think he was wrong. The Einsatzkommandos needed to be destroyed before they destroyed us. I just didn't want to be the one responsible for destroying them. Was I supposed to sneak into their lair with only a knife for protection? Five days ago an account of this expedition would have seemed like the great adventure I'd been waiting for since the war began. But now, in the middle of it, I wished I'd left in September with my mother and sister.

"Do you remember the end of book one of *The Courtyard Hound*? When Radchenko sees his old professor stumbling down the street, muttering at the pigeons?"

"Worst scene in the history of literature."

"Oh, forgive me, you've never read the book."

There was something oddly comforting in Kolya's consistency, his willingness to make the same jokes—if you could call them jokes—over and over again. He was like a cheerful senile grandfather who sat at the dinner table with beet soup splattered on his collar, telling once more the story of his encounter with the emperor, though everyone in his family could recite it now from memory.

"One of the most beautiful passages in literature, you know. His professor had been a famous writer back in his day, but now he's completely forgotten. Radchenko feels ashamed for the old man. He watches him through his bedroom window— Radchenko never leaves his apartment; remember, he hasn't left in seven years—he watches the professor walk out of sight, kicking at the pigeons and cursing them." Kolya cleared his throat and switched to his declamatory tone. *"Talent must be a fanatical mistress. She's beautiful; when you're with her, people watch you, they notice. But she bangs on your door at odd hours, and she disappears for long stretches, and she has no patience for the rest of your existence: your wife, your children, your friends. She is the most thrilling evening of your week, but some day she will leave you for good. One night, after she's been gone for years, you will see her on the arm of a younger man, and she will pretend not to recognize you."*

Kolya's apparent immunity to exhaustion aggravated and amazed me. I could keep moving only by sighting a distant tree and promising myself that I would not quit before I reached it—and when we got to that tree, I would find another and swear this was the last one. But Kolya seemed capable of traipsing through the woods, orating with a stage whisper, for hours at a time.

I waited a moment to make sure he was finished before I nodded. "That's nice."

"Isn't it?" he said quickly, pleased to hear it. The way he responded made me study his moonlit face.

"You've got most of the book memorized?"

"Oh, I don't know about that. Passages here and there."

The snow was deeper as we crossed a ridge, making each step more of a chore, and I huffed and wheezed like an old man with one lung as I staggered toward the next tree.

"Can I ask you something?"

"You just did," he said, with his annoyingly pleased smile.

"What do you write when you write in your journal?"

"Depends on the day. Sometimes just notes on what I've seen. Sometimes I hear someone say something, a line or two, and I like the way it sounds."

I nodded and experimented by keeping one eye closed for ten seconds, then the other, alternating in a bid to give them some rest and spare them from the wind.

"Why do you ask?"

"I think you're writing *The Courtyard Hound*."

"You think . . . you mean a critique of *The Courtyard Hound*? Well, I am. I told you that. Someday I'll give lectures on the book. Maybe seven men in Russia know more about Ushakovo than I do."

"I don't think there is an Ushakovo." I pushed up my cap so I could get a better look at him. "You keep telling me it's this classic and I've never heard of it. And you were very happy when I told you I liked that bit, you were proud of it. If I quoted Pushkin for you, and you said the writing was good, it wouldn't make me proud, would it? They're not my lines."

Kolya's expression never changed. His face admitted nothing, denied nothing. "But you did like it?"

"It's not bad. You just came up with that?"

"Over the last few hours. You know what inspired me? That poem of your father's. 'An Old Poet, Once Famous, Seen at a Café.'"

"That was another clue. You robbed him blind."

He laughed, blowing a great gust of vapor into the frigid air.

"This is literature. We don't call it robbery; we

call it homage. What about the first line of the book? You like that, too?"

"I don't remember the first line of the book."

"In the slaughterhouse where we first kissed, the air still stank from the blood of the lambs."

"A little melodramatic, isn't it?"

"What's wrong with drama? All these contemporary writers are such timid little fish—"

"*Melo*drama, I said."

"—but if the subject demands intensity, it should get intensity."

"So this whole time . . . Why didn't you just tell me you were writing a novel?"

Kolya stared at the moon, sinking now toward the fringe of pine tops. Soon it would be down and we'd be walking in true darkness, tripping over roots and slipping on patches of black ice.

"The truth is, that first night I met you? In the Crosses? I thought they were going to shoot us in the morning. So what did it matter what I told you? I said whatever popped into my head."

"You told me they weren't going to shoot us!"

"Well, you seemed a little frightened. But come on, think about it: a deserter and a looter? What were our chances?"

The next tree I had chosen as a way station seemed impossibly far away, a silhouetted pine that loomed above its brothers, a silent sentinel older than all the rest. While I panted, Kolya sipped tea from his canteen, a naturalist out for an evening hike. Army rations greatly exceeded civilian rations—that was my rationale for his superior energy, ignoring the fact that we had eaten the same meals for the last several days.

"You said you left your unit so you could defend your thesis on Ushakovo's *The Courtyard Hound*," I said, pausing between each sentence to regain my breath. "And now you're admitting there is no Ushakovo and there is no *Courtyard Hound*. "

"But there will be. If I live long enough."

"Why did you leave your unit?"

"It's complicated."

"You two about to fuck in the bushes?"

Kolya and I wheeled around. Vika had crept up behind us without a sound, close enough that I could have reached out and touched her cheek. She glared into our faces with contempt, obviously disgusted to be in the company of such miserable soldiers.

"You were told to march single file with a nine-stride gap." Her voice was very low for such a small girl, hoarse, as if she had been sick the week before and her larynx hadn't recovered yet. She was a practiced whisperer, able to enunciate each quiet word so that we could understand everything yet anyone standing five meters away would not hear a thing.

"You're strolling along like a couple of faggots, chatting about books. You realize we've got German camps within two kilometers of where we stand? You want to end up in a ditch with all the Communists and Jews, that's your business, but I plan on seeing Berlin next year."

"He's a Jew," said Kolya, jabbing at me with his thumb, ignoring the angry look I directed his way.

"Are you? Well, you're the first dumb Jew I ever met. Either turn around and go back to Piter or else shut your mouths and follow our rules. There's a reason we haven't lost a man in two months. Now go on, move."

With a hand on each of our backs she shoved us forward and we resumed our places in the single file, nine strides between us, shamed into silence.

I thought about the nonexistent author Ushakovo and his nonexistent masterpiece, *The Courtyard Hound*. For some reason I wasn't angry at Kolya. It was a strange lie but a harmless one, and the farther I walked the more I understood his motivation. Kolya seemed fearless, but everyone has fear in them somewhere; fear is part of our inheritance. Aren't we descended from timid little shrews who cowered in the shadows while the great beasts stomped past? Cannibals and Nazis didn't make Kolya nervous, but the threat of embarrassment did—the possibility that a stranger might laugh at the lines he'd written.

My father had many friends, most of them writers, and they chose our apartment as their clubhouse because of my mother's cooking and my father's unwillingness to throw anyone out. My mother complained that she was running the Hotel Literati. The place stank of cigarette smoke and the butts were everywhere, in the potted plants and half-drunk glasses of tea. One night an experimental playwright stuck dozens of the butts into gobs of melted candle wax on the kitchen table, representing Roman and Carthaginian forces, so he could demonstrate Hannibal's double envelopment maneuver at the battle of Cannae. My mother griped about the noise, the broken glasses, the rugs stained with cheap Ukrainian wine, but I knew she liked hosting the crowds of poets and novelists, loved it when they devoured her stews and raved about her cakes. When she was young, she was a pretty woman, and if she wasn't a flirt herself she liked it when good-looking men flirted with her. She would sit beside my father on the sofa and listen to the debates and rants and decrials, saying nothing but hearing everything, saving it all for the debriefing she would have with my father when the last drunk finally staggered out the door. She was not a writer herself, but she was a very good reader, passionate and eclectic in her tastes, and my father had great faith in her judgments. When one of the great men came to the apartment, a Mandelstam or Chukovksy, she didn't treat them with any special favors, but I could tell she watched them more carefully, evaluating how they behaved with my father. In her mind the literary community was ranked as precisely as the army; the ranks might not have titles and insignia, but they were ranks all the same, and she wanted to know where my father stood.

Sometimes, when enough bottles of wine had been drained, a poet would stand, swaying slightly as if a strong wind were blowing, and recite a new poem he had written. As an eight-year-old peering into the living room from the hallway, knowing I'd be caught soon and hoping it would be my father to catch me (he was almost impossible to anger, while my mother was quick with a hard hand to the backside), the poems meant nothing to me. Most of the poets wanted to be Mayakovsky, and while they couldn't match his talent they could mimic his opacity, shouting out verses that made no sense to me at eight and probably made just as little sense to everyone else in the room. But even if the poems didn't impress me, the performances did—these huge men with their shaggy eyebrows, always holding cigarettes between their fingers, the long stems of ash breaking and drifting toward the floor whenever they gestured too wildly. On rare occasions a woman would rise and face the staring eyes—once even Akhmatova herself, according to my mother, though I don't remember seeing her.

Sometimes the poets read from scribbled notes, sometimes they spoke from memory. When they were finished, too conscious of all the faces watching them, they reached for the nearest glass of wine or vodka—not only for the drink's support, but to give themselves something to do, a simple action to occupy the hands and eyes while waiting for the crowd's reaction. This was an audience of fellow professionals, competitors, and the usual response was modest approval, signaled by nodding heads, smiles, slaps on the back. Once or twice I saw these jaundiced men of letters erupt with euphoria, so moved by the power of the work that they forgot their jealousy as they shouted out, "Bravo! Bravo!" and charged at the dazed, happy poet, kissing his cheeks with sloppy wet lips, mussing his hair, repeating their favorite lines, and shaking their heads with admiration.

Far more common, though, was the reaction of disdainful silence, nobody willing to meet the poet's eye, to feign interest in the subject matter, or halfheartedly compliment the use of a jaunty metaphor. When a reading failed, the poet knew it quickly. He would down his glass of alcohol, the red flush of shame spreading across his face as he wiped his mouth dry with his sleeve and shuffled off to the far side of the apartment, taking great interest in the books on my father's bookshelves—Balzac and Stendhal, Yeats and Baudelaire. The defeated man would leave the party soon, but leaving too quickly would seem like bad sportsmanship, a sulking form of cowardice, so he would wait an agonizing twenty minutes while everyone around him studiously avoided mentioning his poem, as if it were a brutal fart that no one was rude enough to acknowledge. Finally he would thank my mother for her food and hospitality, smiling but not looking her in the eye, and hustle out the door, knowing that the minute he left everyone would joke about the atrocity he'd unveiled, what a horror, what a lumpy sack of pretension and artifice.

Kolya protected himself by inventing Ushakovo. The make-believe writer gave cover so that Kolya could test his opening line, his protagonist's philosophy, even the title of the book, gauging my reaction without fear of derision. As scams go it wasn't the most elaborate one, but he had pulled it off nicely, and I decided that Kolya could probably write a decent novel someday, if he survived the war and ditched the bombastic first sentence.

The talk with Kolya and the encounter with Vika had jolted me awake again and I peered around the forest, hoping the men in front of me and behind me had better eyes for the darkness than I did. The moon had drifted below the tree line; the sun would not rise for hours; the night was truly black now. Twice I nearly walked into trees. The stars were out in their millions, but they were only for decoration, and I wondered why those distant suns appeared as pinpricks of light. If the astronomers were right and the universe is clogged with stars, many of them far larger than our sun, and if light traveled forever without slowing or fading, why didn't the sky shine every minute of the day? The answer must have been obvious, but I couldn't figure it out. For thirty minutes I didn't worry about the Einsaztkommandos and their leader Abendroth; I forgot about the muscles cramping in my legs; I didn't notice the cold. Were stars like flashlights, unable to project past a certain distance? From the rooftop of the Kirov I could spot a soldier's glowing flashlight from a few kilometers away, even though the beam could not illuminate my face from that distance. But then again, why did a flashlight's beam lose power over distance? Did the light particles spread out like pellets in a shotgun blast? Was light even made of particles?

My semilucid wonderings finally ended when I collided with Kolya's back, banging my nose and crying out in surprise. A dozen voices shushed me. Squinting at the dim shapes in front of me, I saw that everyone had gathered beside a massive, snow-crusted boulder. Vika was already on top of the rock; I don't know how she managed to clamber up its slick, frozen sides in the dark.

"They're burning the villages," she called down to Korsakov.

The moment she spoke the words I smelled smoke in the air.

"They found the bodies," said Korsakov.

The Germans had made their philosophy of retribution very clear to the civilians in occupied territory. They nailed posters to the walls; they issued proclamations in their Russian-language radio broadcasts; they spread the word through their collaborators: kill one of our soldiers and we'll kill thirty Russians. Tracking down partisans was difficult work, but rounding up large numbers of old men, women, and children was easy, even now with half the nation on the run.

If Korsakov and his men were bothered by the

210 ■ David Benioff

knowledge that their raid earlier in the night had triggered a slaughter of innocents, I heard no indication in their whispered exchanges. The enemy had declared total war when they invaded our country. They had vowed, repeatedly and in print, to incinerate our cities and enslave the populace. We could not fight them in moderation. We could not fight total war with half war. The partisans would continue picking off Nazis; the Nazis would continue massacring noncombatants; and eventually the Fascists would learn that they could not win the war even if they killed thirty civilians for every one of their dead soldiers. The arithmetic was brutal, but brutal arithmetic always worked in Russia's favor.

Vika scrambled down from the boulder. Korsakov walked over to confer with her. As he passed us he muttered to Kolya, "So much for Novoye Koshkino."

"We're not going?"

"Why would we? The whole point was to get there before sunrise and hunt for Einsatz. You smell that smoke? The Einsatz are hunting us."

18

The partisans kept a safe house a few kilometers inland from Lake Ladoga, a long-deserted trapper's cabin on a hillside dense with fir trees. We finally got there an hour before dawn, the sky shifting patiently from black to gray, a light snow falling as the air brightened. Everyone seemed to think the snow was a good omen, covering our tracks and signaling a warmer day.

On the way to the cabin we had walked along a ridgeline overlooking another burning village. The fire was silent, the little houses collapsing into the flames without complaint, flocks of sparks rising to the sky. At a distance it seemed beautiful, and I thought it was strange that powerful violence is often so pleasing to the eye, like tracer bullets at night. As we passed the village we heard a burst of gunfire, no more than a kilometer away, seven or eight machine guns firing in concert. We all knew what the shots signified and we all kept walking.

The trapper's cabin looked like it had been hammered together from old planks and rusted nails by a man with little skill for carpentry and no patience for the job. The door hung crooked on its hinges. There were no windows, just a pipe jutting out of the rooftop to vent smoke, and no floor but hard-packed dirt.

Inside the smell of human shit was almost too much to stand. The walls were gouged as if by claws, and I wondered if the ghosts of all the skinned martens and foxes still haunted the place, eager to flay their guests alive when the candles burned out.

As cold as it was outside, inside offered only respite from the wind and no added warmth. Korsakov elected one unlucky man to take the first guard shift. The partisan in the Finnish ski patrol uniform removed his pack and set up a little "bourgeois stove," filling it with scraps of wood that they had left in the cabin earlier. When the stove was lit, all of us crowded as close together as we could, thirteen men and a woman—or twelve men, a woman, and a boy, if we were being honest about it. I wondered, for the hundredth time that night, what she would look like with the filthy coveralls stripped off, her pale dirty skin stretched taut over the blue tracery of her veins. Did she have breasts or was she flat chested as a boy? Her hips were as narrow as mine, I was fairly sure of that, but even with her cropped hair and mud-stained neck there was something undeniably feminine about that proud jutting lower lip. Did the other men in the group lust for her, too, or did they all see her as Korsakov saw her, as a sexless sniper with an uncanny eye? Were they idiots or was I?

The shit stench made my eyes water, but soon smoke from the stove camouflaged the worst of the smell, and the fire and our body heat made the cabin comfortable enough. At that point I could have slept anywhere, and with my father's navy coat laid flat beneath me and my folded scarf as a pillow, for once I slipped into unconsciousness within seconds of resting my head.

A moment later Kolya nudged me.

"Hey," he whispered. "Hey, are you awake?"

I kept my eyes clenched shut, hoping he would leave me alone.

"Are you mad at me?" he asked. His mouth was next to my ear, allowing him to whisper directly into my skull without bothering any of the others. I wanted to punch him to make him shut up, but I did not want him to punch me back.

"No," I said. "Go to sleep."

"I'm sorry I lied to you. Even if I thought we were dead, it doesn't matter. It was wrong of me."

"Thank you," I told him, and shifted onto my side, hoping he would get the hint.

"You like the title, though? *The Courtyard Hound*? Do you know what it means?"

"Please . . . please let me sleep."

"I'm sorry. Sleep, of course."

Thirty seconds passed in silence, but I could not relax because I knew he was fully awake, staring at the ceiling, waiting to ask me another question.

"You want to know the truth, don't you? About why I left my battalion."

"You can tell me tomorrow."

"I hadn't been with a girl in four months. My balls were ringing like a couple of church bells. You think I'm joking? I'm not like you. I don't have your discipline. I fucked my first girl three days after the first time I came. Twelve years old, didn't have a hair on my sack, but I stuck it in Klava Stepanovich down in the boiler room, *boing boing boing*."

Boing boing boing?

"I get this hunger, I'm telling you. I go a week without it and I can't concentrate, my brain doesn't work, I'm walking around the trenches with a hard-on out to here."

Kolya's hot breath was on my ear and I tried to turn farther away, but we were all squeezed to-gether on the earth floor like cigarettes in a pack.

"We had a party planned for New Year's Eve, the whole battalion. There was vodka; there was going to be some singing; I heard a rumor someone found a few pigs stashed away in a barn somewhere and we were going to roast them. All-night affair, right? So I figured, this is good, let them celebrate with their vodka and their pigs, I've got other business. We were less than an hour from Piter, by car. I had a friend de-livering messages to headquarters. He was going to be in the city for three, four hours. Perfect. So I ride with him, he drops me off at a friend's building—"

"Sonya?"

"No, a girl named Yulia. Not the most beautiful girl in the world, not even pretty, really. But listen, Lev, this girl made me hard when she filed her nails. Her pussy was magic. It really was. She lived on the sixth floor and the whole way up I'm getting myself ready. Already decided the position—just toss her over the back of the sofa, ass in the air, go in deep. I don't know if you've got much going on down-stairs, by the way, but if you don't, that's a good po-sition for you. Gets you all the way in. Anyway, I finally get to her apartment, I'm starting to unbuckle my belt, I bang on the door, an old woman opens up. Barely bigger than a midget this woman, looks about two hundred years old. I tell her I'm a friend of Yulia's and she says, 'God forgive me, Yulia's been dead a month now.' God forgive me! Fuck! So I say my sorrys to this crone, give her a piece of bread because she's barely able to stand up, and run downstairs. Time's running out. There's another girl who lives close by, one of the ballerinas I told you about. A little bit of an ice queen, but the best legs in Piter. I have to climb over a gate to get into her building, nearly get an iron spike up my asshole, but I make it, get to her apartment door, bang on it, 'It's me, Nikolai Alexandrovich, let me in!' Door opens, her fat rat-eyed husband's staring me down. Vile turd's never home, except this time. Party man, of course, usually down at the offices figuring out new regulations for the Army, but tonight he decides to stay home and torture his wife for New Year's. 'Who are you? What is this?' he says to me, indignant, as if I've somehow insulted him by banging on his door and demanding his wife's wet twat on a plate. I wanted to knock him on his dimpled ass, but that would have been the end of me, so I give him a salute, the civilian cunt, tell him I knocked on the wrong door, and disappear. Now I'm fucked. The only other girl I know on that side of town is Roza, but she's a professional and I've got no money on me. But I'm a good customer, maybe she trusts me, maybe she'll take whatever food I've got left in exchange, right? It's a couple of kilometers away. I'm sprinting now, sweating, first sweat since October. There's not much time left before my friend's driving back. I make it there, out of breath, up four flights to Roza's apartment; door's unlocked, I let myself in, and there's three soldiers waiting in her kitchen, passing around a bottle of vodka. I can hear her groaning away in the other room and these drunk morons are singing peasant songs and slapping each other on the back. 'Don't worry,' says the one who's last in line, 'I'll be quick.'

"I offered them money to cut the line, except I didn't have any money and they weren't such morons they were going to take a note from me. I told them I had to get back to battalion and one of them said, 'It's New Year's Eve! They're all drunk! Long as you get back by morning you'll be fine.' That sounded right to me, and they kept passing the bottle around, so I drank with them and pretty soon I was singing their fucking peasant songs louder than all of them. And an hour later I finally got to lie down with Roza. She's a sweet girl—I don't care what anyone says about whores—she let me in for the rest of the bread I had in my pocket, and it wasn't a lot. But she said her pussy was hurting so she sucked me off instead. Fifteen minutes later I'm ready again, she grins and says, 'Oh, I love you young ones,' and lets me go inside her, very slow, very gentle. And then again, half an hour later. I must have sprayed a liter of come inside her, north and south."

I had the uncomfortable feeling that Kolya was making himself aroused all over again as he told the story.

"So you missed your ride back."

"Oh, I missed it by hours. But I wasn't worried, I'd find another car heading back to the battalion. I knew most of those boys delivering messages, it wouldn't be a tough trick. You should have seen me walking out of Roza's building. Different human being from the one who walked in. Relaxed, big smile on my face, bit of bounce in my stride. I step out the front door, I'm practically skipping down the sidewalk, and an NKVD patrol, four of the dirty bitches, stops me. Man asks to see my LOA papers. I don't have any LOA papers, I tell him. I'm delivering messages for General Stelmakh—the man's planning a battle, he needs rifles, he needs mortars, he doesn't have time to sign some shit-stained LOA. Stelmakh's one of your tribe, I think. Did you know that?"

"Does this story ever end? Are you going to keep talking for the rest of my life?"

"This little glorified policeman interrogating me, he's still got a Hitler mustache. You'd think everyone in Russia with a Hitler mustache would have shaved it by now, but no, this dank cunt thinks it's a good look for him. He asks me why I'm delivering messages from General Stelmakh to an apartment building in the Vyborg section. I decide a little bit of truth never hurt, decide to appeal to the man's humanity. I give him a wink, tell him I got myself a bit of ass while I waited for my ride back to the general's HQ. You'd think he'd grin and slap my back and tell me to get my LOA in order next time I left my battalion. Four months I'd been on the front line while this mustachioed dwarf minced around Piter, arresting soldiers for bringing a bit of meat home to their parents, a bag of rice. This was my mistake. I appealed to a bureaucrat's humanity. He has his men slap the manacles around my wrists and then he gives me this little superior smile and tells me General Stelmakh is in Tikhvin, two hundred kilometers away, he's just won an important battle."

"You shouldn't have said Stelmakh. That was stupid of you."

"Of course it was stupid! My cock was still wet!" Several of the partisans muttered at Kolya to shut up and he lowered his voice. "My brain wasn't working right. I couldn't believe this man was accusing me. Do you understand how fast it changes? I was a soldier in good standing in the afternoon, and there I am, five hours later, accused of desertion. I thought they'd shoot me right there in the street. But they took me to the Crosses instead. And then I met you, my moody little Hebrew."

"How did Yulia die?"

"What? I don't know. I suppose she starved."

We lay quietly for several minutes, listening to the men around us sleep, some of them quiet, some rasping and nasal, some *shooshing* like wind in a chimney. I tried to distinguish Vika's breathing from the others', curious what sounds she made in the night, but it was impossible to tell.

I had been annoyed with Kolya for keeping me awake with his endless talk, but in the silence I was suddenly lonely.

"Are you asleep?" I asked.

"Hm?" he murmured, groggy, the fast sleeper— his story told—already sailing away into his dreams.

"Why is it dark at night?"

"What?"

"If there are billions of stars, and most of them are just as bright as the sun, and light travels forever, how comes it's not bright all the time?"

I wasn't really expecting an answer. I figured he would snort and tell me to go to sleep, or give some pat reply like, "It's dark at night because the sun is down." Instead he sat up and stared down at me. I could see the frown on his face by the fluttering light of the bourgeois stove.

"That's an excellent question," he said. He thought about it some more, peering into the darkness outside of the stove's circle of light. Finally, he shook his head, yawned, and lowered himself to the ground again. Ten seconds later he was asleep, snoring, the *whoosh* of his inhalations followed by the chuffing of his exhales.

I was still awake when the guard outside came in from his shift, woke up his replacement, refilled the stove with some twigs he'd gathered, and lay down in the circle of huddled bodies. For another hour I listened to the wood knots popping, thinking about starlight and Vika, until I finally fell asleep and dreamed of a sky raining fat girls.

19

The partisan on guard duty woke us before noon, crashing in through the cabin door, trying to keep his voice down despite his panic.

"They're coming," he said. We were on our feet before he could get his second sentence out, gathering our gear, instantly alert with the news of real danger. We had slept in our boots and were ready to move. "Looks like a whole company. With prisoners."

Korsakov slipped his rifle strap over his shoulder. "Infantry?"

"Didn't see any armor."

Thirty seconds later we streamed out the crooked door into the hostile sunshine. The windowless cabin had been dark as a crypt and I could barely open my eyes in the noontime glare. We followed Korsakov and the unspoken order was simple: run.

We never had a chance. Even before the last man was out of the cabin I could hear German voices shouting. I became like an animal, with no thoughts in my head, nothing but fear to drive me. The air had grown warmer and the snow was heavy and wet, grabbing at my boots, sucking me down.

When I was nine, a delegation of famous French Communists visited Piter and the Party spruced up the streets. Workmen with cigarettes dangling from their lips poured fresh tar onto Voinova Street and leveled it with long-handled trowels, making my street look like a boulevard of melted chocolate. I had been watching all morning with the Antokolsky twins, just in front of the Kirov gates. I don't remember anything triggering our collective decision. Without saying a word, without even a glance at one another, we pulled off our shoes, tossed them into the courtyard, and sprinted across the street. We could have burned the soles off our feet, but we didn't care; we left our footprints in the soft road and kept running when we reached the far side, while the workmen cursed and shook their trowels at us, not caring enough to chase us, knowing we could never be caught.

My mother needed an hour that night to scrub my feet clean, angrily scouring them with soap and pumice. My father stood by the window, his hands behind his back, suppressing a smile as he looked down at Voinova. Beneath the streetlights the road was glossy and perfect, save for three pairs of little footprints marring the surface like seagull tracks on the wet sand.

Running across drying tar was not like running through the melting snow; I don't know why the memories linger side by side, but they do.

Gunshots echoed among the firs. One whistled past, so loud and close I touched the side of my head to see if I'd been hit. I saw the man in front of me tumble to the ground and I could tell from the way he fell that he would never stand again. I could not move any faster and I could not be more afraid; watching the man go down changed nothing in me. At that moment I was no longer Lev Abramovich

Beniov. I did not have a living mother in Vyazma or a dead father in some unmarked patch of dirt. I was not descended from black-hatted Torah scholars on my father's side or petit bourgeois Muscovites on my mother's. If a German had caught me by the collar at that moment, shaken me, and demanded my name in perfect Russian, I could not have answered him, could not have framed a single sentence to plead for mercy.

I saw Korsakov turn to fire at our pursuers. Before he could let off a shot, a bullet cleaved his lower jaw from his skull. He blinked, his eyes still alert though half his face was gone. I ran past him, up a steep ravine and down the other side, where a stream had formed in a narrow gully, the meltwater gurgling as it snaked past tumbled rocks and fallen branches.

Following some unarticulated instinct, I veered off my course to follow the stream, running downhill along the slippery stones, faster now that I was out of the snow. My body waited for the inevitable bullet, the railroad spike hammered between my shoulder blades, slamming me face-first into the cold water. Despite everything, I was strangely nimble, my feet picking their next step without consulting my brain, my boots splashing in icy water, never stumbling.

I don't know how long I ran or how far, but finally I had to stop. I ducked behind the trunk of an ancient larch, its drooping branches heavy with melting snow, and sat in the shadows trying to breathe. My legs would not stop trembling even after I pressed my mittened hands down on my thighs to calm them. When my lungs stopped hurting, I peered around the trunk and looked uphill.

Three men were coming my way, rifles in hand, jogging at a deliberate rate. None of them wore German uniforms. The closest man wore a ski soldier's winter whites, and I realized it was the partisan I had seen sucking a dead man's wedding ring off his finger. Markov, the others had called him. I loved him at that moment, loved his blunted red face, the deep-set eyes that had seemed murderous the night before.

Behind him came Kolya and I laughed aloud at the sight of him. I had met him on Friday night and didn't even like him until Monday, and now, Tuesday afternoon, seeing him alive made me want to cry with happiness. He had lost his Astrakhan hat during his flight and his blond hair hung over his forehead until he pushed it back. He turned to say something to the man beside him, grinning as he spoke, and I knew he thought he was making a very funny joke.

The man beside him turned out to be Vika. Unlike Kolya, she had held on to her fur cap; it was pulled down to her eyebrows and even from a distance I could see her wolfish blue eyes roving just below the fringe of rabbit fur. Whatever Kolya said did not amuse her. She did not even seem to be listening. She turned every few paces to check for pursuers.

My run could not have lasted very long (twenty minutes? ten?), but the inside of the trapper's cabin seemed like a memory stolen from a stranger. Real terror—the genuine belief that your life is about to end violently—erases everything but itself from the brain. So even after I saw Kolya and Vika and Markov, even though their three faces seemed to me the most beautiful faces in all of Russia, I wasn't able to call their names or wave my hand. The shadow beneath the sagging arms of the larch tree was my safe place. Nothing evil had happened to me since I got there. The Germans had not found me. I hadn't seen anyone's jawbone blasted off his face, leaving nothing but puzzled eyes over slop from a butcher shop's floor. I could not beckon to Kolya, even though in four days he had become my best friend.

Maybe I shifted my position slightly or shivered—I must have made some slight noise because Vika swiveled toward me, the stock of her rifle pressed against her shoulder, the muzzle pointed at my head. Even then I wasn't able to speak quickly enough to save my life. I could have cried out her name. Any Russian sentence might have helped.

But somehow, though I sat in deep shade, obstructed from view by snow-covered branches, Vika recognized my face and stayed her trigger finger.

"It's your little friend," she told Kolya. "Maybe he's wounded."

Kolya ran over to me, pushing aside the larch branches, seizing the lapels of my greatcoat and tilting my whole body left and then right, searching for bullet holes.

"Are you hurt?"

I shook my head.

"Come on, then." He lifted me to my feet. "They're not far behind."

"It's too late," said Vika. She and Markov had joined us in the cloistered shadows and she gestured uphill with the barrel of her rifle.

Germans in white anoraks had crested the hilltop, less than two hundred meters away, rifles at the ready, advancing cautiously as they scouted the terrain for ambush sites. Only a few soldiers at first, picking their way through the snow, but more and more came bobbing over the rise, until the hillside above swarmed with men who wanted to kill us.

Markov pulled a pair of field glasses from a pocket in his coveralls. He watched the advance scouts descending the hill.

"First Gebirgsjäger Division," he whispered, offering the field glasses to Vika. "You see the edelweiss insignia?"

She nodded, waving away the glasses. Between the lines of uniformed soldiers marched a herd of prisoners, their heads down. Red Army men, their uniforms filthy, trudged alongside stunned civilians, who wore whatever they had managed to grab when the Germans raided their villages. Some poor souls marched in their shirtsleeves, without coats or gloves or hats. They sloshed through the snow, never looking up or saying a word, heading directly for us.

"Looks like a whole company coming this way," said Markov, pocketing the field glasses and readying his rifle. "Figures it happens now, when I've got a pocketful of gold."

Vika put a hand on Markov's arm. "You're so quick to be a martyr?"

He glanced at her, the steel sights of his rifle already lined up on the closest Nazi.

"Shooting infantry," she said, "that's nothing. We're after Einsatz."

He scowled and pushed away her hand as if she were a crazy woman on the street who had come begging for money.

"We don't get to choose. All I see is mountain rangers."

"Einsatzgruppe A travels with the First Gebirgsjäger. You know that. Abendroth has to be close."

Kolya and I glanced at each other. Last night we had heard the name Abendroth for the first time; the syllables were already edged with dread. I could not expel the mental image of Zoya writhing on the floor beside her severed feet. The man himself I could not picture, the girls had not described him, but I imagined his hands—freckled with blood, the nails filed and immaculate—as he rested the saw on the wood floor of the farmhouse.

"It's over," said Markov. "No more running."

"I never said anything about running. They've got more than a hundred prisoners. We mix in with them—"

"Have you gone soft, you silly cunt? You think you walk out there with your rifle in the air, Fritz will let you surrender?"

"We're not surrendering." She wrapped one gloved hand around a low-hanging branch, pulled herself up, and wedged her rifle into the gap between trunk and branch. Lowering herself to the ground, she slapped the snow from her gloves and motioned for Markov to hide his rifle, too.

"We're going to mix in with the prisoners and wait for the right moment. They've already searched those sheep for weapons. You've got a pistol on you somewhere, don't you? Come on, hurry. Get rid of the rifle."

"They might search them again."

"They won't."

The closest Germans were less than one hundred meters away, their hoods cinched tight over their field caps. Markov stared at them, their pink faces easy targets for a skilled marksman.

"They'll kill half those prisoners by nightfall."

"So we'll be in the other half."

Kolya smiled and nodded, warming up to the idea. It was the kind of ludicrous scheme he might have devised himself and it didn't surprise me he was pleased with it.

"It's worth trying," he whispered. "If we get in with the rest of them, there's still a chance. And if they spot us, all right, we'll have our shoot-out then. It's a good plan."

"It's a horseshit plan," said Markov. "How are we going to get in there without them seeing us?"

"You still have a few grenades, don't you?" asked Vika.

Markov stared at her. He looked like the kind of man who had been punched in the face many times, his nose flat as a boxer's, half his teeth missing from the lower row. Finally, he shook his head, strapped his rifle to the hilt of a broken branch, and peered out at the approaching column.

"You're a real cunt louse, you know that?"

"Take off your whites," she replied. "You look like a ski soldier. They'll notice you."

Markov quickly unbuttoned his coveralls, sat in the snow, and pulled them over his boots. Below his whites he wore a quilted canvas hunting vest, several layers of woolen sweaters, and a pair of paint-splattered workman's pants. He pulled a stick grenade from a canvas pouch, unwrapped a cigarette-size fuze, and inserted it into the head of the grenade.

"We'll have to time it just right," he said.

We huddled around the broad larch trunk, crouched and still, holding our breath as the first German soldiers passed by less than twenty meters away.

Nobody had bothered consulting with me,

which made sense because I hadn't opened my mouth to offer any suggestions. I hadn't said a word since running out the door of the trapper's cabin and now it was too late.

I didn't like either of the options. A final shoot-out might have been fine for a hardened guerrilla like Markov, but I wasn't ready for a suicide mission. Posing as a prisoner seemed a bizarre miscalculation—how long did prisoners survive these days? If anybody had asked me, I would have urged either another run, though I wasn't sure if I could run much farther, or to try climbing the tree and waiting while the Germans passed beneath us. Hiding in the branches seemed like a better and better idea as the front end of the Gebirgsjäger company passed by without spotting us.

When the first ranks of Russian prisoners trudged past our tree, Vika nodded at Markov. He took a deep breath, walked toward the edge of the larch's shadow, and hurled the grenade as far as he could.

From my vantage point I couldn't tell if any of the Germans noticed the grenade flying overhead. I didn't hear any shouted warnings. The grenade landed with a muffled *thwup* in the snow thirty meters away. For several seconds I was convinced it must have been a dud, until it exploded with enough force that snow showered down on us from the shaken larch branches.

Everyone marching with the company, mountain rangers and prisoners alike, crouched in momentary panic, looking to the left where a great geyser of snow had shot into the air. We slipped out of the tree's shadow and walked unseen toward the ragged throng of Russians as the German officers began shouting orders, peering into the far woods with their field glasses, looking for snipers in the trees. We were so close to our captive countrymen: fifteen meters away, fourteen, thirteen, stepping softly, resisting the impulse to sprint the last short span. The Germans thought they saw movement in the distant bushes; there was a clamor of cries and directives, fingers pointing, soldiers dropping to their bellies, ready to fire from the prone position.

By the time they realized there were no enemies to the left, we had infiltrated from the right. A few of the prisoners noticed us joining in with them. They gave no sign of camaraderie or welcome. They didn't seem surprised that four newcomers had joined their ranks; the captives, soldiers and civilians both, were so defeated they probably thought it was natural that Russians would emerge from the woods and secretly surrender to the enemy.

All of the prisoners were male, from young boys with missing teeth and frozen strands of snot clinging to their upper lips to old men with crooked backs and white stubble dusting their jaws. Vika had pulled her rabbit fur cap even lower; in her formless coveralls she looked enough like an adolescent boy that nobody glanced at her twice.

At least two of the Red Army men wore no boots, only their torn wool socks to keep their feet warm. The Germans considered a pair of Soviet-issue felt-lined leather boots a great prize, far warmer and more durable than their own footwear. The soldiers' wool socks must have been soaked through with melted snow. When the temperature dropped and the socks froze, the two of them would have to walk with blocks of ice on their feet. I wondered how much farther they could go, how many kilometers, the numbness spreading from their toes to their calves to their knees. Their eyes were as dull and miserable as the eyes of the draft horses that dragged sledges through the snowy streets of Piter before the food ran out and the horses were slaughtered for their meat.

The Germans chattered in their own tongue. None of them seemed badly wounded by the fragmentation, though one young trooper with a thin red gash across his cheek had pulled off his glove so he could dab at the blood with his thumb and show it to his comrades, pleased with his first war wound.

"They think it was a land mine," Kolya whispered. He squinted as he listened to the officers' commands. "They must be Tyrolean. The accents are tricky. Yes, they're saying it was a land mine."

The orders from the officers trickled down to the troopers, who turned back to the meekly waiting prisoners and signaled with their rifles for the march to continue.

"Wait!" shouted one of the Russians, a thick-lipped civilian in his forties wearing a quilted down cap, the earflaps tied under his chin. "This man is a partisan!"

He pointed at Markov. Everyone else on the hillside had gone silent.

"He came to my house a month ago, stole all my potatoes, every bit of food in the place, said they needed it for the war! You hear? He is a partisan! He has killed many Germans!"

Markov stared at the civilian, his head cocked to one side like a fighting dog.

"Shut your mouth," he said, keeping his voice low, his face bright red with anger.

"You don't tell me what to do anymore! You don't tell me what to do!"

A Leutnant stomped over, trailed by three troopers, shoving through the crowd of prisoners that had circled around Markov and his accuser.

"What is this?" he bellowed. He was clearly the translator for the company, speaking Russian with a Ukrainian accent. He looked like a fat man who had recently lost all the fat, his broad cheeks deflated, the heavy skin hanging slack across the bones of his face.

The accuser stood there with his finger pointing, an overgrown child with his earflaps and his trembling lips, addressing the Leutnant but never looking away from Markov.

"He is a murderer, this man! He has murdered your people!"

Kolya opened his mouth to speak out in Markov's defense, but Vika jabbed him in the belly with a sharp elbow and Kolya kept silent. I could see his hand digging into his overcoat pocket, readying the Tokarev in case it was needed.

Markov shook his head, a strange, ugly smile splitting his lips.

"I shit on your mother."

"You don't look so brave now! You don't look so hard! Sure, you're the tough man when you're stealing potatoes from common people, but now what are you? Eh? What are you?"

Markov snarled and snatched a small pistol from the pocket of his hunting vest. Burly as he was, he drew with the speed of an American gunslinger, raising the muzzle as his accuser stumbled backward and the prisoners gathered around dove out of the way.

The Germans were even faster. Before Markov could pull the trigger, a burst of automatic fire from the troopers' MP40s punched a cluster of little holes through the front of his vest. He stumbled, frowning as if he'd forgotten an important name, and toppled backward, landing in the soft snow, wisps of down floating up from the perforated quilting of his vest.

The accuser stared down at Markov's body. He must have known what his denunciation would lead to, but now that the act was done he seemed stunned by the outcome. The Leutnant considered him briefly, trying to decide whether to reward or punish the man. In the end he snatched up Markov's pistol for a souvenir and walked away, leaving the whole mess behind. His young troopers followed behind him, glancing briefly at Markov's body, wondering, perhaps, which one of them had fired the shot that actually killed him.

Soon the company was marching again. A change had been made, however. Six Russians now walked in the front, ten meters ahead of the closest Germans, serving as human minesweepers. Each step was a harrowing experience for them, waiting for the snapped tripwire, the sprung spring. It must have been tempting to run, but they wouldn't have gotten three steps before the troopers gunned them down.

Nobody walked near Markov's accuser. He was a man infected, a carrier of plague. He talked quietly to himself, a long and unheard argument, his eyes flashing left and right as he waited for reprisal.

I was a dozen men behind him, slogging through the slush between Vika and Kolya. If any of the pris-

oners spoke loudly enough for the Germans to hear,
one of the troopers would snap, *"Halts Maul!"* Nobody needed a translator to understand the senti-
ment and the Russian in question would quickly
shut his mouth, lower his head, and walk a little
faster. Still, it was possible to carry on a conversation if you kept your voice very low and one eye on
the guards.

"I'm sorry about your friend," I murmured to
Vika.

She kept walking without answering or ac-
knowledging that she had heard me. I thought I
might have offended her.

"He seemed like a good man," I added. Both
sentences were utterly banal, the kind of lazy senti-
ments you might use at the funeral of a distant rela-
tive you never really liked. I couldn't blame her for
ignoring me.

"He wasn't," she said at last. "But I liked him
anyway."

"That traitor ought to be dangling from a tree,"
whispered Kolya, dipping his head so his voice
wouldn't carry. He glared at the back of the betrayer's head. "I could break his neck with my bare
hands. I know how to do it."

"Leave it alone," said Vika. "He doesn't
matter."

"He mattered to Markov," I said.

Vika glanced up at me and smiled. It wasn't the
cold carnivorous smile I had seen before. She
seemed surprised by my comment, as if she had just
heard a mongoloid whistle *Für Elise* without missing a note.

"Yes, he mattered to Markov. You're a strange
one."

"Why?"

"He's a twisty little devil," said Kolya, giving me an affectionate punch in the kidney. "But he plays a nice game of chess."

"Why am I a strange one?"

"Markov's not important," she said. "I'm not important. You're not important. Winning the war, that's the only important thing."

"No," I said, "I disagree. Markov was important. So am I and so are you. That's why we have to win."

Kolya raised his eyebrows, impressed that I was standing up to the little fanatic.

"I'm especially important," he announced. "I'm writing the great novel of the twentieth century."

"You two are half in love," she said. "Do you know that?"

The grim procession of weary men had bogged down in front of us, the foot traffic stalled, confused prisoners trying to figure out why we weren't moving anymore. One of the bootless Russian soldiers had stopped walking. Other men from his captured unit begged him to move, pleading and cursing. He shook his head, never saying a word, his feet rooted in the snow. A friend tried to shove him forward, but it was useless; he had chosen his spot. When the troopers rushed over, waving their submachine guns and hollering in their own language, the Red Army men reluctantly backed away from their doomed comrade. He smiled at the Germans and raised one hand in a mock Nazi salute. I looked away just in time.

20

An hour before sunset the company halted beside a forbidding redbrick schoolhouse, one of the People's Projects built during the second Five-Year Plan, the lead glass windows narrow as medieval embrasures. Two-foot-high bronze letters above the front door spelled out Lenin's famous line: GIVEUSTHECHILDFOREIGHTYEARSANDITWILLBEA BOLSHEVIKFOREVER. One of the Russophone invaders had scrawled a rejoinder in white paint that had dripped before the words had dried: GIVE US YOUR CHILDRENFOREIGHTSECONDSANDTHEREWILLBENOMORE BOLSHEVIKS.

The Wehrmacht had seized the schoolhouse for use as a command center. Six Kübelwagens were parked near the entryway and a bareheaded trooper, his blond hair as short and yellow as a newborn chick's, refueled one of them with a green steel jerrycan. He watched with no apparent interest as the company approached with its convoy of prisoners.

Officers gave orders, ranks broke, most of the Germans headed inside, already shrugging out of their heavy packs, gabbing with each other, loud and happy, ready for the showers (if the water was running) and a hot meal. The remainder of the Gebirgsjäger, a platoon of forty soldiers, irritated that

236 ■ David Benioff

they were still on duty, surly now with hunger and fatigue after a long day hiking through the endless Russian forest, prodded us along to the side of the building.

A German officer waited for us there, reclining in a folding chair, reading a newspaper while he smoked. He glanced up with an idle smile when we walked into view, happy to see us, as if we were friends he had invited over for supper. Setting aside his newspaper, he finally stood, nodding, inspecting our faces, the state of our clothing, the quality of our boots. He wore a gray Waffen-SS uniform with green cuffs on the sleeves, his gray overcoat hanging on the back of the folding chair. Vika, walking beside me, murmured, "Einsatzkommando."

When we had been formed into rough lines, the Einsatzkommando dropped his cigarette into the snow and nodded at the Gebirgsjäger's slack-skinned translator. They spoke together in confident Russian, as if showing off for their eavesdropping captives.

"How many?"

"Ninety-four. No, ninety-two."

"Yes? And two who could not join us? Very good."

The Einsatzkommando faced us, gazing from man to man, looking us in the eyes. He was a handsome man, his black field cap tilted back from his sunburned forehead, his delicate mustache giving him the air of a jazz singer.

"Don't be afraid," he told us. "I know you've been reading the propaganda. The Communists want you to think we're barbarians, here to destroy you. But I'm looking at your faces and I see good, honest workmen and farmers. Is there even a single Bolshevik among you?"

No one raised his hand. The German smiled.

"I didn't think so. You are smarter than that. You understand that Bolshevism is simply the most radical expression of the eternal Jewish quest for world domination."

He looked over the blank faces of the Russian men arrayed before him and gave a good-humored shrug.

"But we don't need the fancy talk. You understand the truth in your bones and that is what matters. There is no reason for conflict between our peoples. Both of us have a common enemy."

He signaled to one of the troopers, who picked up a stack of newspapers from a wood pallet beside the folding chair and divvied them out to five of his fellow mountain rangers. They walked down the rows of prisoners, handing one newspaper to each Russian. My copy was *Komsomol's Truth*; Vika and Kolya had *Red Star*.

"I understand this is a difficult concept to grasp, after so many years of propaganda. But believe this for the truth: the German victory will be a victory for the Russian people. If you don't understand this now, you will understand it soon, and your children will grow up knowing it."

The sinking sun made giants of our shadows. The Einsatz officer enjoyed the sound of his own words and the impression he made upon us. His Russian was technically perfect, though he made no attempt to hide his accent. I wondered where he had learned the language, if he'd been born in one of the Deutschvolk colonies in Melitopol or Bessarabia. He looked up at an ellipsis of three little clouds far above us in the silvering sky.

"I do love this country. Beautiful land." He low-

ered his head and gave another apologetic shrug.
"All this talk, you are thinking, but we are still fighting a war, aren't we? The truth is, my friends, we
need you. Each of you will serve the cause. In your
hands you hold copies of your illustrious regime's
printed lies. You know how honest these papers
are! They told you this war would never happen,
and here we are! They told you the Germans would
be expelled by August, but tell me"—and here he
gave a stage shiver—"does it feel like August to
you? But never mind that, never mind. Each of you
will read aloud one paragraph. Those we judge literate will come with us to Vyborg, where I can
promise you three meals a day while you translate
documents for the provisional government. Working in a heated building! Those who fail, well . . .
The work will be a little rougher. I have never been
to the steel mills in Estonia, but I hear they can be
dangerous places. Still, we'll give you better grub
than whatever slop the Red Army was handing
out—and I will not even try to guess what you civilians have been eating these past few months."

Some of the older peasants groaned and shook
their heads, making eye contact with one another,
exchanging shrugs. The Einsatzkommando nodded
to the Gebirgsjäger translator and within seconds
the two Germans began testing the prisoners. They
needed to hear only a few sentences to judge the
Russians' literacy. I looked at my copy of *Pravda*.
Atop the lead article was a bold-faced exhortation
fromStalinhimself.COMPATRIOTS!COMRADES!ETERNAL
GLORYTOTHEHEROESWHOHAVEGIVENTHEIRLIVESFOR
FREEDOM AND THE HAPPINESS OF OUR NATION!

The old peasants shrugged and handed their
copies back to the Germans without looking at the

text. Many of the younger men from the collectives struggled to form a few words. These prisoners took the test seriously, frowning as they tried to decipher the letters. The Germans laughed kindly at the mistakes, slapping the illiterates on their shoulders, joking with them.

"You never bothered with the books, did you? Too busy chasing the girls, eh?"

Soon the prisoners relaxed and shouted at their friends on the other end of the line. They laughed along with their captors when they stuttered out the words. A few made up their own articles, pretending to read while inventing accounts of battles outside Moscow or the bombing of Pearl Harbor, doing a passable job of imitating the reporting style they'd heard on the radio. The Germans seemed to enjoy the ruse; both sides knew nobody was fooled.

The Germans asked each failure to step to the left. The first few men to stand there looked embarrassed about their public humiliation, but they cheered up as the ranks of the unlettered grew.

"Ah, Sasha, you too? I thought you were the bright one!"

"Look at him squirming over there in front of the officer! Come on, come on, it's the steel mills with us! What, you thought you might get the office job? What a joker; look at him, still at it!"

"Old Edik, you think you can walk all the way to Estonia? Eh? Come on, cheer up, we'll give you a hand!"

The men who could read wanted to impress the Germans. They recited the lines like actors delivering monologues. Many of them kept going after they were told to stop, giving little flourishes to the

bigger words, demonstrating their ease with the vocabulary. They stepped to the right, proud and
beaming, nodding to their educated fellows, pleased
with how the day had gone. Vyborg wasn't so far,
and working in a heated building with three meals
a day was a better deal than sitting in a trench all
night waiting for the mortars to drop.

Kolya rolled his eyes, watching the literates con-
gratulate each other. "Look at them," he muttered
under his breath. "They want a prize because they
can read the newspaper. And look how condescend-
ing those Fritzes are. Maybe I'll give them the first
chapter of *Eugene Onegin*. Think that would impress
them? Sixty stanzas, *rat-tat-tat-tat-tat*. They think
they're the only culture in Europe? They really want
to match Goethe and Heine against Pushkin and
Tolstoy? I'll give them music. It's closer than they
think, but I'll give them music. And philosophy. But
literature? No, I think not."

The black-capped Einsaztkommando was only
two men down the line from Kolya, who stood to
my left. I felt a gloved hand squeezing my right
hand and I turned to see Vika, her pale face tilted up
toward mine, her fierce eyes unblinking even
through the slanting rays of sunlight. She had taken
my hand to alert me of something, but she did not
let go as quickly as she might have—or at least this
is what I told myself. I could make her love me.
Why not? So what if her general attitude toward me
was bored disgust?

"You don't read," she informed me with that
practiced whisper, too quiet for anyone else to hear.
She kept watching me to make sure I understood.
For once in my life, I didn't need an explanation.

The Einsatzkommando, as patient and benevolent as a professor, stood listening to the Red Army man beside Kolya.

"Soon, Europe will fly the great flag of freedom for the nations—"

"Good."

"—and peace between the nations."

"Good, good. To the right."

I elbowed Kolya's arm. He glanced at me, impatient, ready to show this patronizing Fascist the real face of Russian letters. I shook my head once. The Einsatzkommando walked up to him. There was no chance to say anything. All I could do was stare into Kolya's eyes and hope he understood.

"Ah, here's a fine-looking man of the steppes. Have a bit of the Don Cossack in you?"

Kolya stood straight. He was taller than the Einsatz man and for a few seconds he looked down at the German without opening his mouth.

"I wouldn't know. Born and bred in Piter."

"Beautiful city. Seems a shame calling it Leningrad. Ugly name, isn't it? I mean aside from all the politics. Just seems wrong to me. Saint Petersburg, that's a name that resonates. All the history! I've been there, you know. Moscow, too. Expect I'll visit them again before too long. Now, show me what you can do."

Kolya held up the newspaper and studied the print. He took a deep breath, opened his mouth to begin—and laughed, shaking his head, offering the newspaper to the German.

"I can't even fake it, I'm sorry."

"Don't apologize! Shoulders like yours would be wasted at a desk. Good man, you'll be fine."

Kolya nodded, smiling at the officer like a handsome idiot. He was supposed to join the group of illiterates, but he lingered next to me, his hands in his pockets.

"I want to see if my friend can do any better," he said.

"Well, he can't do any worse," said the Einsatz-kommando with a smile of his own. He stepped in front of me and looked me over. "How old are you? Fifteen?"

I nodded. I didn't know if it was safer to be fifteen or seventeen; I lied on instinct.

"Where were your grandparents from?"

"Moscow."

"All four of them?"

"Yes." I was lying automatically now, not even thinking about the words before I said them. "My parents met there."

"You don't look Russian to me. If I had to guess, I'd say you were a Jew."

"We call him that all the time," said Kolya, ruffling my hair and grinning. "Our little Jew! Makes him crazy. But look at that nose! If I didn't know his family, I'd swear he was a Yid."

"There are Jews with small noses," said the German, "and Gentiles with large ones. We can't be careless with our assumptions. I saw a Jewess in Warsaw a few months ago, her hair was blonder than yours."

He gestured at Kolya's bare head, smiled, and winked.

"And it wasn't dyed. You understand?"

"I do," said Kolya, smiling back.

"Don't be too worried," the German told me. "You're young, still. We all had our awkward years. So tell me, are you any better than your friend here?"

I looked down at the newspaper in my hand.

"I know this says *Stalin*." I pointed to the word. "And *comrade*?"

"Yes, well that's a start."

He gave me an avuncular smile, patted my cheek, and took the paper. I thought he might have felt bad for saying I looked like a Jew.

"Very good. You'll keep your friend here company in Estonia. A few months of hard work never hurt anyone. This will all be over soon. And you," he added, moving down to Vika, the last in the line. "Another child. What do you have for me?"

Vika shrugged and shook her head, never looking up, offering the unread paper to the Einsatzkommando.

"Right, another victory for the Bolshevik education system. Good, all three of you to the left."

We joined the group of grinning illiterates. One of them had worked in a steel mill before and the others were gathered around him, listening to him describe the terrible heat and the danger in handling molten metal. Markov's betrayer stood just outside this circle, rubbing his bare hands to keep them warm, ignored by everyone.

"Was that Abendroth?" I whispered to Vika. She shook her head.

"Abendroth's rank is Sturmbannführer. Four silver pips on the collar tabs. This one only had three."

The company translator was counting each group of prisoners, pointing at heads and moving his lips. When he was finished, he announced to the Einsatzkommando, "Fifty-seven readers. Thirty-eight nonreaders."

"Very good."

The sun was down and the air was getting colder. The Einsatzkommando walked over to the folding chair, where his overcoat waited, while the troopers formed the literate prisoners into two rows and ordered them to march. The Russians gave cheerful waves to their less-educated comrades across the way. They marched with precision now, far different from our stumbling procession earlier in the day. Boots rose and fell on the beat: left, right, left, right. The prisoners wanted to impress their German masters, to prove they deserved this chance to serve out their time clipping newspapers in Vyborg.

The Einsatzkommando wasn't watching them anymore. He buttoned his coat, slipped on his leather gloves, and headed off toward the parked Kübels. The literate prisoners marched to the windowless brick sidewall of the school building, where they halted and faced front. Even then they didn't understand what was happening to them. How could they? They were good students; they had passed the test and been rewarded.

I looked at Vika, but she was staring off into the distance, refusing to watch.

The German troopers leveled their submachine guns and fired at the line of Russians. They kept their fingers on the triggers until the magazines were empty and the Russian men lay splayed and shredded on the ground, smoke rising from their singed coats. The Germans reloaded, walked over to the wall, and fired single shots into the heads of anyone still breathing.

In front of the schoolhouse I saw the Einsatz-kommando greet the young bareheaded soldier who had been filling the fuel tanks. Whatever the officer said must have been funny; the young soldier laughed and nodded in agreement. The Einsatzkommando stepped into one of the Kübels and drove away. The young soldier picked up the empty jerrycans and lugged them toward the schoolhouse. Before he got very far he paused and looked into the sky. I could hear it now, the purr of airplane engines above us. The silver Junkers flew west, in pointed formations of three, for the first bombing raid of the evening. Three after three after three, filling the sky like migrating birds. All of us, the surviving prisoners and the mountain rangers, stood in silence and watched the planes pass.

21

We slept in a toolshed behind the schoolhouse, thirty-five of us jammed into a space eight men might have slept in comfortably. No one could lie down flat. I sat folded into a corner with Kolya on one side of me and Vika on the other. This was bad for my back but good for my breathing—the gaps between the wallboards provided the only ventilation and if I got too claustrophobic, I could turn my head and suck clean, cold air.

There was no light. The German troopers had nailed the shed door shut; we could hear the guards outside talking and lighting cigarettes, but the prisoners still talked of escape. I couldn't see their faces and the effect was like listening to one of the radio plays my mother used to like.

"I'm telling you, we could crack it open like a walnut shell. One man puts his shoulder into it, he'd bust right through the wall."

"You think so? You a carpenter? I am. When they shoved us in here, I got a look at the walls. That's silver birch. That's strong wood."

"And what happens to the man busting through the wall? There's guards out there waiting with machine guns."

"How many? Two, three? We rush them, they'll take a few of us, but we'll get them."

"Can anyone see how many are out there?"

I dipped my head and peered through the gap.

"I *see only* two. But there might be more on the other side."

"Long as I don't go first."

"We all go together."

"There's still got to be a first man out and a last man out."

"I say we wait and do what they say. The war won't last forever."

"Who is that, Edik? Why don't you burn in hell, you old bitch? Didn't you see what happened out there today? You still trust these pig fuckers?"

"If they wanted to shoot us, they would have shot us. It was only the fancy boys they wanted, the ones in the Party."

"Ah . . . you're a miserable old bastard, you know that? I hope your children shit in your soup."

Kolya leaned across me so he could whisper to Vika in the darkness, out of earshot of the squabbling peasants.

"That Einsatzkommando . . . he was right next to us. You told Markov we weren't going to shoot troopers, we were holding out for Einsatz. So?"

For a long count Vika did not respond and I thought she must have been angered by the insinuation, but when she did speak, her tone was thoughtful.

"Maybe I was afraid. And you?"

Kolya sighed. "It didn't seem like the moment. Shoot one man and get blasted to pieces?"

"No. But maybe we waited too long. That might have been our best chance."

I had known her for only a day, but Vika's comments surprised me. She did not seem the sort to admit doubt, and yet here she was using the word *maybe* twice in a row.

"I almost did it," said Kolya, nudging my shoulder. "When he was asking you about your grandparents. I thought he might make you drop your pants, take a look at your meat. I had my hand on the butt of my gun. But we talked him out of it, didn't we? You like what I came up with?"

"You were good," I said. "Very quick."

"I think he wanted to fuck me, to be honest. He had that look."

"What I said before about Jews," whispered Vika, touching my knee in the darkness, "just so you know—anyone the Nazis hate so much is a friend of mine."

"He's only half a Jew," said Kolya. He meant it as a compliment.

"The better half," I replied. Vika laughed. Until that moment I hadn't known she was capable of laughter and it was a strange sound, but not because there was anything odd about her laugh. She laughed like a normal girl.

"What were you doing before the war?" I asked her.

"I was a student."

"Mm," said Kolya. I was hoping he would fall asleep, but he sounded alert, ready for a long conversation. "So was I. What did you study? Agriculture?"

"Why agriculture?"

"Aren't you from a collective?"

"Do I look like I'm from a fucking collective? I'm from Archangel."

"Ah, a northern girl. That explains everything." He elbowed me in the side. "She really is Viking spawn. So you're in the university up there? Studying wood sap and beavers?"

"Astronomy."

"I'm a literature man, myself. Leningrad State." He rambled on about Shchedrin and Turgenev and their flaws for a few minutes before abruptly falling asleep, his long legs stretched out in front of him, forcing me to keep my own legs doubled up against my chest. The peasants began to drop off, too, though here and there I could still hear a whispered argument.

The heat from all the huddled bodies kept the shed warm enough. Before they shoved us inside I had managed to grab a few handfuls of snow to sip at in the darkness. I hadn't eaten anything since the trapper's cabin, where Kolya and I had shared a pocketful of walnuts we'd taken from the farmhouse, but a full day without food was nothing new. During the siege all of us in Piter became hunger experts, with different techniques to distract ourselves from our want. Back in my apartment in the Kirov I had spent many famished nights studying Tarrasch's *Three Hundred Chess Games*. "Always put the rook behind the pawn," he instructed his students. "Except when it is incorrect to do so."

Without a chess book to study or a radio to listen to, I had to find another way to occupy my brain during the long wait for sleep. As the shed grew quieter, I became more and more aware of Vika's body pressed up against mine. When she shifted her head to take a gulp of air from the gap in the wallboards, her hair brushed against my nose. She smelled like a wet dog. I had been raised to be finicky—my mother never tolerated a dirty dish in the sink, an unfolded towel in the bathroom, or an unmade bed. When we were little and she scrubbed us in the bathtub, her rough sponging left my skin raw. Sometimes, if my mother was getting dinner ready for a party, my father would bathe me, and it was like a reprieve from a whipping as he splashed warm water at me, distracted by whatever story he was telling. I loved "The Tale of Cross-eyed Lefty from Tula and the Steel Flea" and he would give it to me from memory time and again.

I was raised to be clean and it bothered me when others were not, when the Antokolsky twins had dirt under their nails or a teacher at school had a soup stain on his collar. But Vika's wet dog smell did not offend me. All of us were slathered in grime by that point, of course—I must have stunk like week-old fish myself—but this wasn't about being inured to foul odors. The tang off her body made me want to lick her clean.

"Do you think they'll really take us to Estonia?" I asked her. Thinking about Vika had been a distraction from my hunger; now I needed a distraction from my distraction. I was not sitting in a comfortable position to have the thoughts I was having.

"I don't know."

"I've never been to Archangel. It must be very cold up there."

In the silence of her nonanswer, I considered the possibility that I was a very boring person. Who else but a boring person would utter such meaningless trifles? If a brilliant pig, the prodigy of the barnyard, spent his entire life learning Russian, and on finally becoming proficient the first words he heard were my own, he would wonder why he had wasted his best years when he could have been lolling in the mud, eating slop with the other dumb beasts.

"You studied astronomy?"

"Yes."

"All right, so I have a question. There are billions of stars in the universe, right? We're surrounded by stars. And all of them emit light, and the light travels forever. So why—"

"Why isn't the sky bright at night?"

"Yes! You've thought about it, too?"

"People have been thinking about it for a long time."

"Oh. I thought maybe I was the first."

"No," she said, and from the way she said it I knew she was smiling.

"So how come it's dark at night?"

"The universe is expanding."

"Really?"

"Mm."

"No, I mean I knew the universe was expanding," I lied. How could the universe expand? Wasn't the universe everything? How does everything stretch out any farther? What does it stretch into? "I just don't see how that explains the starlight."

"It's complicated," she said. "Open your mouth."

"What?"

"*Shh.* Open your mouth."

I did as I was told and she slipped a crust of rye bread through my lips. Unlike the tooth-breaking loaves given out as rations in Piter, this tasted like real bread, like caraway seeds and yeast and scalded milk.

"Good?"

"Yes."

Piece by piece she fed me a full slice of the bread. When she was finished, I licked my lips and waited for more, even though I knew no more was coming.

"That's it. I have to save the rest for tomorrow. Your friend will be hungry."

"Thank you."

She grunted in response and shifted her position, trying to get comfortable.

"His name is Kolya. Just so you know. And I'm Lev."

She seemed to respond to only half the comments I made and this wasn't one of them. I had hoped she would say, 'I'm Vika,' so I could reply, 'Yes, I know. Short for Viktoriya, is it?' For some reason I thought that would be a clever remark, even though every Vika is a Viktoriya.

I listened to her breathing, trying to judge whether or not she had fallen asleep. I tested her by whispering one last question.

"So if you were an astronomy student, I don't really understand. . . . How did you become a sniper?"

"I started shooting people."

That sounded like the end of the conversation to me, so I shut my mouth and let her sleep.

Later in the night I woke up when one of the old peasants on the other side of the shed had a coughing fit. Listening to him hacking up phlegm that had probably been inside his lungs since the reign of Alexander III, I realized that Vika had slipped against me in her sleep, her cheek resting on my shoulder. I could feel her chest rise and fall, the tick of the inhale, the tock of the exhale. For the rest of the night I stayed as still as I possibly could, trying not to disturb her, trying very hard to keep her close.

22

The Germans woke us by prying the nails out of the planks they had hammered over the doorway. Sunlight shot through the gaps in the wallboards, tiny spotlights shining on a greasy forehead, a leather boot with the sole curling away from the toe, the horn buttons of an old man's coat.

Vika sat next to me, chewing on her fingernails. She chewed methodically, not an anxious person with a nervous habit but a butcher sharpening his knives. At some point in the night she had moved away from me and I hadn't felt her leave. She looked up when she sensed I was watching and there was no trace of affection in her eyes. Any glimmer of intimacy I felt in the darkness was gone in the daylight.

The door opened, the Germans shouted at us to move, and the peasants disentangled themselves from one another. I saw the old man Edik press a gnarled forefinger against one nostril and blow a gob of snot to the floor, barely missing another man's face.

"Ah," grumbled Kolya, wrapping his scarf around his neck, "don't you wish you grew up with our comrade farmers on a collective?"

As the prisoners began to file out the door, a man

on the far side of the shed cried out. Those around
him turned to see what had frightened him and soon
they were anxiously whispering among themselves.
From our corner all we could see were peasants'
backs. Kolya and I stood, curious about the commotion. Vika, uninterested, headed for the door.

We stepped to the other side of the shed, sidled
around the muttering peasants, and looked down at
the man still lying there. It was Markov's accuser,
his throat slashed, the blood long drained from his
body, and his face chalk white. He must have been
murdered in his sleep or we would have heard him
cry out, but his eyes had popped open when the
knife cut his skin; they bulged from their sockets,
staring with horror at our downturned faces.

One of the peasants yanked off the dead man's
boots; a second took his sheepskin gloves; a third
pulled the tooled leather belt from the belt loops on
his pants. Kolya knelt down and snatched the
quilted down cap before anyone else could. I turned
and saw Vika adjusting her own rabbit fur cap, setting it very low on her forehead. She looked back at
me for a second and walked out of the toolshed. A
moment later a German trooper stepped inside, angry at the delay, ready to fire his weapon. He saw
the corpse, the gaping throat, the bloodstain that
started under the dead man's back and spread
across the floorboards like a pair of monstrous black
wings. The murder irritated the trooper—this re-
quired an explanation for the officers. He asked a
question in German, more to himself than any of us,
not expecting an answer. Kolya cleared his throat
and replied. I couldn't judge Kolya's German, but
the trooper seemed amazed to hear his own language spoken by a prisoner.

The German shook his head, gave a curt response, and gestured with his thumb for us to leave the shed. When we were outside, I asked Kolya what he had said.

"I told him the peasants hate the Jews even more than your people do."

"And what did he say?"

"'There is a proper way of doing things.' Very Germanic." He was trying to fit his new cap onto his bare head; it wasn't really big enough, but he managed to yank the earflaps down far enough so he could tie the drawstrings together.

"You think it's smart to let them know you speak German? After what they did yesterday?"

"No, I think it's dangerous. But at least now they won't ask any more questions."

The prisoners had been organized into a single-file line; we shuffled forward, squinting in the bright morning sun, toward a hulking, hungover trooper, his eyes still crusted with sleep, who handed each of us a single round biscuit, hard and dry as a lump of coal.

"A good sign," muttered Kolya, tapping at his biscuit with his fingernail.

Soon we were marching south with the Gebirgsjäger company, heads bowed against the wind. Today we walked on the road, though the pavement was hidden beneath layers of tread-marked snow. A few kilometers from the schoolhouse we passed a sign for Mga and I pointed it out to Kolya.

"Huh. What day is today?"

I had to think about it, counting backward in my head to Saturday.

"Wednesday. We're supposed to show up with the eggs tomorrow."

"Wednesday. . . . I haven't shit in thirteen days. Thirteen days. . . . What happens to it all? It's not like I haven't eaten anything. Darling soup and some sausages, those buttered potatoes with the girls, ration bread . . . What's it doing, just sitting in my belly, a fucking lump?"

"You want to shit?" asked Edik, the old bearded peasant, who had heard Kolya's complaints and now turned to give advice. "Boil some buckthorn bark and drink the water. Never fails."

"Wonderful. You see any buckthorns around here?"

Edik glanced at the roadside pines and shook his head. "I'll give a whistle if we pass any."

"Many thanks. Maybe you can find me the boiling water, too."

Edik had already faced front and resumed his place in the line, mindful that one of the troopers had looked our way.

"Stalin goes to visit one of the collectives outside of Moscow," began Kolya in his joke-telling voice. "Wants to see how they're getting on with the latest Five-Year Plan. 'Tell me, comrade,' he asks one farmer. 'How did the potatoes do this year?' 'Very well, Comrade Stalin. If we piled them up, they would reach God.' 'But God does not exist, Comrade Farmer.' 'Nor do the potatoes, Comrade Stalin.'"

"Old one."

"Jokes only get old if they're good. Otherwise, who keeps telling them?"

"People like you who aren't funny?"

"I can't help it if you never laugh. I make the girls laugh, that's what matters."

"You think she did it?" I asked him. He glanced

at me, confused for a moment, until he saw that I
was watching Vika, who marched apart from us today, near the front of the procession.

"Of course she did it."

"I just . . . She was squeezed up against me all
night. When I fell asleep, her head was on my
shoulder—"

"That's as close to sex as you've ever been. You
see that? You've listened to me, you've learned."

"—and somehow she managed to get away from
me, and I'm a very light sleeper, crawl around thirty
peasants in total darkness, cut the man's throat, and
come back? Without waking a single person?"

Kolya nodded, still watching Vika, who walked
alone, scanning the roadside and the position of the
German troops.

"She's a talented killer."

"Especially for an astronomer."

"Ha. Don't believe everything you hear."

"You think she's lying?"

"I'm sure she went to university for a while.
That's where they recruit. But come, little lion, you
think she learned to shoot like that in astronomy
class? She's NKVD. They have agents in every partisan cell."

"You don't know that."

He stopped for a few seconds to kick one boot
against the other, knocking off snow trapped in the
sole, holding my arm to balance himself.

"I don't know anything. Maybe your name isn't
Lev. Maybe you're the greatest lover in the history
of Russia. But I consider the facts and I make an educated guess. The partisans are local fighters. That's
why they're so effective—they know the land better
than the Germans ever will. They have friends in

the area, family, people who can give them food, a safe place to sleep. Now, tell me, how far are we from Archangel?"

"I don't know."

"I don't know, either. Seven, eight hundred kilometers? The German border is probably closer. You think the local partisans just decided to trust some girl who showed up out of nowhere? No, she was sent to them."

She plodded through the snow ahead, her hands jammed into the pockets of her coveralls. From behind she looked like a twelve-year-old boy wearing a stolen mechanic's uniform.

"I wonder if she has any tits," said Kolya.

His crudity annoyed me, though I had wondered the same thing. Judging her body beneath the oversize coveralls was impossible, but from what I could tell she was curveless and slender as a blade of grass.

He noticed the expression on my face and smiled.

"Did I offend you? I apologize. You really like this one, don't you?"

"I don't know."

"I won't talk about her that way anymore. Will you forgive me?"

"You can talk about her any way you want."

"No, no. I understand now. But listen, this isn't an easy fish to hook."

"Are you going to give me more advice from your made-up book?"

"Just listen. Make your jokes, fine, but I know more about these things than you. My guess is she was a little bit in love with that Korsakov. And he was a tougher man than you, so you can't impress her with toughness."

"She wasn't in love with him."

"Just a little bit."

"I never thought I was going to impress her with toughness. Do you think I'm that stupid?"

"So the question is, what *do* you impress her with?"

Here Kolya went silent for a long time, eyes scrunched up, forehead creased with worry lines as he pondered my assets. Before he could think of any we heard shouts behind us and turned to see the troopers waving us to the side of the road. A convoy of Mercedes half-tracks with tarpaulin-covered flat-beds rumbled past, hauling provisions and materiel to the front lines. We stood watching for five minutes and still there was no end to the slow-rolling convoy. The Germans could not have cared less about impressing their prisoners, but I was impressed. Fuel rationing in Piter meant that I rarely saw more than four or five moving vehicles in a day. I had already counted forty of the hybrid trucks, with their rubber tires in front and tank tracks in the rear, three-pointed stars on their grilles and white-bordered black crosses painted on their backsides.

Behind the half-tracks came eight-wheeled ar-mored cars, caterpillar-tracked heavy mortars, and light trucks carrying troopers seated on parallel benches, faces weary and unshaven, rifles strapped to their shoulders, huddled up in their white anoraks.

We heard curses from the front of the convoy, drivers leaning out of their windows to find out what the trouble was. One of the self-propelled ar-

tillery pieces had slipped a tread, and while its op-
erators scurried to fix it, the howitzer blocked
everything behind it. The infantrymen took the opportunity to jump out of their trucks and piss along
the side of the road. Soon there was a line of several
hundred troopers and half-track drivers and artillerymen stamping their boots and hollering to their
friends, leaning back to see who could launch their
stream the farthest. Steam rose from the yellow
snow.

"Look at these ass-lickers pissing on our land,"
muttered Kolya. "They won't be laughing so loud
when I squat down to shit in the middle of Berlin."
The thought cheered him. "Maybe that's why I can't
squeeze one out. My bowels are waiting for
victory."

"Patriotic bowels."

"Every part of me is patriotic. My cock whistles
the 'Soviet Hymn' when it comes."

"Whenever I hear you two talking, it's always
cocks and asses," said Vika. She had crept up behind us in her usual silent way, startling me when
she spoke. "Why don't you both strip naked and get
it over with?"

"It's not me he wants to strip naked," Kolya said
with a leer.

I felt a rush of anger and embarrassment, but
Vika ignored the comment, keeping an eye out for
watchful guards and other prisoners as she slipped
us both half slices of her good rye bread.

"You see the officers' cars at the end of the convoy?" she asked, looking in that direction but not
raising a hand to point.

"That's the best bread I've had since summer,"
Kolya said, his portion already devoured.

"You see the Kommandeurwagen with the swastika fender pendants? That's Abendroth's car."

"How do you know?" I asked her.

"Because we've been tracking him for three months. I almost had a shot at him outside Budogoshch. That's his car."

"What's the plan?" asked Kolya, picking at a caraway seed stuck between his teeth.

"When the convoy starts moving again, I'll wait till he's close and I'll take my shot. Shouldn't be hard."

I looked up and down the road. We stood in the middle of what seemed like a full battalion, surrounded by hundreds of rifle-toting Germans on foot and in armored vehicles. Vika's pronouncement meant that we would die in a few minutes, whether or not she hit her target.

"I'll take the shot," said Kolya. "You and Lev stand over there with those cretins from the collective. No point bringing us all down."

Vika curled her lips in her half smile and shook her head. "I'm the better shooter."

"You've never seen me shoot."

"True. And I'm the better shooter."

"It doesn't matter," I told them. "Both of you shoot, what difference does it make? You think they'll let any of us live after that?"

"The boy has a point," said Kolya. He surveyed the illiterate prisoners standing around us, shuffling their feet and clapping their hands to keep warm, most of them farmers who had never before traveled more than a few kilometers from their collectives. A few Red Army privates were mixed into the lot. One or two of them, I was sure, could read just as well as I could.

"How many prisoners did they say? Thirty-eight?"

"Thirty-seven now," said Vika. She saw me staring at her and she stared right back with those pitiless blue eyes. "How long do you think you'll last before one of these peasants notices you're missing a few bits down there"—and here she pointed at my crotch—"and turns you in for an extra bowl of soup?"

"Thirty-seven. . . . It seems like too many to sacrifice for one German," said Kolya.

"Thirty-seven prisoners headed to the steel mills? These men aren't Russian assets anymore," she said in her quiet, uninflected tone. "They're German labor. And Abendroth is worth sacrificing for."

Kolya nodded, peering at the Kommandeurwagen in the distance.

"We're pawns and he's a rook, that's what you're saying."

"We're less than pawns. Pawns have value."

"If we can take a rook, we have value, too."

Saying this, Kolya blinked and looked at me. He flashed a sudden and certain smile; his whole Cossack face lit up with the grandeur of a new idea.

"Maybe there's another way. Wait here a minute."

"What are you doing?" asked Vika, but it was too late; he had already started toward the closest cluster of troopers. The Germans narrowed their eyes when they saw him coming and moved their fingers toward their trigger guards, but Kolya held up his hands and began chattering to them in their native tongue, as cheerful and relaxed as if we were all gathered together to watch a parade. After thirty seconds they were laughing at whatever jokes he was telling. One of the troopers even let him take a long drag off the man's cigarette.

"He has charm," said Vika. She sounded like an entomologist discussing a beetle's carapace.

"They probably think he's their long-lost Aryan brother."

"The two of you are a strange couple."

"We're not a couple."

"I don't mean it like that. Don't worry, Lyova. I know you like girls."

My father had called me Lyova and hearing the nickname coming from her mouth—so unexpected but so natural, as if she had been calling me that for years—almost made me want to cry.

"He made you angry before, didn't he? When he said that about wanting to see me naked."

"He says a lot of stupid things."

"So you don't want to see me naked?"

Vika wore her mocking smile now, standing with her feet wide apart, her hands jammed into the pockets of her coveralls.

"I don't know." Yes, it was a stupid and cowardly response, but I could not handle the morning's peaks and valleys. One moment I thought I had a few minutes left to live; the next a sniper from Archangel was flirting with me. Was she flirting with me? The days had become a confusion of catastrophes; what seemed impossible in the afternoon was blunt fact by the evening. German corpses fell from the sky; cannibals sold sausage links made from ground human in the Haymarket; apartment blocs collapsed to the ground; dogs became bombs; frozen soldiers became signposts; a partisan with half a face stood swaying in the snow, staring sad-eyed at his killers. I had no food in my belly, no fat on my bones, and no energy to reflect on this parade of atrocities. I just kept moving, hoping to find another half slice of bread for myself and a dozen eggs for the colonel's daughter.

"He told me your father was a famous poet."

"He wasn't that famous."

"Is that what you want to be? A poet?"

"No. I don't have any talent for it."

"What do you have talent for?"

"I don't know. Not everybody has talent."

"That's true. Despite what they always told us."

From the look of things, Kolya was delivering a grand lecture to the troopers arrayed around him in a semicircle, making elaborate hand gestures to punctuate his sentences. He pointed at me and I felt my throat constrict as the German soldiers turned and glanced my way, curious and amused.

"What the hell is he telling them?"

Vika shrugged. "He'll get himself shot if he's not careful."

The troopers seemed doubtful, but Kolya kept cajoling them and finally one of them, shaking his head as if he couldn't quite believe he was listening to this lunatic Russian, adjusted the strap of his MP40 and hustled toward the back of the convoy. Kolya nodded to the remaining men gathered around him, made some final joke that had them grinning again, and ambled back to us.

"The Nazis adore you," said Vika. "Were you quoting *Mein Kampf*?"

"Tried to read it once. Very dull."

"What did you say to them?"

"I told them I had a wager for Herr Abendroth.

That my friend here, a fifteen-year-old boy from the less-fashionable side of Leningrad, could play without a queen and still beat the Sturmbannführer in a game of chess."

"I'm seventeen."

"Oh. Well, fifteen is more of an insult."

"Is this a joke?" asked Vika, head tilted to one side, watching Kolya and waiting for him to smile and explain that he had done no such stupid thing.

"No joke."

"You don't think he'll wonder how you knew he was here? Knew his rank, knew that he played chess?"

"I think he'll wonder all of those things. And that will make him curious, and that will make him come to us."

"What's the bet?" I asked him.

"If he wins, he can shoot us dead on the spot."

"He can shoot us dead whenever he wants, you thick-headed fool."

"That's what the troopers said. Of course he can. But I told them that the Sturmbannführer is a man of honor, a man of principle. I told them I trust his word and I trust his spirit of competition. They love all that blood and honor horseshit."

"What do we get if I win?"

"First, he sets all three of us free." He saw our expressions and cut us off before we could speak. "Yes, yes, you think I'm an idiot, but you two are the slow ones. We can't play now, with the convoy moving. With any luck the game happens tonight, inside, away from all of this." Kolya waved his hand, indicating the German soldiers standing in loose circles, chatting and smoking; the half-tracks loaded with provisions; the heavy artillery.

"He'll never set us free."

"Obviously he'll never set us free. But we'll have a much easier shot at him. And if the gods are smiling, maybe we'll even have a chance to run."

"'If the gods are smiling,'" said Vika, mocking Kolya's pomposity. "Have you been paying attention to this war?"

The mechanics had reset the track on the self-propelled howitzer. The driver and his crew hopped into the hatch. Moments later the engine coughed back to life and the long-turreted beast groaned into motion, cracking through the ice that had formed around its cast-steel track pads. The infantrymen didn't seem in any rush to get back to their trucks, but after their final hoarse-voiced good-byes, with the officers shouting and the convoy beginning to snake forward, they took long last drags on their cigarettes, flicked them away, and hopped back onto the tarpaulin-covered flatbeds.

The trooper who had set off with the message for Abendroth jogged back to his unit. When he saw us watching him, he nodded and smiled. His face was pink and hairless, his cheeks round, and it was easy to picture him as a baby bald and bawling. He hollered at us, a single German word, before catching up to his already rolling truck, reaching out a hand, and letting one of his compatriots haul him onboard.

"Tonight," said Kolya.

Our guards had already barked at us, knowing we didn't understand and not caring. The message was simple enough. The prisoners formed into lines again, Vika drifted away from us, and we waited for the long convoy to pass. When the Kommandeurwagen motored by, I tried to spot Abendroth, but the window glass was frosted over.

I remembered something that had been bothering me and I turned to Kolya.

"What's the second thing you asked for?"

"Hm?"

"You said if I win, first he sets us free. So what's the second thing you asked for?"

He looked down at me, his eyebrows tilted toward each other, incredulous that I could not guess.

"Isn't it obvious? A dozen eggs."

23

That evening we sat with the other prisoners in a sheep barn just outside of Krasnogvardeysk. The air smelled of wet wool and dung. The Germans had given us a few twigs for firewood and most of the men were gathered around a timid little fire in the center of the barn. Tonight they were too tired to talk of escape. They complained with little vigor that the Germans hadn't fed us since the morning biscuit, they muttered predictions about the next day's weather, and soon all of them were sleeping on the cold ground, spooned together for warmth. Vika, Kolya, and I sat with our backs against the splintering wood wall, shivering, debating whether or not the game would happen.

"If he sends for us," Vika said, "if they bring us to him, I promise you, they will search us for weapons."

"They already searched the prisoners. What are they going to think, we found guns in the sheep barn?"

"The man knows he's a target. He's very careful. They'll find the guns."

Kolya responded with a mournful fart, low and solemn as a single note from a baritone horn. Vika shut her eyes for a few seconds, breathing through her mouth. I studied her pale red lashes in the firelight.

"All the same," she said at last, "they will find the guns."

"So what should we do, strangle the man?"

She reached into her coveralls, pulled her Finnish knife from the sheath on her belt, and began carving a little grave in the frozen dirt. When it was deep enough, she buried her pistol and held out her hand for Kolya's.

"I want to keep it."

She waited with her outstretched hand and finally he handed it over. When both pistols were covered with soil, she unbuttoned her coveralls and unbuckled her belt. Kolya gave me a little nudge. The coveralls had slipped off Vika's shoulders; beneath them she wore a heavy wool woodcutter's shirt and two layers of long underwear, but for a moment I saw her collarbone shifting beneath skin speckled with dirt. I had never before given any conscious thought to another human's collarbone; hers looked like the wings of a gliding seagull. She yanked off her canvas belt, lifted her woodcutter's shirt and the two undershirts to just below her breasts, held the shirts in place with her chin, and strapped the belt to her bare skin. The knife sheath now rested against her sternum, and when she pulled down the undershirts and the woodcutter's shirt and rebuttoned her coveralls, it was impossible to detect its shape.

She took my hand and placed it against her chest. "Do you feel anything?"

I shook my head and Kolya laughed. "Wrong answer."

Vika smiled at me. My hand still rested on her

padded chest. I was scared to move it and scared to keep it there. "Don't listen to him, Lyova. He was born from his mother's ass."

"You two want some privacy? I could cuddle up with old Edik over there. He looks lonely."

"What about my knife?" I asked her.

"I forgot about your knife."

"Let me have it," said Kolya. "I know how to use it."

"No," said Vika. "They'll search you the most carefully. You're the only one who looks like a soldier." She leaned forward and I pulled away my hand, certain that I had somehow missed an opportunity even if I didn't know what it was or where it went. She unclipped the sheath from my boot and hefted it in her hand for a moment, pondering its size and shape. Finally, she slipped it deep inside my boot, under my sock. She examined the boot again. Nothing was visible. She patted the leather and seemed satisfied.

"Can you walk normally?"

I stood and took a few steps. I could feel the sheath point digging into my foot, but it seemed secure, held firmly in place by my sock and my boot.

"Look at him," said Kolya. "The silent killer."

I sat down beside Vika again. She touched the soft spot below my ear and drew her finger across my throat, stopping below the other ear.

"You cut that open," she told me, "and no one can ever close it."

The senior officers of Einsatzgruppe A had commandeered the Krasnogvardeysk party headquarters, a grubby warren of small offices with peeling linoleum floors above the blackened husk of the police station. The building stank of smoke and diesel fumes but the Germans had already restored electricity and fired up the furnaces; the second floor was warm and comfortable, aside from the occasional brushstroke of dried blood on the walls. A few hours after we buried the pistols, two troopers from the Gebirgsjäger battalion escorted the three of us into the conference room, where before the town fell the planning committee members had met to discuss orders from above and commands for below. Four-paned windows overlooked the unlit main street of Krasnogvardeysk. Posters of Lenin and Zhdanov still hung from the walls, unmolested, as if their stern expressions bothered the Germans so little they weren't worth tearing down or defacing.

Abendroth sat at the far end of the long table, drinking clear liquor from a cut-crystal tumbler. He nodded when we walked into the room, but made no move to stand. His gray peaked hat—banded in black, with a silver death's head below the German eagle—rested on the tabletop. A traveling chessboard, the pieces already arranged, waited between the hat and an unlabeled, nearly empty bottle of liquor.

I had been expecting a slender aesthete, a professorial type, but Abendroth was a big man, built like a hammer thrower, his collar digging into the veins of his thick neck. The heavy tumbler seemed dainty as a doll's cup in the palm of his hand. He didn't look older than thirty, but the close-cropped hair on the sides of his head was white, as was the stubble on his chin. SS lightning bolt runes gleamed on his right collar tab; four silver pips indicated his rank on the left tab; and a black-and-silver Knight's Cross hung in between.

He was at least a little drunk, though his movements remained perfectly coordinated. I had learned at an early age how to spot a drunk, even the skillful drunks who held their liquor well. My father wasn't a big drinker, but his friends all were, poets and playwrights who had never gone to bed sober in their adult lives. Some were sloppy with their affection, kissing my cheeks and mussing my hair while they told me what a lucky little man I was to have a father like him. Others were cold and distant as orbiting moons, waiting for me to return to the room I shared with my sister, to leave the adults alone so they could resume their debates about the Litburo or Mandelstam's latest provocation. Some slurred their words after a single glass of vodka and some became articulate only after draining their first bottle.

Abendroth's eyes shined a little too brightly. He smiled from time to time for no apparent reason, amused by whatever joke he told himself. He watched us and didn't say a word until he had finished his glass of liquor, wiped his hands together, and shrugged.

"Plum schnapps," he told us, his Russian quite precise, though like his fellow Einsatz officer at the schoolhouse he made no effort to approximate the accent. "An old man I know makes it by hand, best stuff in the world, and now I bring a case with me wherever I go. One of you speaks German?"

"I do," said Kolya.

"Where did you learn it?"

"My grandmother was from Vienna." Whether this was true or not I had no idea, but he said it with such conviction Abendroth seemed to accept it.

"Waren Sie schon einmal in Wien?"

"*Nein.*"

"Too bad. Beautiful city. And no one has bombed it yet, but that will not last. I expect the English will get to it before the year is out. Someone told you I play chess?"

"One of your colleagues back at the schoolhouse. An Obersturmführer, I believe? He speaks Russian almost as well as you."

"Kuefer? With the little mustache?"

"That's the one. He was very . . ." Kolya hesitated as if he were not sure how to proceed without saying something offensive. ". . . friendly."

Abendroth stared at Kolya for several seconds before snorting, amused and disgusted. He covered his mouth with the back of his hand and burped before pouring himself another glass of the schnapps.

"I am sure he was. Yes, he is very friendly, Kuefer. And how did your conversation turn to me?"

"I told him my friend here is one of the best players in Leningrad and he said—"

"Your Jewish friend here?"

"Ha, that was his joke, too, but no, Lev's no Jew. He got the curse of the nose and none of the money."

"I am surprised Kuefer did not inspect the boy's cock to verify his race."

Still looking at me, Abendroth commented in German for the benefit of the troopers, who glanced my way, curious.

"Did you understand what I just said?" he asked Kolya.

"Yes."

"Translate for your friends."

" 'It is my business to know a Jew when I see one.' "

"Very good. And unlike our friend Kuefer, I can spot a girl, too. Take off your hat, my dear."

For a long count Vika did not move. I did not dare to look at her, but I knew she was debating whether or not to go for her knife. It would have been a pointless gesture, the troopers would have gunned her down before she had taken a step, but pointless gestures seemed like all we had left. I could feel Kolya tensing beside me—if Vika went for her knife, he would lunge for the nearest trooper, and then everything would end very quickly.

The imminence of death did not frighten me as much as it should have. I had been too afraid for too long; I was too exhausted, too hungry, to feel anything with proper intensity. But if my fear had diminished, it was not because my courage had increased. My body was so weak, so spent, that my legs trembled from the effort of standing upright. I could summon no great concern for anything, including the fate of Lev Beniov.

Vika finally removed her rabbit fur cap and held it between her hands. Abendroth downed half his glass with a single swallow, pursed his lips, and nodded.

"You will be pretty when your hair grows out. Now everything is in the open, yes? Tell me something," he said to Kolya. "You speak German quite well, but you cannot read Russian?"

"It always gives me a headache, trying to read."

"Of course. And you," he said to me, "you are one of the best chess players in Leningrad, but you cannot read either? It is a strange combination, yes? Most of the chess players I know are quite literate."

I opened my mouth, hoping lies would flow

forth as quickly as they did for Kolya, but Abendroth raised one palm and shook his head.

"Do not bother. You passed Kuefer's test, good, I respect that. You are survivors. But I am not a stupid man. One of you is a Jew posing as a Gentile; one is a girl posing as a boy; all of you, I assume, are literates posing as illiterate. And despite the attentions of our vigilant mountain rangers and the esteemed Obersturmführer Kuefer, all these ruses have succeeded. And yet you asked to come here for a game of chess. You asked for me to notice you. This is very strange. You are not fools, that is clear, or you would already be dead. You do not really expect that I would set you free if you win this game, do you? And the dozen eggs . . . the dozen eggs is the strangest part of the whole equation."

"I realize you don't have the power to free us," said Kolya, "but I thought, if my friend wins, perhaps you could put in a good word with your superiors—"

"Of course I have the power to free you. It is not a question of—ah." Abendroth pointed at Kolya and nodded, almost smiling. "Very good. You are a clever one. Play on the German's vanity. Yes, no wonder Kuefer was so fond of you. Explain the eggs."

"I haven't had one since August. We're always talking about the food we're craving, and I couldn't get the idea of fried eggs out of my head. The whole day, marching in the snow, that's all I could think about."

Abendroth tapped the tabletop with his fingertips. "So, let's consider the situation. The three of you are confirmed liars. You come up with a dubious story that gets you a private audience—" Abendroth glanced at the troopers and shrugged. "A semiprivate audience with a senior officer of the despised Einsatzgruppe A. Obviously you have information you wish to trade."

There was a moment's silence before Kolya said, "I don't understand."

"I think you do. You know which of the prisoners are Bolsheviks, perhaps, or you have heard plans for Red Army troop movements. You cannot deliver this information in front of the other Russians so you arrange for this meeting. It happens very often, you know. Your countrymen seem eager to betray Comrade Stalin."

"We're not traitors," said Kolya. "The boy happens to be very good at chess. I heard you're a player. I saw an opportunity."

"This is the answer I hoped for," said Abendroth with a smile. He gulped down the rest of his tumbler of schnapps and poured out the final glass, holding it to the light to examine the liquor.

"My God, this is the stuff. Seven years in an oak cask . . ."

He took another small sip, patient now, not wanting to rush the last glass. After a moment to savor the schnapps, he spoke a few quiet words in German. One of the troopers leveled his MP40 at us while the other stepped closer and began patting me down.

The knife had seemed well hidden back in the sheep barn, but standing there while the soldier searched me, I could think of nothing but the hard leather sheath digging into the top of my foot. He searched the pockets of my father's old greatcoat, checked beneath my armpits, under my belt, down my legs. He dug his fingers into my boots and my fear returned, a jolt of pure terror, mocking me for the numbness I had felt five minutes before. I tried to breathe normally, to keep a calm expression on my face. He prodded around my shins, found nothing, and moved on to Kolya.

I wonder how much he missed it by, how many millimeters separated his fingertips from the sheath. He was a boy, a year or two older than I was, his face constellated with small brown moles. His classmates had teased him about those moles, that was certain. He had stared at them in the mirror, sullen and ashamed, wondering if he could shave them off with his father's razor. If he had gotten another fifteen minutes of sleep the night before, if he had swallowed another spoonful of soup, he might have had the energy to do his job properly and find the knife. But he did not, and his carelessness changed everything for both of us.

When he finished searching Kolya, he stepped over to Vika. His fellow ranger made a joke and chuckled at his own wit. Maybe he wanted to goad the boy into slapping Vika's ass or pinching a nipple, but she watched him with her cold unblinking eyes and he seemed unnerved, inspecting her far less thoroughly than he had Kolya and me. I realized the boy must be a virgin; he was as nervous around a woman's body as I was.

After he timidly patted down her legs, he stood, nodded to Abendroth, and backed away. The Sturmbannführer watched the boy for a moment, a slight smile curling his lips.

"I think he is afraid of you," he told Vika. He waited a few seconds to see if she would respond and when she didn't, he turned his attention to Kolya. "You are a soldier, I cannot release you or you will rejoin the Red Army, and if you kill a German, his parents would have me to blame." He looked at me. "And you are a Jew; releasing you goes against my conscience. But if you win, I will let the girl go home. That is the best offer I can make."

"I have your word you'll let her go?" I asked him.

Abendroth rubbed the silver stubble on his chin with his knuckles. A gold wedding band on his ring finger caught the light from the bulb overhead.

"You like the girl. Interesting. And you, little redhead, do you like the Jew? Never mind, never mind, no need to be vulgar. So . . . you are in no position to make demands, but yes, you have my word. I have been looking for a good game since Leipzig. This country has the best chess players in the world and I have not seen anyone competent."

"Maybe you shot them before you could find out," said Kolya. I held my breath, quite certain this was a step too far, but Abendroth nodded.

"It is possible. Work comes before play. Come," he said to me, "sit. If you are as good as your friend says, I might keep you around for the competition."

"Wait," said Kolya. "If he wins, you let her go and you give us the eggs."

Abendroth's patience with the back and forth began to fade. His nostrils flared as he leaned forward, though he did not raise his voice.

"What I have offered is more than generous. You wish to continue with this stupidity?"

"I believe in my friend. If he loses, put bullets in our heads. But if he wins, we'd like to fry up some eggs for supper."

Abendroth spoke again in German and the older

trooper jammed the muzzle of his gun against the base of Kolya's skull.

"You like to negotiate?" asked Abendroth. "Good, we negotiate. You seem to think you have leverage. You have no leverage. I say two words and you become a corpse. Yes? Two words. Do you understand how fast it happens? You are a corpse, they drag your body outside, I play chess with your friend. Later on, maybe I take the little red-head back to my room, give her a bath, see what she looks like without all the dirt. Or maybe not, maybe no bath, maybe tonight I want to fuck an animal. When in Rome, yes? Now think, boy, think very carefully before you open your mouth. For your own sake, for your mother's sake if the bitch still lives, think."

Another man would have decided to leave it alone and shut up for good. Kolya did not hesitate for more than a second.

"Of course, you can kill me whenever you'd like. This is undeniable. But do you think my best friend here will have a decent game left in him after he sees my brains on the table? Do you want to play Leningrad's best or a scared boy with piss running down his leg? If he can't win our freedom, very well, I understand, this is war. But at least give him the chance to win the supper we've been dreaming about."

Abendroth stared at Kolya, his fingertip slowly drumming the tabletop, the only sound in the room. Finally, he turned to the trooper with the moles and uttered a clipped command. After the young German saluted and left the room, the Sturmbannführer gestured for me to sit in the chair at the corner of the table beside him. He nodded to

Kolya and Vika and pointed to the chairs at the far end of the table.

"Sit," he ordered them. "You have been walking all day, yes? Sit, sit. Should we flip a coin?" he asked me. Without waiting for a response he pulled one from his pocket and showed me the swastika-clutching eagle on one side and the fifty Reichspfennig marking on the other. He flicked the coin in the air with his thumb, caught it, slapped it down on the back of his other hand, and looked up at me. "Bird or numbers?"

"Numbers."

"You do not like our bird?" he asked with a slight smile. He removed his hand and showed me the Nazi eagle. "I'll play white. And do not worry—you can keep your queen."

He slid his queen's pawn forward two spaces and nodded when I mirrored the move.

"One day I will choose a different opening." He moved his c-pawn up two, offering the sacrifice. The Queen's Gambit. At least half the games I played started with these moves. Weekend players and grand masters alike began with the combination; it was still too early to tell if the German knew what he was doing. I declined the Gambit and moved my king's pawn forward a space.

Over the years I've played thousands of games against hundreds of opponents. I've played on a blanket in the Summer Gardens, in tournaments at the Palace of the Pioneers, in the courtyard of the Kirov with my father. When I played for the Spartak club, I kept records of all my games, but I threw them away when I quit competition. I was never going to study my old matches, not after I realized I was only a middling player. But if you gave me a piece of paper and a pen, even today, I could write out the algebraic notation of my entire game with Abendroth.

I sprang my queen from the back row on the sixth move, which seemed to surprise him. He frowned, scratching the stubble along his upper lip with his thumbnail. I chose the move because I thought it was a good one, but also because it might appear to be a bad one—neither of us yet had any sense of our opponent's skill, and if he believed I was a poor player, I could lure him into committing a critical mistake.

He murmured something in German and moved his kingside knight, a reasonable response but not the one I had feared. If he had taken my pawn, he would have kept the initiative, forcing me to respond to his aggression. Instead he played defensively, and I took advantage by moving my bishop into his territory.

Abendroth leaned back in his chair, studying the board. After a minute's worth of contemplation, he smiled and looked up at me.

"It has been a long time since I had a good game."

I said nothing, watching the board, visualizing potential sequences of moves.

"You do not need to worry," he continued. "Win or lose, you are safe. A good game every night will keep me sane."

He sat forward again and moved his queen. While I deliberated, the young trooper returned carrying a slatted wood box stuffed with straw. Abendroth asked him a question and the trooper nodded, placing the box on the table.

"You've put me in the mood," Abendroth said

to Kolya. "If I win, I might eat a twelve-egg omelet."

Kolya, sitting at the far end of the table, grinned at the sight of the box of eggs. Both troopers now stood behind him and Vika, their hands never straying from the butts of their submachine guns. Kolya had been trying to follow the game from a distance, but Vika stared at the table. Her face never gave much away, but I could tell she was irritated and I realized, far too late, that I had missed an opportunity. When the trooper had gone to fetch the eggs, we briefly outnumbered the Germans; they had guns and we had only knives, but it might have been our best chance.

Eight moves into the game the Sturmbannführer and I began exchanging pieces. I took a pawn; he took a knight. I took a bishop; he took a pawn. At the end of this flurry our forces were still evenly matched, but the board had opened up and I judged my position stronger.

"Violinists and chess players, eh?"

I had been afraid to look at him before, but now I stole a glance as he analyzed our formations. Sitting so close, I could see the dark, swollen crescents below his hazel eyes. His jaw line was strong and right-angled, in profile a capital L. He noticed that I was watching him and he raised his massive skull to stare back at me. I lowered my eyes quickly.

"Your race," he said. "Despite everything, you make wonderful violinists and chess players."

I pulled back my queen and for the next twelve moves we gathered our forces, avoiding direct confrontation. Both of us castled, protecting our kings as we prepared for the next battle, massing toward the center, trying to claim the best ground. On the twenty-first move I nearly fell for an elegant little trap he had set for me. I was ready to snatch an exposed pawn when I realized what the German had planned. I returned my bishop and moved my queen to give her a better angle of attack.

"Too bad," said Abendroth. "That would have been a pretty little maneuver."

I looked over and saw that Kolya and Vika were staring at me. The plan had never been spelled out, but now it seemed obvious. I wriggled my foot in my boot and felt the dead pilot's sheath digging into my ankle. How quickly could I pull the blade? It didn't seem possible that I could get the knife free and slash Abendroth's throat before the troopers gunned me down. Even without his soldiers protecting him, Abendroth looked far too powerful for me to kill. When I was little, I had seen a strongman in a circus with hands like the Sturmbannführer's— he had twisted a heavy steel wrench into a knot, and because it was my birthday, I got to keep it. For years I saved the knotted wrench, showed it to my friends in the Kirov, bragged about how the strongman had tousled my hair and winked at my mother. One day I looked for it and could not find it; I suspected Oleg Antokolsky stole it, but I never had any proof.

The idea of pulling a knife on a man that big panicked me, so I stopped thinking about it for a few minutes and concentrated on the game. A few moves later I saw an opportunity to exchange knights. My position seemed a little cramped, so I forced the trade. Abendroth sighed when he took my piece.

"I should not have allowed that."

"Well played," cried Kolya from the far end of

the table. I turned that way, saw that he and Vika were still watching me, and quickly returned my focus to the board. How had I become the chosen assassin? Didn't Kolya know me by now? Abendroth should die, I knew that—I had wanted him dead since I heard Zoya's story. Without doubt he had slaughtered thousands of men, women, and children as he followed the Wehrmacht across Europe. Berlin awarded him shiny medals for executing the Jews, Communists, and partisans of occupied countries. He was my enemy. But facing him now across the chessboard, watching him worry his wedding ring as he contemplated his next move, I didn't believe I was capable of murdering him.

The sheath dug into my ankle. The Sturmbannführer sat across from me, the collar of his jacket digging into a blue vein on the side of his broad neck. Kolya and Vika sat at the far end of the table, waiting for me to act. Given the weight of these distractions, I managed to play decent chess. As meaningless as the outcome might have been, the game mattered to me.

I sat with my elbow on the table, my head propped on my palm so that my hand blocked my view of Kolya and Vika. On the twenty-eighth move I pushed my c-pawn to the fifth row, an aggressive advance. Abendroth could take the piece with his b- or d-pawns. There is an old rule in chess that players should "capture toward the center." Abendroth followed classical strategy, using his b-pawn, establishing dominance in the middle of the board. But just as Tarrasch said, "Always put the rook behind the pawns, except when it is incorrect to do so," capturing toward the center is the right move except when it is wrong. When the sequence was over, we had exchanged two pawns each, our piece count was still even, and like a man who has swallowed poison but continues to chew his meat, not realizing his death is now certain, Abendroth had no idea he had committed a fatal error.

Far from tipping over his king, the German thought he held the superior position. As we neared the endgame, his a-pawn was alone on the edge of the board, racing toward the eighth row, where he could transform into a queen and batter my defenses. Abendroth was so intent on getting a second queen he gladly accepted the various exchanges I proposed. How could he lose with two queens on the attack? Focused on his a-pawn, he didn't realize until too late that I had my own passed pawn in the center of the board. In the end, my d-pawn earned its promotion one move before his a-pawn. Two queens are tough to beat unless your opponent gets his second queen first.

Abendroth still did not realize the game was over, but it was over. I glanced at Vika, stupidly proud of my imminent victory, and saw that her hand had slipped inside her coveralls. She would wait no longer for me to act, she was reaching for her knife; and Kolya had his hands on the edge of the table, ready to shove himself to his feet and attack when she did. My eyes met Vika's and I knew with sudden clarity that if I sat still, her tattered body would soon be dripping out its last on the peeling linoleum floor.

While Abendroth considered the board and the rare mob of queens, I pretended to itch my calf, dipping my fingers slowly inside my boot. This was not a surge of courage, but the opposite—my fear of Vika's death overpowered all my other fears. Abendroth squinted at his king and I saw his expression shift as he understood the truth about his position. I expected defeat to anger him. Instead a smile brightened his face and for a moment I could see what he must have looked like as a young boy.

"That was beautiful," he said, raising his head to look at me. "Next time I won't drink so much."

Whatever he saw in my own expression troubled him. He peered around the table and saw my hand digging inside my boot. I fumbled with the hilt and finally yanked the knife free of its sheath. Before I could swing at him Abendroth lunged forward, knocking me out of my chair and onto the floor, pinning my knife hand down with his left hand and reaching for his holstered pistol with his right.

If I had managed to free my knife faster, if I had lucked into slashing his jugular, if this miracle had happened, Vika and Kolya and I would have died. The troopers would have raised their MP40s and blasted us from existence. Abendroth's alertness—or my clumsiness, depending on how you look at it—saved us. As the troopers charged forward to help the Sturmbannführer, who needed no help, they neglected their other prisoners. Only for a moment, but that was enough.

Abendroth drew his automatic. Hearing the clamor at the far end of the room, he looked that way. Whatever he saw worried him more than this feeble, emaciated Jew writhing beneath him. He aimed at his target—Vika or Kolya, I could not see. I cried out and reached for the barrel of the gun with my left hand, slapping the muzzle just as he pulled the trigger. The pistol kicked and the report nearly deafened me. Abendroth snarled and tried to pull the gun away from my grasping fingers. Fighting

him was as pointless as fighting a bear, but I clung
to the barrel of that gun with all the strength left in
me. Those seconds were a tumult of noise and violence, hollered German and flashing muzzles, the
drumming of boot heels on linoleum.

Frustrated by my stubborn grip, Abendroth
punched me hard in the side of the head with his left
hand. I had been in a few scrapes and tussles growing up in the Kirov, but they were the brand of
sloppy, bloodless fights you'd expect from boys who
belong to chess clubs. No one had ever hit me in the
face. The room went blurry, fireflies darting across
my field of vision, as Abendroth ripped his automatic out of my hand and pointed it at my eyes.

I sat up and shoved the point of my knife deep
into his chest, through the breast pocket of his jacket,
below the cluster of medals, the blade sliding in all
the way to the silver finger guard.

Abendroth shuddered and blinked, looking
down at the black hilt. He still could have shot a
bullet through my brain, but avenging his own
murder did not seem important to him. He looked
disappointed, his lips curling downward, and finally he looked confused, blinking steadily, his
breath gone ragged. He wanted to stand, but his
legs gave way and he toppled over sideways, falling off of the knife in my hand, his pistol dropping
from his slack fingers. He opened his eyes wide—a
sleepy man forcing himself awake—placed his
palms on the linoleum, and tried to crawl away
from the sordid tableau, ignoring the commotion
around him. He did not get far.

I turned and saw Kolya struggling on the floor
with one of the troopers, both men trying to gain
control of the German's submachine gun. By that

point I considered Kolya a champion fighter, but no one had told the trooper and he seemed to have the upper hand. I don't remember getting to my feet or running over to help, but before the trooper could level his MP40 and empty his magazine into Kolya's chest, I was on the man's back, plunging the knife in and pulling it out, again and again.

Vika finally pulled me off the dead man. Her coveralls were drenched with blood and before logic could assert itself, I assumed she had been shot in the gut. I don't think I said anything coherent, but she shook her head, hushed me, and said, "I'm not hurt. Here, let me see your hand."

I didn't understand the request. I raised my right hand, still clutching the bloody knife, but she gently pushed it down, took my other wrist, and held my left hand between her palms. For the first time I realized that I was missing half of my index finger. Vika knelt beside one of the dead troopers—the boy with the moles, who stared blindly at the ceiling, his throat split open—and cut a strip of wool from his pants. She came back to me and tied it around my finger, a tourniquet to staunch the bleeding.

Kolya had grabbed the MP40s. He tossed one to Vika, kept the other for himself, and snatched the egg crate off the table. We could hear German voices calling out from elsewhere in the building, confused officers wondering if the gunshot they heard in their sleep was dreamed or real. Kolya slid open one of the four-paned windows and crawled onto the ledge.

"Hurry," he said, beckoning for us to follow him. He jumped and I rushed to follow him. The drop from the second floor wasn't very far and the snow below the window was a meter deep. I lost my balance on landing and tumbling face-first into the snow. Kolya hauled me to my feet and brushed the snow from my face. We heard a burst of gunfire from the conference room. A moment later Vika leaped from the window, smoke rising from the muzzle of her submachine gun.

We ran from the burned-out police station. Unlit streetlamps curled above us like question marks. The shouting from the old Party headquarters intensified and I expected bullets to start ripping through the air, but none ever came. The guards stationed at the front door must have run inside when they heard the gunfire; by the time they realized their mistake we were lost in the darkness.

Soon we reached the edge of the small town. We turned off the road and ran through the frozen farm fields, past the silhouettes of abandoned tractors. Back in Krasnogvardeysk we could hear car engines revving and chain-wrapped tires trundling over the snow. In the murky distance ahead we could see the black edge of the great forest waiting to receive us, to cloak us from the eyes of our enemies.

I have never been much of a patriot. My father would not have allowed such a thing while he lived, and his death insured that his wish was carried out. Piter commanded far more affection and loyalty from me than the nation as a whole. But that night, running across the unplowed fields of winter wheat, with the Fascist invaders behind us and the dark Russian woods before us, I felt a surge of pure love for my country.

We ran for the forest, crashing through the stalks of wheat, beneath the rising moon and the stars spinning farther and farther away, alone beneath the godless sky.

24

An hour later we still looked over our shoulders, listening for tracked vehicles, but the deeper into the woods we went, the more likely our escape began to seem. We sucked on icicles snapped off pine branches, but the night was so cold we couldn't bear to keep ice in our mouths for very long. The stump of my finger began to throb in time with my pulse.

Kolya had unbuttoned his army coat and shoved the straw-stuffed box under his sweater to keep the eggs from freezing. Over the last few kilometers he had slapped my shoulder repeatedly, grinning wildly beneath his stolen down cap with the silly drawstring tied beneath his chin.

"You really showed me something back there," he told me four separate times.

Now I was a killer of men and the German knife stuffed in my boot was an actual weapon, not just a boy's memento. Perhaps it would reflect better on me to tell you I felt a certain sadness, a solidarity with the dead men despite the necessity of the violence. The mole-strewn face of the dead boy stayed with me for a long time, until finally I forgot what he actually looked like and could remember only the memory. The Sturmbannführer crawling toward nowhere is an image still vivid in my mind. I could mouth all sorts of pieties to convince you that I'm a sensitive man, and I believe that I am a sensitive man. Even so, that night I felt nothing but exhilaration about my actions. I had *acted*, against all expectation, against my own history of cowardice. In the end, killing Abendroth had nothing to do with avenging Zoya or eliminating a vital Einsatz officer. I had kept Kolya and Vika alive. I had kept myself alive. Our warm breath rising above our heads, our grunts as our boots sunk deep in the snow, every sensation we experienced on our long march—experience itself—all of it was because finally, my back against the wall, I had shown a bit of courage. The proudest moment of my life came when we paused to catch our wind and Vika, checking my finger to make sure the bleeding had stopped, whispered in my ear, "Thank you."

At one point Vika and Kolya argued about which direction to walk. Vika ended the discussion with an impatient shake of her head, marching off without checking to see if we would follow. After the Mga debacle I had no faith in Kolya's ability to navigate; I followed her. Kolya held his ground for all of eight seconds before hurrying after us.

Somewhere along the way I told her the true story of why Kolya and I had snuck out of Piter, crossed enemy lines, and eventually stumbled onto the farmhouse beneath the larches. I kept my voice low so Kolya would not hear, though I couldn't imagine whom I was betraying. I told her about the colonel's daughter, skating on the Neva; the cannibals and their grisly wares hanging from the ceiling chains; the dying boy Vadim and his rooster, Darling; the antitank dog bleeding in the snow; and the dead Russian soldier rooted in the ice. When I finished the story, Vika shook her head but said nothing, and I worried that I had told her too much.

Watching her march through the woods, silent and tireless, the submachine gun strapped to her shoulder, I remembered what Kolya had told me the previous morning. The war had changed everyone, but still, it was difficult to believe she had been an astronomy student seven months earlier.

"May I ask you something?"

She kept walking, not bothering to answer. She didn't have time for inane questions like "May I ask you something?"

"Kolya says you're NKVD."

"Are you asking?"

"I guess so."

"What do you think?"

"I don't know," I said, but the moment I spoke the words I realized I did know. "I think he's right."

She peered through the darkness, looking for some kind of landmark to clarify which way we were going.

"Does it bother you?"

"Yes."

"Why?"

"Because of my father." I realized she didn't know what happened to my father, so I added, quietly, "They took him."

For nearly a minute we walked in silence, climbing a slowly sloping hill. I began to pant, the weakness returning to my legs as we moved farther from the victory at Krasnogvardeysk.

"Your father was a writer, yes? Then the odds

are very good other writers turned him in. The police were just doing their jobs."

"Yes. And the Einsatz, as well. Of course, they chose their jobs."

"If it changes anything, they took my father, too."

"Really? Was he a writer?"

"No. He was NKVD."

Cresting the long hill took us nearly an hour and stole all the spring from my legs, but when we finally got to the top of the treeless rise, I saw why Vika had chosen to come this way. The half-moon shone across the outstretched hectares of forest and farmland, all of it shimmering beneath a layer of frost and snow.

"Look," she said, pointing north. "Do you see it?"

Far beyond the valley below us, past the hills that blocked the horizon in the shadowy distance, a slender pillar of light rose to the sky, bright enough to spotlight the cloud far above. The powerful beam began to move, a brilliant saber carving the night, and I realized I was looking at an antiaircraft searchlight.

"That's Piter," she told us. "You get lost on your way home, that's your North Star."

I turned to look at her. "You're not coming with us?"

"There's a band of partisans outside of Chudovo. I know the commander. I'll try to connect with them."

"I'm sure the colonel can give us an extra ration card if you come with us. I'll tell him you helped us and he'll—"

She smiled and spat on the ground. "Fuck the

ration card. Piter's not my city. I'm needed out here."

"Don't get killed," said Kolya. "I think the boy is in love."

"Stay off the roads on your way back. And be careful getting into the city. We've got mines everywhere."

Kolya extended his gloved hand. Vika rolled her eyes at the formality but shook it. "I hope we meet again," he told her. "In Berlin."

She smiled and turned to me. I knew I would never see her again. When she saw the look on my face, something human entered those wolfish blue eyes. She touched my cheek with her gloved hand.

"Don't look so sad. You saved my life tonight."

I shrugged. I was afraid that if I opened my mouth I would say something mawkish and stupid, or worse, that I would start to cry. Five years had passed since I had cried, but I had never lived through a night like this one, and I was convinced that the sniper from Archangel was the only girl I would ever love.

Her gloved hand still rested on my cheek. "Tell me your last name."

"Beniov."

"I'll track you down, Lyova Beniov. All I need is the name." She leaned forward and kissed me on the lips. Her mouth was cold, her lips rough from the winter wind, and if the mystics are right and we are doomed to repeat our squalid lives ad infinitum, at least I will always return to that kiss.

A moment later she walked away from us, head down, rabbit fur cap brimmed low, chin tucked into her scarf, her little body in the oversize coveralls dwarfed by the ancient pines around her. I knew she would not look back at me, but I watched her anyway until she was gone.

"Come," said Kolya, wrapping his arm around my shoulders. "We have a wedding to attend."

25

The snow had melted in the daylight and frozen again at night, making for a treacherous walk, a skin of frost cracking with every step we took. My finger hurt so much it was hard to think about anything else. We kept walking because we had to keep walking, because we had come too far to stop now, but I do not know where the energy for each footfall came from. There is a place beyond hunger, beyond fatigue, where time no longer seems to move and the body's misery no longer seems fully your own.

None of this applied to Kolya. He had eaten as little as I had, though he had slept better the night before in the toolshed with the illiterates, as comfortable as if he lay on a feather bed in the Europa Hotel. While I slogged north with my head down, Kolya gazed around at the moonlit countryside like an artist on a stroll. We seemed to have all of Russia to ourselves. For hours we saw no sign of humanity aside from the abandoned farm fields.

Every few minutes he would reach inside his coat, making sure that his sweater remained tucked inside his belted pants and the box of eggs was secure.

"Have I told you the story of the courtyard hound?"

"Your novel?"

"Yes, but where the title comes from."

"Probably."

"No, I don't think I have. The hero, Radchenko, lives in an old building on Vasilevsky Island. A house really, built for one of Alexander's generals, but now it's falling apart, eight different families living there and none of them like one another. One night, the middle of winter, an old dog walks into the court-yard, lies down by the gate, and makes the place his home. A big old beast, his muzzle gone gray, one of his ears chewed off in some fight ages ago. Rad-chenko wakes up late the next morning, looks out his window, and sees the dog lying there with his head between his paws. He feels sorry for the poor fucker; it's cold and there's nothing to eat. So he finds a bit of dry sausage and opens his window, just as the church bells start ringing for noontime."

"What year is this?"

"What? I don't know. 1883. Radchenko whistles and the dog looks up at him. He tosses down the sausage, dog gobbles it down, Radchenko smiles, closes the window, and gets back in bed. Now re-member, at this point he hasn't left his apartment in five years. The next day, Radchenko's still sleeping when the church bells ring at noon. When the bells go quiet, he hears a bark outside. And then another one. Finally, he crawls out of bed, opens the win-dow, looks down to the courtyard, and sees the hound staring up at him, tongue dangling from his mouth, waiting to be fed. So Radchenko finds some-thing to toss the old boy, and from then on, every time the church bells ring at noon the dog waits be-neath the window for his lunch."

"Like Pavlov's dog."

"Yes," said Kolya, a little annoyed. "Like Pavlov's dog, except with poetry. Two years go by. The courtyard hound knows everyone in the building, he lets them pass without trouble, but if a stranger comes to the gates, the old boy's a terror, growling and gnashing his teeth. The residents love him, he's their guardian, they don't even lock their doors anymore. Sometimes Radchenko wastes a whole afternoon, sitting in a chair by the window, watching the dog watching the people streaming past the gates. He never forgets the noontime ritual, always makes sure he has plenty of good meats to toss down. One morning Radchenko's in bed, having a wonderful dream about a woman he admired when he was little, a close friend of his mother's. The church bells ring and Radchenko wakes with a smile, stretches his arms, walks to the window, slides it open, and looks down to the courtyard. The hound's lying on his side by the gate, very still, and right away Radchenko knows the beast is dead. Remember, Radchenko had never touched him, never scratched behind his ear or rubbed his belly or any of that, but still, he came to love the old mutt, considered him a loyal friend. For almost an hour Radchenko stares at the dead hound and finally he realizes no one's going to bury him. He's a stray; whose job is it? Radchenko hasn't left the apartment in seven years; the thought of stepping outside makes him nauseous, but even worse is the thought of leaving the hound to rot in the sun. Do you understand how dramatic this is? He walks out of his apartment, down the stairs, out the front door of the building, steps into sunlight—first time in seven years!—picks up the big dog, and carries him out of the courtyard."

"Where does he bury him?"

"I don't know. In one of the university gardens, maybe."

"They wouldn't let him do that."

"I haven't figured that part out yet. You're missing the point of the story—"

"And he needs a shovel."

"Yes, he needs a shovel. You've got all the romance of a train station whore, you know that? Maybe I won't even write the burial scene, how would that be? Leave it to your imagination."

"Probably a good idea. Could be a little maudlin. Dead dogs, I don't know."

"But you like it?"

"I think so."

"You think so? It's a beautiful story."

"It's good, I like it."

"And the title? *The Courtyard Hound*? Now you understand why it's such a great title? All these women come over to Radchenko's, constantly trying to get him to go outside with them, and he never does. It's almost like a game for them; they all want to be the first one to lure him out the gates, but none of them can make him go. Only the dog, an old dumb dog with no master."

"*The Courtyard Dog* wouldn't be nearly as good."

"No."

"What's the difference between a dog and a hound?"

"Hounds hunt." Kolya grabbed my arm, his eyes gone wide, forcing me to stop walking. At first I thought he had heard something, a growling Panzer engine or the calls of distant soldiers, but whatever demanded his attention seemed internal. He held my arm very tight, his lips slightly parted, a look of intense concentration on his face, as if he needed to remember a girl's name but he only had the first letter.

"What?" I asked. He held up his hand and I waited. Stopping for even ten seconds made me want to lie down in the snow and close my eyes, only for a few minutes, just long enough to take the weight off my feet and wriggle my toes back to life.

"It's coming," he said. "I can feel it."

"What's coming?"

"My shit! Oh, come on now, you bastard, come on!"

He hurried off behind a tree and I waited for him, swaying in the wind. I wanted to sit, but some irritating voice within my skull told me that sitting was dangerous, that if I sat I would never stand again.

By the time Kolya returned I was sleeping on my feet, a montage of incoherent dream images flashing through my mind. He grabbed my arm, startling me, and shined his Cossack grin.

"My friend, I am no longer an atheist. Come on, I want to show you."

"Are you joking? I don't want to see."

"You have to look at this. It must be a record."

He tugged on my arm, trying to get me to follow him, but I dug my boots into the snow and leaned my weight backward.

"No, no, let's go; we don't have time."

"Are you afraid to see my record-breaking shit?"

"If we don't get to the colonel by dawn—"

"This is something extraordinary! Something you'll tell your children about."

Kolya pulled with his superior strength and I could feel myself beginning to topple, when his gloved hands slipped off my coat sleeve and he fell onto the ice-skinned snow. His first reaction was to laugh, but he quit laughing when he remembered the eggs.

"Fuck," he said, staring up at me. For the first time in our journey I saw something close to genuine fear in his eyes.

"Don't tell me you broke them. Don't tell me that."

"*I* broke them? Why is it only me? Why didn't you just come and look at the shit?"

"I didn't want to look at your shit!" I shouted at him, no longer mindful of enemies that might be moving through these same woods. "Tell me if they're broken!"

Sitting on the ground, he unbuttoned his coat, pulled out the box, and inspected it for damage, running his hand over the wood slats. He took a deep breath, pulled off his right glove, and gingerly felt inside the straw-stuffed box with his bare fingers.

"Well?"

"They're good."

After the box was warm and secure beneath Kolya's sweater, we resumed our northward march. He didn't mention the historic shit again, but I could tell that he was irritated I hadn't gone with him to bear witness. Now when he told the story to his friends, he wouldn't have any verification to back up his claims.

Every minute I'd look for the powerful searchlight roving through the sky. Sometimes we'd lose sight of it for a kilometer or two, our view blocked by trees or hills, but we always found it again. As we got closer to Piter we saw more of the searchlights, but the first one was the most powerful, strong enough that it seemed to brighten the moon when the light passed over those cold distant craters.

"I bet the colonel will be surprised to see us," said Kolya. "He must think we're dead by now. He'll be so happy with the eggs, I'll ask him for an invite to the daughter's wedding. Why not? His wife's going to love us. And maybe I'll get a dance with the bride, show her a few steps, let her know I'm not averse to married women."

"I don't even know where I'm going to sleep tonight."

"We'll go to Sonya's. Don't even think about it. I'm sure the colonel will give us some food for our troubles, we'll share it with her, try to get a little fire going. And tomorrow I'll have to track down my battalion. Ha, the boys will be surprised to see me."

"She doesn't even know me, I can't stay there."

"Of course you can. We're friends now, Lev, am I right? Sonya is my friend, you're my friend; don't worry, she has plenty of room. Though staying with her might not be so exciting now that you've met Vika, eh?"

"Vika scares me."

"She scares me, too. But you like her quite a bit, admit it."

I smiled, thinking about Vika's eyes, her fat lower lip, the precise curve of her collarbone.

"She probably thinks I'm too young for her."

"Maybe. But you saved her life back there. That bullet was heading straight for her head."

"I saved your life, too."

"No, I had that Fritz under control."

"You did not, he had that gun—"

"The day some Bavarian goose-stepper beats me in a fight—"

The argument kept going, veering from an analysis of the chess game and my supposed mistakes to the likely guests at the colonel's daughter's wedding to the fate of the four girls we met at the farmhouse. The conversation kept me awake, kept my mind off my numb feet and my legs stiff as stilts beneath me. The sky brightened, shade by imperceptible shade, and we stumbled upon a paved road where the snow was tamped down and the walking was easier. Before the sun had risen to the east, we saw the outer ring of Piter's fortifications: the trenches like dark gashes in the snow; the cement block dragon's teeth; the thickets of rusted railroad irons sprouting from the cold ground; kilometer after kilometer of barbed wire wrapped around wood posts.

"I'll tell you one thing," said Kolya. "I want a slice of this fucking wedding cake. What we've gone through, it's only fair."

A moment later he said, "What are they doing?" and a moment after that I heard the gunshot. Kolya grabbed my coat and shoved me to the ground. Bullets twanged overhead. "They're shooting at us," he said, answering his own question. "Hey! Hey! We're Russian! We're Russian, don't shoot!" More bullets ripped through the air above us. "We're Russians, damn your mothers, listen to me! Do you hear my voice! Do you hear me! We have papers from Colonel Grechko! Colonel Grechko! Do you hear?"

The rifles went quiet, but we stayed on our bellies, our arms over our heads. Behind the fortifications we could hear an officer shouting to his men. Kolya lifted his head and peered toward the trenches, several hundred meters to the north.

"Haven't they heard of warning shots?"

"Maybe those were warning shots."

"No, they were aiming for our heads. They don't know how to shoot, that's all. Bunch of slobs from the Works, I bet. Probably got their rifles a week ago." He cupped his hands around his mouth and yelled. "Hey! Can you hear me? You want to save your bullets for Fritz?"

"Put your hands in the air and walk slowly toward us!" came the hollered reply.

"You're not going to shoot us if we stand up?"

"Not if we like the looks of you."

"Your mother likes the looks of me," Kolya muttered. "You ready, little lion?"

As we stood, Kolya grimaced and stumbled, nearly falling. I grabbed his arm to steady him. Frowning, he brushed the snow off the front of his greatcoat before twisting to examine his lower back. We both saw the bullet hole punched through the thick wool at hip height.

"Throw down your weapons!" the officer shouted from the distant trench. Kolya tossed aside his MP40.

"I'm shot!" he yelled back. He unbuttoned his coat and studied the hole in the seat of his pants. "Do you believe this? Those cunts shot me in the ass."

"Walk toward us with your hands in the air!"

"You shot me in the ass, you fucking idiot! I can't walk anywhere!"

I had my hand on Kolya's arm, helping him stay upright; he couldn't put any weight on his right leg.

"You should sit," I told him.

"I can't sit. How am I going to sit, I have a bullet in my ass! Do you believe this?"

"Can you kneel? I don't think you should be on your feet."

"You know how much shit I'm going to get from my battalion? Shot in the ass by fucking amateurs straight off the assembly line?"

I helped as he lowered himself to the ground. He winced when his right knee hit the snow, jarring his leg. The officers in the trench must have held an impromptu conference. A new voice called to us now, an older voice with more authority.

"Stay where you are! We're coming to you!"

Kolya grunted. "Stay where you are, he tells us. Yes, I think I'll do that, now that I've got one of your fucking rifle bullets in my ass."

"Maybe it went straight through. That's better, isn't it, if it went straight through?"

"You want to pull down my pants and check?" he asked, giving me a pained grin.

"Should I do something? What do I do?"

"Pressure, they say. Don't worry, I'll do it." He untied the drawstring of his down hat, took it off, and pressed it against the bullet hole. He had to close his eyes for a moment, inhaling deeply. When he opened them again, he seemed to remember something; with his free hand he reached under his sweater and pulled out the straw-stuffed box of eggs.

"Put it under your coat," he ordered. "We don't want them freezing. And don't drop them, please."

A few minutes later we saw a GAZ rolling toward us, an armored model with thick-nubbed snow tires and a heavy machine gun mounted in the back. The gunner kept the wide-mouthed muzzle aimed at our heads as the car braked beside us.

A sergeant and a lieutenant hopped out and walked over to us, their hands on the butts of their holstered pistols. The sergeant paused beside the discarded MP40 lying in the snow. He considered the submachine gun for a moment before looking at Kolya.

"Our snipers saw the German gun. They did the right thing."

"Snipers, is that what you call them? Are they trained to shoot men in the ass?"

"Why do you have a German gun?"

"He's bleeding, he needs help," I told them. "Can't you ask these questions later?"

The lieutenant glanced at me, his flat, bored face devoid of all emotion save mild hostility. His head was shaved and he wore no hat, as if he didn't notice the cold wind gusting around us.

"You're a civilian? You're giving me orders? I could execute you right now for violating curfew and exiting the city limits without a permit."

"Please. Comrade Officer. We stay out here much longer, he'll bleed to death."

Kolya dug into his pocket, pulled out the colonel's letter, and offered it to the officers. The lieutenant read it, disdainful at first but stiffening when he saw whose signature was on the bottom of the page.

"You should have said something," he muttered. He waved his hand for the driver and the gunner to come help.

"I should have— I was screaming the colonel's name while you shot at us!"

"My men did the right thing. You were advanc-

ing with enemy hardware, we had no advance
warning—"

"Kolya," I said, my hand on his shoulder. He
looked up at me, his mouth already open, ready to
verbally fillet the lieutenant. For once in his life he
understood that it was time to shut up. He smiled,
rolling his eyes a little, but then he saw the troubled
expression cross my face. He followed my gaze
down to where the blood was seeping into the snow,
his pants leg drenched. The stained snow looked
like the cherry ices my father used to buy me at
summer fairs.

"Don't worry," Kolya said, staring at the blood.
"That's not so much, don't worry."

The driver grabbed him under the armpits, the
gunner held him under his knees, and they carried
him to the backseat of the still-idling GAZ. I crouched
in the space between the driver's seat and the backseat while Kolya lay on his stomach, his greatcoat
draped over him for warmth. We drove toward the
trenches, Kolya closing his eyes each time the car
jolted over a bump in the road. I had taken the blood-
soaked cap from him and I pressed it against the bullet wound, trying to maintain enough pressure to
slow the bleeding without hurting him.

He smiled, his eyes closed. "I'd rather Vika was
the one with her hand on my ass."

"Does it hurt very much?"

"Have you ever been shot in the ass?"

"No."

"Well the answer is yes, it hurts. I'm just happy
they didn't hit the other side. Please, Lieutenant,"
Kolya said loudly, "will you thank your snipers for
not shooting my balls off?"

The lieutenant, sitting in the passenger seat,

stared at the road ahead and did not answer, his bare scalp flecked with small white scars.

"The women of Leningrad thank them, too."

"We're taking you to the hospital at the Works," said the lieutenant. "That's where the best surgeons are."

"Very good, I'm sure the NKVD will give you a medal. And when you've dropped me off, please take my little friend here to Kamenny Island. He has an important package for the colonel."

The lieutenant sat in sullen silence, angry that he had to take orders from a private but unwilling to risk making a powerful enemy. We stopped at a sandbagged barricade and lost nearly two minutes as soldiers lowered a wooden platform across the trench so we could cross. The driver barked at them to hurry, but even so the soldiers drifted about, weary and nonchalant, arguing about the proper way to position the bridge. Finally, we made it to the other side. The driver stepped on the gas and we sped past machine-gun emplacements festooned with sandbags.

"How far to the hospital?" I asked the driver.

"Ten minutes. Eight, if we're lucky."

"Try to be lucky," said Kolya. His eyes were clenched shut now, his face pressed against the seat, his blond hair hanging over his forehead. In the last minute he had gotten very pale and could not stop shivering. I rested my free hand on the back of his neck and his skin was cool to the touch.

"Don't worry," he told me. "I've seen friends bleeding worse than this and they were back a week later, all stitched up."

"I'm not worried."

"There's so much blood in a human body. What is it, five liters?"

"I don't know."

"It looks like so much, but I bet I haven't even lost a liter. Maybe one."

"Maybe you shouldn't talk."

"Why not? What's wrong with talking? Listen, you go to the wedding. Dance with the colonel's daughter, and then come to the hospital and tell me about it. I want details. What she's wearing, what she smells like, all that. I've been jerking off to her for five days straight, you know that? Well, once to Vika. My apologies. But what she did in the sheep barn, tightening the belt around her chest? You saw that. Can you blame me?"

"When did you have time to do that?"

"On the endless fucking march to here. You learn how to jerk it on the move when you're in the army. Hand in the pocket, it's no big trick."

"You jerked off to Vika while we were walking last night?"

"I wasn't going to tell you. You were sleepwalking half the night, I was bored, I had to do something. Now you're angry. Don't be angry with me."

"Of course I'm not angry."

The driver hit the brakes hard and Kolya would have tumbled off the backseat if I hadn't been holding him. I sat up and peered through the windshield. We had reached the edge of the sprawling Kirov Works, a city in itself, where tens of thousands labored night and day. Artillery shells and Luftwaffe bombs had flattened some of the brick-walled machine shops; empty windows throughout the complex had been covered with plastic tarps;

310 ■ David Benioff

ice-filled craters pockmarked the yards. But even now, with thousands of workers evacuated and thousands more dead or waiting to die on the front lines, even now the chimneys still smoked, the alleyways bustled with women pushing carts filled with coal, the air was loud with the clamor of whirring lathes and rolling mills and hydraulic presses shaping steel.

A line of newly completed T-34 tanks had trundled out of an assembly shop as big as an airplane hangar. Eight of the tanks, their steel unpainted, rumbled slowly over the dirty snow, blocking off the road.

"Why did we stop?" Kolya asked. His voice sounded much weaker than it had a minute before and it made me afraid to hear him like that.

"Some tanks are going by."

"T-thirty-fours?"

"Yes."

"Good tanks."

Finally, the tanks passed and we shot forward. The driver had a heavy foot on the accelerator, a sure hand on the wheel, and he knew the Works well—cutting through back alleys behind turbine shops; blasting down unpaved paths alongside the workers' housing, tin-roofed sheds with squat little stovepipes—but even with an expert it took time to get to the far side of the rambling factory town.

"There," said the lieutenant at last, pointing to a brick warehouse that had been converted into the local hospital. He turned in his seat and looked at Kolya. When he couldn't see Kolya's face, he looked at me, questioning. I shrugged to say, *I don't know.*

"Devils!" shouted the driver, slapping the steering wheel and hitting the brakes again. A small lo-

comotive chugged across the tracks that bisected
the Works, tugging boxcars loaded with scrap metal
for the foundry.

"Lev?"

"Yes?"

"Are we close?"

"I think we're very close."

Kolya's lips had gone blue, his breathing rapid
and shallow.

"Is there any water?" he asked.

"Does anyone have water?" My voice broke as I
asked the question. I sounded like a frightened
child.

The gunner passed forward a canteen. I unscrewed the cap, shifted Kolya's head sideways,
and tried to pour water in his mouth, but it ended
up spilling onto the seat. He managed to lift his
head a little and I got some down his throat, but he
choked and spat it up. When I tried to give him
more, he refused with a slight shake of the head and
I handed the canteen back to the gunner.

Realizing Kolya's head must be cold, I tore off
my hat and put it on him, ashamed that I hadn't
thought to do that before. Even though he shivered,
his face was damp with sweat, his skin pale and
mottled with coin-size scarlet patches.

I could see the doors of the hospital, less than a
hundred meters away, through the gaps between
the rolling boxcars. Our driver sat hunched forward
in his seat, his arms draped around the wheel, nodding his head impatiently as he waited. The lieutenant kept glancing back at Kolya, more and more
worried.

"Lev? You like the title?"

"What title?"

"*The Courtyard Hound.*"

"It's a good title."

"I could just call it *Radchenko.*"

"*The Courtyard Hound* is better."

"I think so, too."

He opened his eyes, those pale blue Cossack eyes, and smiled at me. We both knew he was going to die. He trembled, lying on the backseat beneath his greatcoat, his teeth very white against his blue lips. I have always believed that smile was a gift for me. Kolya had no faith in the divine or the afterlife; he didn't think he was going to a better place, or any place at all. No angels waited to collect him. He smiled because he knew how terrified I was of dying. This is what I believe. He knew I was terrified and he wanted to make it a little easier for me.

"Can you believe it? Shot in the ass by my own people."

I wanted to say something, to make some stupid joke to distract him. I should have said something, I wish that I had, even though I still can't think of the right words. If I told him that I loved him, would he have winked and said, "No wonder your hand's on my ass?"

Even Kolya couldn't hold the smile for long. He closed his eyes again. When he spoke, his mouth was very dry, his lips sticking together as he tried to form the words.

"It's not the way I pictured it," he told me.

26

Officers in uniform and stern-faced civilians hurried in and out of the mansion on Kamenny Island, shoving through the front door beneath the white-columned portico. Behind the old house the Neva lay coiled, frozen and dusted with snow, a white snake slithering through the broken city.

The bald lieutenant escorted me to one of the machine-gun emplacements in front of the mansion, where a band of soldiers sat behind stacked sandbags, sipping weak tea from tin cups. The sergeant in charge read the colonel's letter, glanced at me, and said, "You have something for him?"

I nodded and he beckoned for me to follow him. The lieutenant turned and walked away, never looking back, eager to escape what had turned into an unfortunate morning for him.

We finally found Grechko downstairs in the mansion's wine cellar. All the grand old bottles of wine had been drunk long ago, but the walls were still honeycombed with terra-cotta racks. The colonel stood beside one of his subordinate officers, who checked items off a list. Young soldiers opened wood crates with crowbars. They dipped their arms into the shredded paper protecting the contents, pulling out tins and jars and burlap sacks and calling out the contents.

"Two kilos of smoked ham."

"Five hundred grams of black caviar."

"Kilo of jellied beef."

"Garlic and onions . . . no weight listed."

"Kilo of white sugar."

"Kilo salted herring."

"Boiled tongue, no weight listed."

For a minute I stood and watched as the pile of foodstuffs grew, all the ingredients for a legendary feast. Carrots and potatoes, plucked chickens and jars of sour cream, wheat flour, honey, strawberry jam, jugs of fermented cherry juice, canned borovik mushrooms, blocks of butter wrapped in wax paper, a two-hundred-gram bar of Swiss chocolate.

The sergeant escorting me whispered a word to the officer standing beside Grechko. The colonel heard him and turned my way. For a few seconds he frowned, unable to place me, the deep furrows splitting his forehead.

"Ah," he said, his strange, beautiful smile emerging. "The looter! Where's your friend, the deserter?"

I don't know how my face reacted to this question, but the colonel saw and understood.

"Too bad," he said. "I liked that boy."

He waited for me to do something and for a long count I couldn't remember why I was there. When it came back to me, I unbuttoned my coat, pulled the slatted, straw-stuffed box out from under my sweater, and handed it over.

"A dozen eggs," I told him.

"Wonderful, wonderful." He gave the box to his underling without looking at it and gestured to the delicacies heaped on the stone floor. "Airlifted some provisions in last night. Just in time. You know how many owed favors I had to spend on this wedding?"

The subordinate officer handed the egg box to one of the young soldiers and made a mark in his book. "Another dozen eggs."

I watched the soldier walk away with the box.

"You already have eggs?"

The subordinate checked his book. "That's four dozen now."

"The more the better," said the colonel. "Now we can make fish pies. Here, give the boy a Grade One ration card. Ah, give him two; he might as well have his friend's."

The subordinate raised his eyebrows, impressed with this generosity. He pulled two ration cards from a leather wallet and signed them. He took an inkpad from his pocket and stamped the cards before handing them to me.

"You'll be a popular boy," he said.

I stared at the cards in my hand. Each one entitled me to an officer's rations. I looked around the cellar. Kolya would have known which vineyards the Dolgorukovs preferred, the white they chose for sturgeon, the red best paired with venison. Or if he didn't know, he would have made it up. I watched soldiers walk upstairs carrying sacks of rice and long strings of fat sausage.

When I turned toward the colonel, he stared right back at me. Again he understood my expression.

"Those words you want to say right now? Don't say them." He smiled and cuffed my cheek with something close to real affection. "And that, my friend, is the secret to living a long life."

27

On the night of January 27, 1944, more than three hundred cannons fired an hour-long fusillade of white, blue, and red rockets, the brilliant, glittering tails lighting up all of Leningrad, the Russian colors reflected in the gold dome of Saint Isaac's and the two thousand windows of the Winter Palace. The siege was over.

I stood on the rooftop of Sonya's building, drinking bad Ukrainian wine with her and a dozen other friends, toasting the names of Govorov and Meretskov, the generals who had broken through the German lines. By that time I had been in the army for over a year. My superiors had sized me up, decided I didn't have the look of an infantryman, and assigned me to duty at *Red Star*, the army's newspaper. My job that first year was to assist a team of experienced journalists traveling around the front, gathering anecdotes and quotations from soldiers in the various units we visited. I carried a rifle but never used it. My missing half finger bothered me only when I typed. Eventually I earned a promotion and began sending my own reports to the *Red Star* offices, where an editor I never met converted my submissions into sturdy, patriotic prose. My father would have hated all of it.

The night the siege ended, up on Sonya's roof, after we had drunk too much wine and shouted till our throats hurt, I kissed her on the mouth. It was more than friendly and less than erotic. When we stepped apart, smiling to cover our embarrassment, I know we both thought of Kolya. I imagine he would have been delighted to see me kissing a pretty girl, he would have coached me on my technique and insisted on a firmer touch—but still, we thought of him and we never kissed that way again.

A few days after I had returned to Piter with the colonel's eggs, I learned that the Kirov did not collapse until hours after the bombs struck. Most of the residents had survived, including Vera Osipovna and the Antokolsky twins. I ran into each of them eventually, but the winter had changed us all and there was little to say. I had hoped Vera would feel mildly guilty for running away without looking back after I had saved her at the courtyard gates, but she didn't mention it and I didn't bring it up. She had already earned a seat in the city's depleted orchestra and she kept it for the next thirty years. The twins both fought with distinction in General Chuikov's Eighth Guards, making it all the way to Berlin. There is a famous photograph of one of them signing his name on the Reichstag wall, but I could not tell you if it was Oleg or Grisha. Of all the fifth-floor Kirov kids, I suppose I am the least accomplished.

In the summer of 1945 I lived in a large apartment near the Moscow Station with two other young journalists. The evacuees had returned to Piter by then, including my mother and sister, but the city remained far less crowded than it had been before the war. People said water from the Neva still tasted like corpses. Boys ran home from school again, swinging their book bags. The restaurants and shops of Nevsky Prospekt had reopened, even though almost no one had money to spend. On state holidays we all strolled up and down the street, staring through new plate glass windows at the marzipan treats and wristwatches and leather gloves. Those of us who had lived through the siege stayed by habit on the south sidewalk, though no shells had landed for nearly two years.

One cool August night, the north wind blowing down from Finland with the scent of pine needles, I sat alone at the kitchen table of my apartment, reading a Jack London story. My roommates had gone to see a new play at the Pushkin; I'd been invited, but there was no contemporary Russian playwright I liked as much as Jack London. When I finished the story, I decided to read it again from the beginning, this time trying to figure out how he had written it. *Buck did not read the newspapers, or he would have known that trouble was brewing. . . .*

I did not look up from the page at the first knock on the door. The boy who lived a few apartments over entertained himself most evenings running up and down the hallway, banging on each door. Everyone I knew would let himself in, anyway—the lock was broken and we had few visitors. The third knock broke London's spell. A little annoyed, I dropped the book on the kitchen table and went to scold the boy.

A young woman stood in the hallway, a suitcase at her feet, a cardboard carton in her hands. She wore a yellow cotton dress with a white flower print. The silver dragonfly on her necklace hung in the hollow of her collarbone and her thick red hair cascaded past her sunburned shoulders. She will tell you that she hadn't chosen that dress with any care, or the necklace, that she hadn't washed her hair or scrubbed her face, put a little red on her lips. Don't believe it. No one looks that good by accident.

She grinned at me, that infuriating curl of the lips that seemed more smirk than smile, her blue eyes watching mine to see if I recognized her. If I were a little better at playing the game, I might have pretended not to, I might have said, "Hello, are you looking for someone?"

"You're not as skinny as before," she said. "But you're still too skinny."

"You have hair," I replied, and immediately wished I could take it back. For three and a half years I had dreamed of her—literally, she had marched in her oversize coveralls through half the dreams I remembered—and all I could think to say when she finally arrived was, *"You have hair"*?

"I brought you a gift," she said. "Look what they've invented now."

She flipped open the lid of the cardboard carton. Inside twelve eggs nestled in their snug compartments. White eggs, brown eggs, and one that was speckled like an old man's hand. She closed the lid and opened it again, pleased with its functional simplicity.

"Much better than packing them in straw," she added.

"We could make an omelet," I suggested.

"We?" She smiled, handing me the carton, picking up her suitcase, waiting for me to open the door wide and let her inside. "One thing you should know about me, Lyova. I don't cook."

Acknowledgments

Narrison Salisbury's masterpiece, *The 900 Days*, remains the best English-language book on the siege of Leningrad. It was my constant companion while writing *City of Thieves* and I recommend it to anyone wishing to learn more about Piter and its inhabitants during the Great Patriotic War. I am equally indebted to Curzio Malaparte's work of strange genius, *Kaputt*, which provides an entirely different perspective on the conflict. His descriptions of German antipartisan tactics, along with much else, proved essential in composing this narrative. I'd like to thank both of these late gentlemen for their books. If I got the details right, they deserve much of the credit.

By
David Benioff

978-0-452-28295-7

978-0-452-28664-1

Available wherever books are sold.

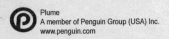

Plume
A member of Penguin Group (USA) Inc.
www.penguin.com